P9-DKF-279

DUALED

DUALED

ELSIE CHAPMAN

RANDOM HOUSE 🏠 NEW YORK

Text copyright © 2013 by Elsie Chapman
Jacket art copyright © 2013 by Michael Heath

All rights reserved. Published in the United States by
Random House Children's Books, a division of Random House, Inc., New York.

Random House and the colophon are registered trademarks of Random House, Inc.

Visit us on the Web! randomhouse.com/teens

Educators and librarians, for a variety of teaching tools,
visit us at RHTeachersLibrarians.com

Library of Congress Cataloging-in-Publication Data
Chapman, Elsie.
Dualed / Elsie Chapman. — 1st ed.
p. cm.
Summary: "West Grayer lives in a world where every person has a twin, or Alt.
Only one can survive to adulthood, and West has just received her
notice to kill her Alt."—Provided by publisher.
ISBN 978-0-307-93154-2 (trade) — ISBN 978-0-375-97093-1 (lib. bdg.) —
ISBN 978-0-307-97536-2 (ebook)
[1. Science fiction.] I. Title.
PZ7.C36665Du 2013   [Fic]—dc23   2011052348

Printed in the United States of America

10 9 8 7 6 5 4 3 2 1

First Edition

Random House Children's Books supports
the First Amendment and celebrates the right to read.

For Jesse, Matthew, and Gillian

CHAPTER 1

I've buried nearly everyone I love.

That's the thought that keeps crossing my mind as I sit in the restaurant, picking at the seam along my sleeve where it's starting to wear thin. Beneath the overly bright lighting, the cheap black cotton of the jacket I usually wear to funerals is faded, gray, nubby with use.

Across the table from me, Luc's staring blankly at the menu. His blacks aren't looking too hot, either. The jacket is too small across the shoulders, stretched tight, his wrists popping out from beneath the cuffs. At seventeen, my brother's taller than Aave was. By default I'm the tallest girl, since Ehm's gone, too.

I toss my menu down. "I guess I'm just going to get the same thing I always do."

Luc shakes his head in puzzled disgust, glances up at me. "Why do we keep coming here, again? The food sucks."

"I think Aave kept making us come back? He always said Balthazar's was one of his favorite restaurants in the Grid. And we just kind of . . . never stopped."

"Yeah, probably. I swear the guy had a stomach lined with steel."

I fiddle with the fork that's lying next to my hand, wondering if any Alt has ever actually used one to complete an assignment. A last-resort-and-being-cornered kind of thing. Would a handful of pointy tines be enough to fend off death if you're the one meant to survive?

"What do you think about your combat classes so far this year?" Luc's voice breaks through the buzz of my thoughts, the clamor of the crowd seated around us.

"Well, I'm already counting down the days until weaponry. You don't know how lucky you are to be in there already."

"Hey, what's wrong with combat?" Luc's dark brown eyes are amused. "At least admit it's not as bad as kinetics."

The study of body and muscle movement, kinetics is the first level of the Alt Skills program, and it makes up year one in school. Learning how to fight effectively with your body is combat, years two and three—though in a battle, given a choice between bare flesh and man-made steel, I know which one I'd pick every single time. An Alt's bullet travels fast, before you can even begin to think about calculating how to form a fist without breaking your bones. It's not until weaponry that you learn the minute mechanics of aiming and firing a gun, the torque and spin of a blade, the balletic beauty of wielding a dagger.

"Okay, fine, nothing's as bad as kinetics," I say to Luc. "But it doesn't change the fact that year two combat's not much more than filler." At fifteen, I'm just starting year three at Torth Prep. In Kersh's citywide school curriculum, weaponry isn't offered until years four and five. "Everyone knows weaponry is the only training class that isn't a total waste of time."

"Well, you've only got this one last year. Then you're good to go."

I pick up the dinner knife, let the muscles of my hand spin it into position.

"Relax, West," Luc says, and gestures to the waitress headed in our direction. "You're going to scare Bren."

Slowly, I put the knife down.

"Two of my favorite customers," Bren says to us, smiling. But I can see the sympathy in her eyes. "I'm so sorry to hear about your dad. Was he sick?"

I look away, not caring if it's rude. Whatever Luc tells her is up to him. All I know is I can't say the words.

It seems like a very long time before he answers. "Yeah, he was sick, Bren."

Close enough to the truth, I guess.

"Can I just get the chicken salad, please?" I ask abruptly. It's late, way past dinnertime, and I don't even know if I feel like eating. But we're here, and I'll do anything to keep her from asking more questions.

"Sure." Bren flicks her eyes at me, uncertain. "You know it's just the culled pigeon, right? Chicken's reserved for completes."

"Until when?"

"Oh, I'm not sure. You know how it is."

"Sure, it's fine," I tell her. It has to be. Completes always get the best food. Idles like Luc and me are served the scraps, remnants, surplus. None of the good stuff until we're completes, too.

"Just the cheeseburger," Luc says to the waitress. "Thanks."

"It won't be too long." She walks away.

"Wow," I say to Luc. "You keep ordering that like you think it's going to taste different each time. It's not even meat; it's straight filler."

"It's not filler. It's . . . protein booster."

I laugh for the first time all day. "Yeah, okay, tell yourself that. You're probably going to sprout a third eye or something."

"Hey, having a third eye when you go active could actually help—"

A sharp crack in the air. It could be mistaken for the boom of thunder, or the sound of a car backfiring. But living where I live, I instantly recognize it.

Gunfire. And it's close by.

"Completion of an assignment," Luc says, looking past my shoulder and out the window, proving my instincts right. "Just across the street."

Breath held, I turn to see the figures of the two Alts outside. Slightly rippled through the bulletproof glass and little more than blurred shadows beneath the hazy glow of the streetlamps, but their movements are familiar, a choreography of steps all citizens of Kersh have seen before. One Alt finally tumbles to the ground. The other crouches over him, checking for vitals. It hits me how their silhouettes could almost be mistaken for lovers'.

But they're not. They're Alts. Enemies from birth. And now

one's dead, which means the survivor has completed his assignment. He takes off down the road, leaving behind his childhood, a past life as easily shed as a prisoner's jumpsuit.

Able to breathe again, I turn back to see Luc still staring out the window, his expression strange, not his own. Around us, the other diners begin talking and eating again. A waitress brings an order to a table in the corner.

"Hey, promise me something," I blurt out. "That if I go first—if I end up being an incomplete—you'll do something for me."

His eyes drift back to mine. I can see the scene still playing out in his head, but it's no longer two strange Alts battling each other. It's friends with theirs, me with mine, him with his.

"A promise?" he asks. Picks up his glass but doesn't drink from it. Puts it back down.

"That when your assignment comes, you'll think about nothing else except how you're going to beat your Alt. That you won't be distracted by anything until you're a complete."

A slight smile at the corner of his mouth. "Well, yeah, why wouldn't—"

"And that you'll go for all that stuff Mom and Dad wanted for you. What you guys used to talk about together—school, a safe desk job that will probably pay way too much for what you actually do. Getting married, old, fat. Buying a nice house somewhere in the suburbs. Kids, if you want."

Luc laughs. His face is his again. "You're crazy, you know that?"

"It's what you want, right?"

"I don't know," he says, shrugging. "Maybe, I guess . . ."

"So, promise that you'll go and do whatever you want, once you're a complete." I mean every word. Suddenly it seems important that he knows that. Luc's as good a brother as they come. He's genuinely nice, not seriously lacking in the brains department, and he can be pretty funny when he decides to be. Add in his height, the clean lines of his features, his dark hair and eyes, and Luc's got everything going for him. Only one last hurdle to overcome.

"Okay, okay." He throws his hands up. "I'll do my best. Not the part about getting fat, but everything else. But it goes both ways, you know."

"What, me? Marriage and kids?" To try to see myself as someone beyond the West I know, to see different depths to the features so familiar to me is . . . hard. Average height, on the skinny side, eyes the same brown as Luc's, long hair a shade closer to black. High cheekbones, rounded chin, a mouth that often says the wrong thing at the wrong time.

Now it's my turn to shrug. "I don't have a clue about any of—"

"No, not that," Luc says. "I mean, what you want to *do*. To be. Something to do with your art, maybe."

At his words, I automatically glance down at my hands, double-checking for any dried paint left under my nails, ink smeared between my fingers. But I did a good job cleaning them off earlier. Much better than normal—whether because of what was in store for today or because I was trying to keep one world from bleeding into the other, I'm not sure.

I clasp my hands together. Only after completing will I dare ask myself what I want.

"It doesn't mean I *know*," I finally say.

"And you're giving *me* a hard time?"

"I'm not," I protest. "It just seems like you have a better idea, that's all."

"Well, since I've already said yes, you have to promise *me* something," Luc says. "If *I* go first."

The very idea of him leaving me alone, the last of us left, is an instant punch of pain. I start folding and unfolding my paper napkin to keep my hands from clenching. "Fair's fair, so shoot."

"When you get your assignment . . . if things turn bad, and you feel like there's no way out . . . tell me you'll turn to Chord for help."

I blink up at Luc. "Chord? What are you talking about?" Chord is Luc's best friend, someone I've known for most of my life. He's never too far away for long, but for Luc to ask this—not just of me, but of Chord . . . "You're not talking about an Assist Kill, are you, Luc? You know it's not allowed. If the Board finds out—"

"No, I don't mean an AK," he says. His jaw's gone tight now, and he looks uncomfortable. "I'm talking about someone having your back, West. You're too stubborn for your own good, always thinking you can do everything alone. But for this, you know Chord wouldn't want you to keep him in the dark."

I frown at him. "Are you serious? You don't think I'm capable of defending myself? You know I'm nearly as accurate with a blade as you are."

"Don't kid yourself. You still need to practice. Your aim sucks."

"Hey, it doesn't suck *all* the time, but fine, I'll let you have that. As long as you admit I'm good with a gun." Better than good, even. Excellent.

A quick grin flashes across Luc's face. "You always were a fast learner. But it's not about that. I'm talking about the fact that having someone in your corner isn't a sign of weakness, okay? So if you need him, you'll ask. And you won't shut yourself off from everyone, like I think you'll want to do." He's thinking about Ehm's and Aave's deaths and how distance was what I sought out first.

"I don't do that," I lie.

"You do, West," he says. Not unkindly. "C'mon."

"I guess I can promise I won't *not* tell him."

He lifts an eyebrow at me, then laughs, shaking his head. "I guess that'll have to do."

The mention of Chord makes me realize he should be here by now.

"Where *is* he, anyway?" I ask Luc. "I know he was stopping by his place first but he's not usually this . . ."

The expression on Luc's face as he stares past me to the door leaves my words hanging. Only a handful of other times have I seen Luc look this way, a terrifying blend of shock and despair. And I know instantly that Chord is right behind me. The room seems to have shifted, the weight of what Chord now carries throwing everything off balance.

He's gotten his assignment.

I slowly turn to face him.

Tall and lanky with just enough muscle so that he's perfectly filled out. His face is all angles and planes, without a trace left of the softness he had a few years ago. Thick hair almost as dark as mine, a mix of his heritage of black and white and everything in between.

One look in his eyes and I've never been more devastated to know I'm right. Dark brown and shot through with bits of amber, just as they were when we parted mere hours ago. But now they're also the eyes of an Alt gone active, no longer an idle. Encoded on each pupil is a black spiral of tiny numbers. The sequence seems random, but their significance is huge—they are Chord's assignment number. And somewhere else in the city, within the heavily guarded borders of Kersh, his Alt has the exact same sequence encoded on his eyes. Eyes that are the same as Chord's, set in a face that's the same, on a body that's the same.

"Sorry I'm late." Chord drags out a chair and sits down at the table next to me. He's also still dressed in his blacks from my father's funeral, and he shoves his hands into the pockets of his pants as he leans back. His face is dark, already hunted. "I got . . . held up for a few minutes."

"No." The word bursts through the air so fast I don't realize at first that it came from me. "Not yet."

"No way," Luc says, his words harsh with disbelief. "Taje just—how could they—"

"The Board can't worry about that," Chord says. His voice is flat. "It's not a factor."

Taje was Chord's little brother. He died a couple of months ago, an incomplete at the age of thirteen. And Chord's right. The Board's system of activating assignments doesn't take into account their timeline within a family. The three of us right here are proof of that—Chord with Taje, me and Luc with Aave and Ehm. Names, ghosts, incompletes.

Bren is back with our food, and Chord only shakes his head when she asks him if he wants to order. As though sensing the tension surrounding the three of us, she's just as quick to leave this time as the last.

"Can I see it, Chord?" I ask him as soon as we're alone again.

He passes his cell to me without a word. I push my plate toward him as I tap open his assignment notice. The thought of eating has become impossible. My heart is racing too fast, the room closing in on me, bearing down so I can't breathe.

The details I bring up on the screen are eerily familiar— except it's Chord's name and address and assignment number this time, not those of my siblings. Dread uncoils in my gut and spreads outward as I scroll and read, rereading what's most vital.

> *Chord Reese Jameson*
> *Assignment Number: 462895103732*
> *Date/Time of Activation: 10/2/18:33*
> *Date/Time of Activation Expiration: 11/2/18:33*
> *Alternate's Point of Origin: 45990 Fireton Street, Jethro Ward*
>
> *Be the one, be worthy.*

The Board's logo is at the bottom: the profiles of two identical teenagers facing each other, their features carefully left androgynous, ambiguous, open to being anyone. Each eye is a black spiral.

Thirty-one days for Chord to kill his Alt before his Alt kills him. If neither one completes by the expiration date, they're both dead, the genetic timer in their shared embedded Alt code triggering it to self-detonate.

Chord's Alt's current address at the bottom. The PO—Point of Origin—is the one piece of information the Board freely gives to an Alt upon activation of an assignment. Just enough to get things started and still ensure there will be a decisive contest. Of course, Chord's Alt has the same information about him.

I scan his assignment again, taking it all in. Such simple sounds and letters strung together to create such life-altering news.

Time is our only advantage.

It's a hard stat that can't be ignored. The majority of fresh actives' responses are neither fight nor flight but freeze. Despite all the training, the initial combination of shock and fear still immobilizes people. Everyone secretly hopes they won't get their assignment until a month before their twentieth birthday, the last possible day to receive it—and sometimes they hope so hard they come to believe it can't be otherwise.

No guarantee Chord's Alt isn't one to break the mold, but odds are that he's sitting in his living room right now, assignment in hand, mind blown into inaction.

I pass the cell to Luc and turn to Chord. "Fireton's the boundary street that runs along the border, out on the east side of the ward," I say to him in a rush. "It wouldn't take us that long to get there, especially if we leave right now."

Chord exhales, swears. "Give me a minute, West. I'm still thinking about what to do."

I can feel my cheeks get hot. "You're *thinking*? Are you kidding me?"

His face is tight, closed off. "I'm right in the middle of packing up Taje's things. I was going to put them in storage; though for what, I have no clue. School admin needs all these documents signed and returned. I still have to talk to the parents of these friends of his, the ones who . . ." His voice trailing off, he turns the full force of his eyes on me. The numbers printed in their depths are jarring, alien, something I'll never get used to. But now I also notice the bags under his eyes, how pale he is, the way his cheekbones are sharper than they've ever been. "I'm wiped, West, okay?"

I swallow my anger and try to inject some give in my voice, when all I want to do is grab him by the hand and start running. "You know you can't just sit and wait for him. We've got to move."

"Not 'we,' West. Whatever I end up doing, you're staying out of it."

"And you're still in the clothes you wore to my father's funeral, Chord," I say to him pointedly. "No way you're leaving us behind so we go crazy with worrying." For a second, Luc's words about not pushing Chord away ring in my head. I made a half-assed promise, and now here I am, begging Chord to not push *me* away.

For a long second, he looks elsewhere, watching without seeing the other people in the restaurant. Most of them are over twenty and complete, the safe ones who aren't counting down the days, hours, minutes, wondering if their next bite will be their last.

"What if I told you a part of me just wants to go home, finish what I need to get done, and hope that fate's on my side when he gets there?" Chord says. His words are soft bullets of defeat, somehow more unsettling than hard anger or fear would have been.

"You'd be as good as incomplete then, wouldn't you?" I snap. "*This* is what you need to get done. What's the matter with you, Chord?"

"I'm just thinking that we don't always win."

"We don't always lose, either. And I'm not letting you give up."

"When *do* you give up, then?" His face is a stark, hard mask, turning him into someone else. "When your entire family's been killed? Is that when it'll finally get too hard for you, West? When Luc is gone, and you're all by yourself? Because I'm already there."

I draw back from his hopelessness, wincing. I haven't forgotten his parents' death in a car accident—but it was so long ago, when he wasn't more than a little kid, that I can't remember it being any other way. Since then, guardianship for him and his brother has been a revolving door of other relatives. Up until Chord turned fifteen, at least. At that age, he was finally allowed to take care of Taje himself.

"It gets easier, Chord," Luc says quietly, giving him back his cell. "About Taje, I mean."

Chord shuts his eyes. When he opens them again, my heart twists to see the memory there. "It was my fault," he says listlessly. "I should have known that school admin would never ask Taje to come back because he left something behind. You know how strict they are about not having assignments completed on school grounds. I should have known his Alt was behind it."

"It's not your—" Luc starts.

"Did I tell you his Alt killed two of his friends?" Chord continues, his guilt too loud to ignore. "They stepped in front of Taje, and his Alt cut them down like they were nothing. He didn't even care about racking up two Peripheral Kills, as long as he completed. It almost makes Taje seem responsible just for being his Alt, if that makes sense."

I nod. It does make sense. Fair or not, Alts are seen as a reflection of each other. It's our shared physical appearance, even if beneath the skin we're not entirely the same. Because if we share the genes that make our eyes the same color, our faces the same shape, our bodies the same type, then who knows how far the overlap goes? However different we are, the Board has meshed together both identities so tightly that it's impossible to see where one ends and the other begins.

"You have to know it doesn't change what we think of Taje," Luc says.

"It's not you guys," Chord says, his voice dull. "It's just . . . I don't know. I'm seventeen. I only had three years left for my assignment to happen, anyway. I knew it was coming. This is what we've been taught to expect. All the training in school, everything we're ever told, just for this one month." He shakes his head. Looks up at us with a bleak expression. "So why don't I care more?"

"Because you're an idiot," I say, struggling to keep my voice from breaking. I can't believe we're having this conversation.

I can't believe we're still in this stupid restaurant, when we should be on the road, racing toward his Alt. "Feeling guilty about Taje isn't going to change anything. And I think he'd be embarrassed that his big brother is copping out."

Chord's eyes flash at me. They've darkened with some nameless emotion, nearly black now, and it's a relief to not be able to see the numbers so easily. That they're almost normal reminds me that, assignment or no assignment, this is the same Chord I've known nearly my whole life—someone with a personality all his own, an identity that goes beyond being classified as just another active.

"West." Luc rubs his hand over his face. "West, just shut up."

"No, I won't. Someone has to wake him up. Or he's dead. Simple as that."

"*West—*"

"It's okay, Luc, let her finish." Chord's watching me so intently that something flexes in my chest, sharp, almost achy. "Whatever she says can't be worse than what I've already told myself."

"I know it's how the filtration system plays out," I say to him, trying to ignore that startling sensation, the unsettling fact of who's causing it. "That the stronger—better—Alt is supposed to win in the end. To be the one worthy of taking up space in Kersh and going all soldier out there in the Surround if it's ever needed. But if you don't even give him a good fight, then it's already over. And no way am I letting you go out like that. That's not who you are."

His eyes narrow, and he leans forward, getting closer to me. "And who is it you think I am, West Grayer?"

"Someone who's not supposed to die yet," I say, scowling at him.

A flicker of a smile on his lips. Not quite his own, but nearly. "If this is your way of telling me you'd miss me, I'll take it."

There's the sense of a weight being lifted—not a lot, but a bit—and I know Chord has turned some dark corner that exists only in his head. "All that to hear me say I'll miss you?" I push his foot with mine. "You could have just asked."

Now he's grinning for real, and the sight is almost enough to obliterate the panic running through me. Almost.

Luc's voice breaks the silence. "If you two are done, let's go."

Chord picks up his cell and gets to his feet. "You guys, you shouldn't come with me. Not after what just happened with your dad."

"You need a ride," Luc says mildly, making sure to leave enough cash on the table to cover the bill before standing. "Faster to get to the other side of Jethro than taking an inner ward train."

Chord looks from me to Luc. "You guys are coming no matter what I say, aren't you?"

"Yeah, sorry about that," Luc says. His grim determination is almost disguised by the lightness of his words. He would never let Chord go out there on his own. Chord is as much his brother as Aave was.

"Can't you guys walk and talk at the same time?" I call back to them, already on my way out the door of the restaurant.

It's impossible to miss what's happening across the street. The last stage of an assignment is nothing new, but I pause just the same. Surrounding the dead Alt for site cleanup are members of Jethro Ward's clearing crew. They work in sync, their movements a symphony just as the completion was, flagging the body with a red claim tag, the gun a white. Both will eventually be collected by family, once the Board signs off on the updates to the Alt log.

Luc and Chord come up behind me, and the three of us stand there for another moment, not needing to speak because we know we're all thinking the same thing. The death of an Alt only reminds us that we're still alive . . . for now. But when our turn comes—

I grab Chord's arm. "Let's go."

We're parked around the corner. It's Aave's beater, the one he somehow found time to work on between school, training, and helping our father fix machines out at the plants. Luc took over working on the car after Aave's death, spurred on by a kind of mad grief to finish what his big brother couldn't. Now that it's up and running, he takes care of it like nothing else.

We tear our way out of the Grid and through the streets of Jethro Ward, going against our instincts as we make our way closer to the border. The top edge of the gigantic electrified iron barrier that separates Kersh from the Surround looms high in the sky, a curving ridge of teeth. Pulsing red dots light up the city's night landscape, shrinking and blurring as they peter out into the distance. Strewn throughout the city, they mark the tops of gigantic silver pylons crisscrossed with power lines, the tips of the spinning arms of wind turbines, the edges of broadly sweeping solar panels. They're the veins and nerves that keep this whole place alive. Without them, all of Kersh's four wards—Jethro, Gaslight, Calden, and Leyton—would be cold and dark.

Even without the readings from Chord's cell's shadowing system, we can tell we're nearly there. Jethro is the city's designated industrial zone. It's filled with long, concrete factories, but out here along the eastern fringe of the ward, right where it butts up against the barrier that holds back the Surround, aging factories pump out as much exhaust as they do metal, plastic, and glass. Ugly warehouses built from rusted sheet metal fill the spaces in between, before eventually thinning out to crooked, jagged lots of run-down housing.

All around I can feel the sting of poverty, the ache of wanting more, the danger of the restlessness running throughout. The next time I get antsy in the Grid, the heart of Jethro Ward, I should come back here. The Grid's crowds that suffocate with the constant need to keep pushing, to keep moving, are nothing compared to this kind of life.

"Talk about depressing," Luc says from behind the wheel. He turns to Chord. "Just think—it could have been you out here."

Chord says nothing. I'm sure the thought has already crossed his mind. It has probably crossed the minds of everyone who lives within Kersh's borders.

When the universal cold vaccine had the nasty side effect of irreversible infertility, it was the Board who managed to keep the human race alive through a system of constant and carefully controlled biological intervention. But human nature has a way of disintegrating no matter how many chances it's given, and the world fell into war. An offshoot of the Board broke off, claimed the upper West Coast of North America as its own, and turned its back on everyone else. It called the massive gated city Kersh, the last war-free zone in the world.

The price of living here is high, though. In exchange for relative safety within, we have to be prepared for danger from without. The threat that the war in the Surround will break through to us is constant, always simmering just beneath the surface. So we're bred to be soldiers. Overcoming a city of killers would not be an easy task.

Since the city is closed off to the rest of the world, limiting space and resources, only the best of us are wanted. The Board, in their genius, created Alts, manipulating genes so two identical children are born to two sets of parents. Each couple is tasked with the duty of raising the best killer, the best survivor. Because when their child's assignment kicks in—which happens anytime between the ages of ten and twenty—both active Alts must hunt each other down until only one remains. It's the ultimate survival-of-the-fittest test, allowing only those capable of killing to go on to become adults in Kersh.

All for peace. Fighting ourselves in here, so we don't have to fight the world out there.

Suddenly a flame lights the night sky, turning everything bright crimson for one glorious, suspended instant, before dying away. The echo of it sizzles and hisses, lasting a heartbeat longer. Even inside the car with the windows rolled up, I swear I can taste smoke on my tongue.

"It always looks so nice, don't you think?" I search the darkness for any last lingering light, oddly uneasy to see it go. "When the Surround sets off test flares?"

"Yeah, I guess," Luc says. "Until you remember what they're used for over there."

Signals of distress.

Another flare bursts to life before burning out. The deception of its beauty is nearly cruel.

Chord's cell dings. He glances at the screen before putting the cell in his pocket. "Right at the end of the block, Luc," he says, sounding as tense as I feel.

"Which house?" Luc asks.

"The corner one, left."

I sit up in my seat as Luc pulls over to the far curb and cuts the engine. After the sound of the flares, the quiet is almost too loud.

The house is no different from any of the others around it: gravel patch for a driveway, peeling roof shingles, sagging porch. Though some of the streetlamps are burnt out, I can still see the dingy stains of black factory exhaust streaking the cheap stucco walls. Grim fingerprints, a signature of the way people keep afloat out here.

The air has my nerves tingling. I don't like it. Sometimes such hunger and desperation sparks an even stronger kind of internal drive, one that goes beyond any kind of training. Having little more than a basic ability to handle weapons isn't going to be a problem when something deeper helps you aim your gun, swing your blade, use your fists. Completing means finally being able to grasp what the Board holds just out of reach:

higher education, better-paying jobs, permission to marry and have a family.

I'm strung so tightly I feel like I'm about to snap. Luc and Chord are the same, shoulders stiff with clenched muscle. We're wired on a heightened mix of fear and anticipation. Is this what every assignment feels like? That last second before jumping off a ledge to somewhere unknown?

In the shadowed darkness, Chord utters a short command. "Time." His watch beeps out the answer.

23:00.

"Think he's already sleeping?" he asks.

Luc is staring at the house. "There's no lights in the windows. At least, not through the blinds."

Chord frowns, thinking. "We don't know who else is in there with him."

"Nope. No idea. But he's pretty much you, isn't he? Seventeen, living at home with his family, a student—well, not as of today, I guess. But even if he's decided to co-op somewhere, those jobs usually start in the morning. And chances are good he hasn't gotten around to arranging somewhere else to crash yet."

"If he's not alone in there . . ." Chord doesn't need to finish. He's thinking about Taje's friends, the ones who got caught in the crossfire.

"There's nothing you can do about that," Luc says. His voice reveals nothing, but the memory of our mother circles. She was a PK, too, in the wrong place at the wrong time last fall, hit by a stray bullet at the grocery store. I push the image of her body away. Her being dead can't keep Chord from doing what he needs to do.

Clutching the back of Chord's seat and aiming for a calm I don't feel, I say, "If he's not alone, then he's not alone."

"One-story house, three bedrooms at the most," Luc says, running it down. "Window in the front is the living room, the smaller one next to that probably the kitchen or dining room." He cranes his head to see. "And the one at the side is frosted."

"The bathroom," I say. Like all houses in Kersh, the windows are plain glass, not the bulletproof type businesses are allowed to install to prevent damage during a completion.

"We'll go around back to where his bedroom must be," Luc says. "We might luck out and find an open window. Otherwise, it's the back door." He looks at me in the rearview mirror. "Like we agreed, you stay here. As soon as you see us, start the car."

I can feel my face go stiff. "Actually, we didn't agree. You guys decided."

"Same thing."

"You don't need me to be ready to take off. It's not like anyone's going to chase you guys down afterward for an RK. The Board would never let that slide."

Revenge Kills became so rampant a few decades ago that the Board had to step in. RKs undermine the reason for assignments and the filtration system as a whole, and for an Alt to win only to be mowed down later is seen as a huge waste. Alts who complete their assignments are stronger, smarter, and more skilled—they're supposed to stay alive, just as the weaker, dumber, and less skilled are supposed to die. If someone pulls an RK today, the Board sends a harsh message by shutting all doors: no chance of job advancement, no marriage, no kids. So not much chance that Chord's Alt's family or friends would seek revenge, but I will argue whatever I can to make Luc and Chord let me help.

"West, you're not coming in, and that's it," Luc says, brushing me off. "Besides, I only have one gun."

"Even one gun's too many," I protest. Assist Kills—accidental or not—are punished just the same as RKs. There are EKs, too, the rarest of all unnatural completions. Early Kills are when two Alts happen to meet as idles, before their assignments, and one or the other decides to go for completion. Enough of these happening at the same time and Kersh wouldn't be much different than the Surround, so punishment for AKs, RKs, and EKs is swift.

"You know you can't use a gun," I say.

Luc lifts one eyebrow. "Neither can you."

"Then give it to Chord. It's too risky for you to have it."

"You think I should give the gun to Chord? He's the worst shot in Kersh." Luc looks at Chord.

"Thanks, bud," Chord says.

Luc shrugs, grins. "Sorry, but you know you're way better with a blade." He glances at me in the rearview mirror again. "We don't know what we're walking into. It can't hurt to have the gun with me, even if I only end up using it to scare someone else off."

"So I'm the getaway driver." I hate how I sound. Sulky, childish, whining. But I don't want to be useless. Haven't I already been useless enough, with so many people I care about dying?

"Yeah, exactly." Luc swings the car door open. Takes off his watch and passes it back to me. "Here. So you don't have to keep checking your cell."

"You don't need a driver!" I hiss at his back, tossing the watch up onto the dash. "I'm not even supposed to be driving."

"It's never stopped you before, when I didn't say anything about you sneaking out for a joyride and Mom and Dad didn't happen to notice."

"What if I said I'm starting to feel bad about breaking the law?"

Luc exhales, and I know he's itching to strangle me. "West, listen. I don't want you in there because I don't want you getting hurt, okay? We can't be worrying about you the whole time."

"How very macho, Luc," I mutter.

"Fine. Then you'll just get in the way. How's that for a good reason?"

"I can take care of myself." Why can't he see that just sitting here, waiting for him and Chord to come out alive, is going to drive me insane?

"I know you can. Stay here." With that, Luc steps out of the car and into the night, leaving me to swear at the back of his head.

Chord turns and gives me a smile. It barely reaches his eyes, his mind already racing ahead, already inside the house.

"Don't be so pissed off that you leave without us, okay?" he says. "It's a long walk home from here."

My frustration is nothing in the face of Chord's fear, and soon enough my own dread is back, making my heart thud.

"Well, don't keep me waiting, then," I say evenly. It's like holding on to a ledge and pretending my fingers aren't in agony. "Luc wasn't exaggerating about me sneaking out with the car, you know."

He reaches in, about to playfully mess up my hair the way

he always does. But then at the last second, he hesitates, brushing the nearly black strands from my cheek instead. "I wish you hadn't come, but I'm glad you did," he finally says.

He's gone before I can say anything.

I climb up into the front seat for a better view. I'm not the tallest girl around, so I can't see much over the hood; Luc's pushed the seat way back to make room for his much longer legs. Still annoyed, I yank it as far forward as it'll go.

There. Now to wait. And not think.

Which is impossible. Like trying to quiet my thoughts when they're already awake and shouting at me. Letting Luc and Chord walk away is one of the hardest things I've ever had to do.

It hasn't always been just me and Luc. Our parents went to the Board four times. First for Aave, then Luc, then me, and finally Ehm. Not a typical size for a Kersh family—which usually has two children—but my parents never could measure us in terms of cost, only in the benefits of our being given the chance to grow up.

Aave was the first of us to go. He bled to death behind Slinger's, a club in the Grid that had no problem serving underage actives; the alcohol in his system had dulled his exceptional blade skills and made them merely ordinary. And Ehm . . . I thought I could handle anything after the shock of Aave's death, but her death brought me to my knees. Part of it was the fact that she was only eleven, just a year to really prepare herself for her assignment. But her Alt had been so quick, faster than even Luc and I had been ready for, and Ehm had had her own plans. So while we were figuring out the best way for Ehm to safely complete, her Alt caught her sneaking out of the house to go to her best friend's sleepover party.

She bled out in my arms, and I remember screaming so loudly that Chord came running from his house down the block. He crashed to the ground on the street next to me and grabbed me in a hug and didn't let go. Even after Luc took Ehm from me, Chord didn't let go—

A dog barks, shattering the silence and the drowning pull of my memories. A man yells at it to shut up.

I look around uneasily. Which house is the barking coming from? Not the Alt's, I don't think. If Luc and Chord have been spotted, it's more than barking that I should be hearing.

"Time," I ask out loud.

Luc's watch beeps out the answer: *23:15* already. Not long, but still too long.

Scenario after scenario plays out of my mind's eye, none of them good. What are Luc and Chord doing in there? What's taking them so long? Shouldn't they be back by now?

To keep my hands busy, I strap on Luc's watch, fiddle with the car's mirrors, crank open the window for fresh air.

There's a muffled echo of voices. I can't make out any words, only the rhythms and beats of what sound like shouts.

They're coming from Chord's Alt's house.

I don't even give myself a chance to consider what I'm doing before I hurtle from the car, leaving the door swinging open behind me. No time to care.

In the moonlight, the prickly lanceweeds that make up the front lawn are a mottled gray and black. They catch on my sneakers, my ankles, little swords in their own right, trying to keep me back. Panic is sharp and metallic in my mouth, and it chases me until I reach the back of the house. Where Luc and Chord went.

Through the filtered darkness, I see a patch of a yard, beaten down with neglect. A sad tire swing hangs from the low arm of a thin, scraggly tree; its branches are claws, its trunk a hunkered threat of a body. There is a tricycle in the far corner, half-buried in some stiff grass.

Kids. There are *kids* here.

Alarm floods me. In my head I see Chord's tormented face again; I hear him tell us about what happened to Taje's friends, how they were PKs.

Luc, Chord, did you see? Did you know, when you went inside?

The voices are louder here behind the house, an angry cacophony of sound. They flow out from the crack that separates the back door from its frame. It's unlocked and open.

So I do the only thing I can do. I step up, nudge the door open a bit more, and slide right in.

Dark inside. The air is stuffy and smells like sleep. The scale of everything is too cramped, angles and corners and furniture wherever my eyes touch down. Only my ears tell me something is happening.

There. It's coming from the room down the hall.

It takes me an eternity to cover the few feet that lie between where I came in and the bedroom doorway. When I get there, I see it all, a flash of a nightmare lit by cool moonlight streaming in through open blinds.

A threadbare carpet. Stale bedsheets dotted with cigarette burns and stains. A collection of dirty needles on the bedside table. And people—too many people stuffed into too small a space.

Luc is sprawled on the ground on his back, the handle of a blade sticking out of his side. He's holding his gun in his hands. It's pointed right at Chord's Alt, who's standing in the middle of the room. The Alt's gun is pointed right back at Luc. And Chord, standing behind *him,* his arm clotheslined around his Alt's neck. With his free hand, Chord's pressing the tip of his switchblade into a face too much like his own. Except the eyes are harder, the body addict-thin and running on nothing but pure adrenaline and whatever was in those needles.

"Let me go, or he's as good as dead!" The Alt's voice is a smoker's, rough and guttural . . . but still too much like Chord's. His eyes don't waver from Luc. His hands don't shake. It's the worst kind of courage, built on pills, powders, heated crystals. It doesn't know fear or doubt.

Luc's face is harsh and furious. "Don't, Chord! Don't listen to him!"

The Alt's snarl of a laugh chills me to the bone. It's horrible to hear nuances of Chord in there.

"Time's running out for you, man," Chord's Alt says to Luc. "Look at you. You're bleeding out."

"I have more than enough time to kill you first."

"And make this an AK? Nah, man. You won't go there." The Alt shakes his head in disgust. "Then your life would *really* be over."

"Then I have nothing left to lose, do I?" Luc says. He sounds so calm. How is he so calm?

"So do it. What are you waiting for? Do it!"

"Shut up!" Chord's yell booms throughout the room. With

a flick of his wrist, he slides the blade up to his Alt's temple. "Put the gun down. *Now.*"

"I'll get the first shot off before you can even think about it!" his Alt snaps.

Chord twists the blade, angles it just so. The gesture is almost elegant. *"Put it down."*

A sudden, soft swish against my hip shocks me into taking a breath.

It's a little boy. No more than five or six. Clad in pajamas, his hair wild from sleep, something in his face pulls at the strings of familiarity. Then I realize what it is. He reminds me of Taje, Chord's little brother. In fact, he resembles both Taje and Chord—which in a weird way makes perfect sense.

The next few seconds are chaos.

The boy takes a tentative step into the room.

Instinctively, I reach out to stop him. "No, don't!" I shout. My voice is too thin, too high. The hysteria in it makes all of them turn to stare at me. The expressions on Luc's and Chord's faces are of stunned confusion.

"West?" Luc's eyes widen, shining in the moonlight. His arms drop an inch, his gun now off its aim by a mere fraction. "What are you— *Get out of—*"

He's not able to finish, the warning falling from his lips. Because that's when Chord's Alt squeezes the trigger.

The bullet lodges with dull finality inside Luc's chest.

"Luc!" I hear myself scream. His name is the only thing in my head. *"Luc!"*

In the half light, Chord's face convulses. His eyes go hot

with a pain so great that they're nearly crazed. He doesn't even seem to be breathing as he pulls his Alt's head up by the hair and, before his Alt can begin to bring his gun around, draws the blade across his neck.

A whistle of a scream followed by the sound of blood pouring down on the carpet like rain.

Chord drops his Alt's body to the floor. And then together we're at Luc's side.

Luc's gasps seem to be coming from the depths of him. Blood blooms on his chest, spreading wildly across the floor beneath him. His face is bleached to the color of bone.

"Luc," I sob. This isn't happening. It can't be. We did everything right. It's not supposed to end this way. I crush my palm on top of the wound, only knowing that I'm supposed to put pressure on it. But one look at Chord tells me it's hopeless. The shot was too accurate, its path too destructive.

Luc pushes my hand from his chest. Presses his gun into my palm. Holds it there until I have no choice but to accept it.

"Be careful with it . . . West," he gasps. A ghost of a grin. "You always did . . . move too fast."

It feels too heavy to lift, the fit more cumbersome than I remember. When the time comes, will I be able to use it on my Alt? To not hesitate, even for a second?

"I was too late." Chord's eyes are hollow and dazed. No longer marked by his assignment number. They're his own again. "Luc, I was too late."

"No, man, you did good," Luc whispers. "And you're . . . safe now." Red foam lines his mouth, and he coughs weakly.

The bullet must have hit his lung, too, I think. But the

thought is faint and unimportant and passes like it never was. It won't help.

"Be there for her, okay?" Luc says to Chord. "When she needs you." A hitch of breath.

Chord nods. "I won't forget."

"Love you, Luc," I say. It's all I can do to keep my voice steady. I swipe at the tears that make it hard to see, angry at their existence, their uselessness. "You hear me?"

He coughs again. More red froth. "Got it, West." A huge gasp for air. "Love you, too."

Then he dies.

Chord grabs me as I'm keeling over, wanting to absorb whatever pain of mine that he can take on top of his own. Whatever I'm willing to give up.

Time passes in meaningless chunks, blurs of nothing that makes sense. It might be seconds or minutes or hours. In a different city, a different world, it might not have happened at all.

Numb. A dim awareness that the little boy is still sitting over Chord's Alt, his small hand covered in blood as he tries to wipe his brother's neck clean.

I help Chord with Luc's body. Drape him over Chord's shoulder in a fireman's carry. Except Luc can't be saved now.

And then we're leaving. Stumbling out from the shadow of the house and onto the street and into the car. Trying to leave behind everything that just happened and knowing there's no way we can.

CHAPTER 2

The house is empty. But their ghosts haunt the halls and fill the rooms, their voices echo in my ears.

It's two days after Luc's funeral and already I'm lost.

I'm still lying on the couch. I've slept, woken, slept again. I feel as drugged as Chord's Alt must have been. Not that electric, strung-out high, but a kind of thick, grieving sluggishness. Which one's more of an escape, I don't know.

My cell buzzes. I know it's Chord, but I answer it anyway. I can only avoid him for so long.

"Hello?" The word is dry, rusty. It's so strange not having Luc around to talk to anymore.

"Hey, West."

My throat clenches at the sound of Chord's voice. "Hey."

"I wanted to come by earlier, but I thought maybe you were still asleep."

"I was." A pause. "I kind of still am." *Then I can pretend none of this is real. That I didn't play a hand in his death . . . that it wasn't your Alt that killed him.*

"How about I come pick you up, head out into the Grid

for a bit? Whatever you want to do. Lunch, maybe?" Chord's voice is soft, careful not to say something that'll send me away. He knows me too well, having seen both the best and worst of me over the years. I can't help but think of Luc's words from that day in the restaurant, when he made me promise to keep Chord in my life.

The sudden thought that they might have talked about this earlier makes my gut churn. Half of me is pissed off at them for thinking I'm that helpless; the other half wonders bleakly if maybe they're right.

"No, I don't think so, Chord," I say evenly. "I'm just . . . cleaning the house now. Luc's room." A lie; his room hasn't been touched at all. I haven't been able to go in there yet. But it's the first thing that comes to mind, and anything is better than telling Chord what I've really been doing. Namely, nothing. Haunting the house along with the others, here but not here.

"I can help you," he says, sounding painfully hopeful. "Or just keep you company."

"No, that's okay."

A pause. "You've got to eat, don't you? I bet you're living off . . . I don't know, crackers or dry cereal or something like that."

I can't remember the last time I ate. My stomach still hurts, has ever since Chord began to haltingly deliver Luc's eulogy. "I'm fine. I can cook, you know." Barely, though. Not that I care much right now.

"West." His worry for me is obvious, even through my cell, across the physical distance. "I'd like to see you, okay?"

I shut my eyes tight, and Chord's face fills my mind. It's

changed, somehow. From the one I've known forever to the one that now draws me in, calling me closer, telling me there's more to uncover.

When did it change?

Then his face is his Alt's, the face of Luc's killer, and my eyes flare open.

"West?" Chord says my name again, more roughly this time. "C'mon, I can be there in five—"

"No, Chord, not now. I'll talk to you tomorrow."

He sighs. "You're going to school, then." Not a question but a confirmation. As if asking would make me realize it wasn't necessarily a given. At fifteen, I could opt out. Co-op . . . somewhere. I haven't given school any thought—work, even less. But what else would fill my hours now?

"Yeah, I'll be there," I tell him. "See you." And with that I disconnect.

Silence in the house again, too loud with the fullness of the past. Chord was right, I do need to get out. But not with him, not yet. I'm scared that if I see him right now, it won't be him I'll be seeing.

I leave the house, shutting the front door behind me. I start walking, though I don't exactly know where I'm going. But old habits die hard, and next thing I know I'm blocks and blocks away, back in the Grid.

Bodily, my family lived in our house in the western suburbs of Jethro Ward, but a part of our hearts always stayed behind in the streets of the Grid, holding our place for us, awaiting our return. As the ward's ground zero, its true epicenter, it spreads out over an area just shy of one square mile. The Grid has a life of its own. It has no patience with the slow or naïve. It makes no allowances and stops for no one. The four of us honed our instincts out here, as much our playground as our pretend battlefield. Preparing us.

I look up at the building in front of me.

Kersh's public library, where the city's largest collection of old paper books is stored. Half of the books are actually remnants from the Surround, the Board having claimed them as their own before permanently sealing the border's iron barrier. There's talk about moving them into private Board quarters before long. And even though the public still has access to them, most people don't touch paper books—not when stores stock flexi-readers that can bend without breaking and fold down to the size of your palm. Besides, paper books smell like the past, an alien world.

A brass plate next to the front doors is etched with block letters that are discreet and tasteful, the authoritative voice behind them impossible to miss: REMEMBER FOR YOUR SAFETY AND WELL-BEING DO NOT INTERFERE WITH ANY COMPLETION THAT IS NOT YOUR OWN THANK YOU THE BOARD.

The scents of age and dust assail my nose as soon as I enter. As always, I'm both comforted and confused. The stories bound in paper and ink have always given me a sense of peace, and it's jarring to realize they come from the war-torn Surround.

But I'm not here to lose myself in a story. Not today. That would be asking for the impossible.

By the time I'm upstairs in the Alternate History section,

deep in the stacks, I'm crying silently, blind with hot tears and sudden desperation. Trying to find an answer to a question already decided, a way to change what can't be changed.

Why did they have to leave me all alone? Why am I still here?

The first book falls to the ground with a thump. Then the second. It doesn't matter that I'm not being careful with them, the way I usually am. Not when people haven't been careful with what belongs to me.

I can't stop pulling down the books. They land on and around my feet, a pile of information that has failed me. It's a history that has yet to end, in fact is still happening, will continue to happen.

A hand grabs mine. Stops it from yanking the next book down.

I look up, glaring with burning eyes and trembling mouth. *Who—*

It's a man. Standing over me, with a solid build that leaves no doubt as to his physical strength. Not the kind that comes from bulk or weight, but a fast-moving, compact one. Closely shaved hair the color of rust, skin pitted with faded slashes and scars. Though his features are hard with what has to be annoyance, his pale blue eyes are full of something else. Something very close to sorrow . . . and even closer to understanding.

"Hold on, now," he says in a low voice. "You're making quite the mess, don't you think?"

I rip my hand from his grip. "Yeah. So?"

"Mrs. Silas downstairs won't be too happy if she sees this. Might be about time to start setting this right."

"I will—when I'm done."

A drawn-out sigh. "And you're far from done, aren't you?"

I kick a book across the aisle, wincing and yet enjoying the way it scrapes across the splintery wood floor, the way the ancient cover is getting even more beat-up.

"You have the look of your brothers," he says, startling me.

My brothers? What does this man have to do with them? "What?"

"Exactly what I said. You look like your brothers."

I bend down and begin to pick up the books. Anything to get him to stop talking to me. To just leave me alone. Whatever he thinks he knows, I've never seen him before in my life.

"Aave was a student in my weaponry class," he continues. "For both years four and five. And Luc, of course. Can I assume I'll be seeing you in my classroom soon?"

By now I'm staring at him. So he's the weaponry teacher at Torth Prep, then. And I know his name is Baer—everyone knows his name. Not just because he runs the most popular class at school, but because of his reputation. The strongest complete in all of Torth, and maybe even all of Kersh. The legend is that he killed his Alt with his bare hands at the age of ten. That he was so cool afterward he stuck around for the clearing guys just to see them take the body away.

As a year three student, with most of my friends the same, I don't spend much time in the older year wings. There's no reason why I *would* have recognized him. But now I can see for myself why his class is so popular. It's the look in his eyes as he glares down at you. Like you are finally going to learn how to fight—or die trying. End of story.

"One more," I say.

"Say again?"

"One more year before I can do weaponry. I'm still in year three."

"One more year." Baer's eyes glitter like ice. "Perhaps you'll have found a better use for your anger by then. It doesn't seem as though combat is doing the job as an outlet."

I scowl, hating that I'm so easily baited. "You might have been my brothers' teacher, but you're not mine. Yet."

A hint of a smile. "Well, not yet, that's true."

I say nothing. The conversation is going nowhere. I'm just waiting for him to realize that, as I already have. The pile of books in my arms is growing heavier by the second, and I turn to put them back on the shelf.

"And will you be ready?" Baer asks.

I force a book to fit between two others, not caring if it isn't in the exact right spot. This whole half of the shelf is dedicated to Alternate History, anyway, so I can't be that far off.

"None of those books will help you much, when it comes down to it," he says.

I don't turn to him, just put another book away. If I ignore him for long enough, then he'll have to leave, won't he? Won't we have to deal with each other enough once I'm actually his student?

Baer plucks the top book off the pile I'm still holding and eyes the cover without opening it. His hands are even more scarred than his face. Now that I know who he is, I realize all the marks are battle scars—signatures of years spent teaching others how to fight for their lives.

"This one here?" He holds the book up: *The Cold Vaccine:*

What Went Wrong. "Dull as dirt. There's over a hundred damned pages on what could have gone wrong with the vaccine. Could it have been something in the stabilizer? The particular purification method? A faulty isolation technique?" He shakes his head. "Who cares? Too late." He shoves the book onto the shelf and grabs the next one off the pile in my arms.

"This one?" *Revival of the Gladiator Games.* "Sure, it talks a bit about how they did it back then, when people were pitted against each other for sport and glory. But quick enough it goes on about how the Board has brought those games back to life on a whole new scale. No puny stadium here; instead we get a battlefield as big as this city. How the Board has decided that it must be children who do this, so we can flush out the weak before they grow up and waste our resources and time."

I stare at him. Afraid of interrupting him . . . afraid of *not* interrupting him.

"So only the strongest survive, the smartest, the ones best able to complete. To shape us into a society of killers, all in the name of self-defense." Baer slides *Revival of the Gladiator Games* onto the shelf next to the first book.

He's not done. He's on a roll, pushed along by resentment, disgust. He grabs *Mechanics Behind the Alternate Code.* Baer looks at me from the corner of his eye. "Now, this one's required reading. Worse than watching paint dry, I bet."

I can't help it. My lip twitches. "Yeah, it was pretty boring."

Learning about Alt codes is about as much fun as any in-depth bio or chem or math course in school. Unless you're really into it, it's just another class to get through. When parents want a baby, the Board accesses their individual gene maps and draws up a new, combined one. The next couple that comes in goes through the same procedure. Then the Board takes the gene maps of both babies and creates what is called an Alt code. A synthetic genetic material, it directs the genes responsible for physical traits to match up. In this way, Alts are like twins. It makes it easy for Alts to find each other—they just have to look for their own face.

But often the Alt code oversteps its parameters and talks to other genes, too, so two Alts could have similar reflexes, brain patterns, language proficiencies. To fight yourself and find a way to win is the greatest challenge for any soldier.

Baer tosses *Mechanics Behind the Alternate Code* aside. He picks up *Through the Years: The Origins of Alts.* "Drivel." *Fight Your Alt with Heart, Soul & Spirit.* "Holistic tripe."

It seems wrong, but I can feel a bubble of laughter start up in my chest.

He has *Beyond the Board: Analyzing Assignments* in his hands now. "Complete and utter *garbage.* Can't be said enough about that—"

A shout bursts through the room, followed by the thud of many footsteps. They're heading our way, coming so fast I know we aren't going to be able to avoid it. A completion about to take place. Here in the Grid, where the number of people alone has the odds working against you, there's no way you can stay for any substantial period of time and *not* witness one.

The humor of the moment is instantly replaced by irritation. "I guess Mrs. Silas is going to have bigger things to complain about today," I say to Baer.

I slide the remainder of the books into the gap on the shelf. Done, I drop back against the stack, trying to shrink, disappear. Automatically doing what was drilled into our heads as kids if we are caught near crossfire: Fall Down and Fade Out. FDFO—or, get as low as possible and shut up.

Shots fire. Footsteps pound. Shelves sway. Books drop.

Baer barely flinches, just continues to stand in the middle of the aisle. His cool eyes are distant with listening, and his arms are crossed in front of his chest.

"You should get out of the way," I tell him. The words are urgent and annoyed. "You're going to get hurt. FDFO, remember?"

"I won't get hurt."

A sudden crash on the other side of the stack I'm leaning against makes me jump up.

"See?" he says, raising one eyebrow. "They're over there."

I drop into a crouch again. Fine. If he wants to stand there, let him. It's not my fault if something happens. But I can't do that. Not getting out of the way is the same as volunteering for target practice.

One of them is grunting in pain as his Alt stabs and grazes, stabs and nicks. Just not enough to finish the job. Then there's the sharp crack of a shot, and the other Alt screams. Blood begins to seep past the metal feet of the stack and toward me. I back away from it, but it keeps coming and coming, a living thing that doesn't want to stop until it touches something else alive.

The bullet has hit a nest of arteries, but not vital ones. It'll take a long while for him to bleed out. Now it's a race against time and a question of whose blood flows the fastest. I have no clue which way it's going to go.

"Will they get on with it?" Baer says. He rocks back and forth on his heels impatiently. "Shameful if they're any students of mine."

I don't think they hear him, but it doesn't last for too much longer. The one with the gun eventually manages to get a clean shot off, and with that, it's one more completion for the Board's books. I can hear the squeak of sneaker soles as the surviving Alt makes sure the other is dead. Then the complete stumbles off, the victor of this particular battle between Alternates.

I glance over at Baer. Wondering if I can just leave now, or if that would be rude. The scent of blood from the next aisle is strong enough to make me feel a bit sick.

"There is much to be learned when it comes to weapons," Baer says quietly, now also sidestepping the blood on the ground. "Learning to wield one properly—to maximize efficiency and minimize pain—is what's useful. All this history"—an abrupt gesture toward the books that surround us—"will not change that. *Learning* all this history will not change that. All this has no more need to be heard than bedtime reading when you're already half-asleep and no longer listening." And with that he nods his head. "Good-bye, West Grayer."

My eyes narrow in surprise. How does he—

"I make a point of knowing all my students' names," he says, obviously seeing my confusion.

"I'm not your student," I tell him again.

"Not yet, as you said." He frowns, and then says casually enough, "But I don't think admin would have a problem if a potential student wanted a . . . preview of the class."

My mouth drops open. "Me?"

"Tomorrow after school, year five wing." He starts walking away.

"Hey, I haven't even said yes yet."

Baer turns back to me. "You don't have to. Your answer's on your face. But if you change your mind, I won't hold it against you." He takes a few more steps before coming to a stop again. He looks back, says, "I'm sorry about your brothers. They were good kids."

He walks away and disappears around the corner, gone as quickly as he appeared. Leaving me alone with a dead Alt, shelves of reference materials, and new questions.

Luc.

For just a bit I was able to forget about him. As if he didn't die, his assignment yet to be completed. But Baer's parting words gouge the wound open, and grief makes my stomach ache again . . . even as my mind struggles to clear.

Weaponry. Tomorrow.

I walk home slowly in the settling dusk, the swirl of leaves rushing around my ankles, crunching beneath my feet. Luc's face is still with me, same as Ehm's, always in the shadows, never gone no matter how bright the sun shines. I wonder when my heart will stop hurting with each punishing beat. When my lungs will start taking a full breath again, so I won't feel like I am drowning anymore.

Students are still trickling out of Baer's classroom by the time I get there the next day after school. It's a year five class; other than those who were friends with Luc, I recognize no one.

They walk past me, and I skim each face from the corner of my eye, wondering what it must be like to know you're only counting down the days now. Getting older, getting closer to twenty.

I can hear Baer's rumble of a voice from inside the classroom, calling for all weapons to be handed in before leaving for the day. Metal and steel clang against each other.

I hate waiting, and even more, I hate that I'm nervous. I tuck my hands deep into my pockets so I can't fidget with the straps of my bag anymore.

What if I'm nothing like my brothers? What if I'm not nearly as good as Luc told me I was? What if Baer says, Don't bother, you're obviously the weaker Alt, there's no point?

The last student is leaving, and I make myself move closer to the doorway, just so I can shut up the doubts in my mind.

"So you made it," Baer says from his desk.

He's as intimidating as he was yesterday, maybe even more so beneath the bright lights, his scars all the more vivid. And he's holding a sword in his hand. Three feet of polished steel. Another one sits in front of him on top of his desk.

"Those might not be exactly Board approved." My voice is stiff, awkward.

"I checked. Swords aren't mentioned anywhere in the rules." He brandishes it in front of him, as if testing the blade.

"That's because an active walking down the street with a sword strapped to their side would kind of freak people out. I think the Board knows by now that most Alts want to avoid being noticed."

"True. Not all audiences would appreciate such a show."

Bystanders are a pretty big concern for the Board. Guns and an accurate eye are encouraged over heavy fists and brute force. Always the goal is efficiency, not prolonged or unnecessary pain. A distant second to guns is knives or any kind of weapon made up of a blade. Last is hand-to-hand combat; though lethal if done properly, it can get messy, almost personal. I wonder if it's ever occurred to the Board that an assignment itself is about as personal as it gets.

"So what's with the swords, then?" I ask, feeling stupid, beginning to doubt my decision to come now. I was expecting . . . well, I'm not sure what I was expecting, but not this.

"As beautiful as they are, they're still made to kill. So why not swords?" His look instantly makes me defensive.

"It just seems kind of pointless," I say slowly. "I mean, they make guns and knives available to us for our assignments." Sales of any such weapons in Kersh are tightly controlled, but it's usually no questions asked with the scan of an active's encoded pupils during purchase.

"Learning how to use a weapon is never pointless," Baer says. "Each one of them helps with reflexes, coordination, muscle strength. At all times, you'll need the three to defeat your Alt." He holds the sword out to me, hilt first, obviously expecting me to take it.

I do.

The smooth arc of metal in my hand is heavier than it appears, and I peer down the length of it, marveling at the sleek craftsmanship, the balance of its lines.

Baer picks up the sword on his desk. Slightly longer than mine, the shiny edge just as sharp. His face is as harsh as ever, but a smile twists one side of his mouth up. "Care for a test, West Grayer?"

I stare at him. "You're serious, aren't you?" But I already doubt he can be anything else as I toss my bag onto a desk behind me. With both hands, I grasp the soft leather-covered hilt more tightly.

His eyes have gone even paler with concentration. "I didn't invite you here to help me organize my classroom materials. Head up."

He slices the air between us, the sound of the blade a whoosh in the air, and it's all I can do to fend off flashes of caught light and twisting silver. The world narrows to nothing more than Baer and the thin screaming rasp of steel against steel. I can hear my breathing; I can smell my sweat, sharp and clean and proof that I'm doing my best not to die. I'm moving more by reflex than skill, no time to think between defensive slashes.

"Speed up your recovery," he barks. "It leaves you wide open."

As I joust around Baer's sword, I begin to form an attack of my own. But it's like trying to skewer a fast-moving animal, with a sword that's growing heavier and heavier with each passing second. My arms are soon aching with effort.

How is Baer making this look so easy?

Suddenly he steps back. Lets go of his sword with his right hand, so only his left is wielding it. "Now, just your left arm."

I push my hair back, sweating, both of us knowing my left side is my weakest. "You're crazy, I can't do that."

"Your Alt won't be so generous as to give you a warning. Remember that." He lunges, his blade coming within inches of my neck.

"Watch it—" The words are a stutter on my lips as I scramble to adjust my grip in my already cramping left hand.

Another jab. "Again, will your Alt give you such an allowance?" Baer's voice is made of the same kind of steel as our swords. "This is your life on the line, Grayer."

And we dance, the clang of hammered blades echoing throughout the classroom, each one a reminder of how close we are to death.

"You're trying to kill me, remember, not tickle me with the damn thing!" Baer yells at me, when my sword makes one too many wild swings.

"I'm using my left arm!" I shout back at him as he swings. "What do you expect?" I circle him, my arm on fire, my chest one flaming knot.

Baer stops short. Doesn't even flinch as my sword barely misses his shoulder. His face is stone cold. "I expect you to do whatever it is you need to do to kill your Alt. As you should expect the same of her." He lets his arm fall to his side, his sword at rest.

I do the same, willing myself not to be so winded. Or at least to hide it as best as I can.

"You will do well in this class," Baer says. "I hope to see you here next year."

Of course I will be here. No way can I pay for any kind of training outside of school. And Baer's class could rival any of the paid lessons, I think. A thought hits me. "Well, unless something happens before then."

Baer frowns. "Your assignment, you mean."

I nod.

For a second, Baer says nothing. Then he sheathes his sword, places it on top of his desk, and turns back around to face me. He leans against the desk with his arms crossed in front of his chest.

"What do you know about strikers?" he asks. He could be asking about the weather, his tone is so nonchalant. But I'm caught by surprise. Why is Baer asking me about strikers?

Assassins for hire, strikers are paid by wealthy people to kill their Alts. They mostly stay underground, working contract to contract, loyal to their work if not to each other. Supposedly. As much as Board members stay out of the public eye, strikers are even more mysterious.

"Well?" Baer says.

"I don't know, I guess about the same as everyone else." I shrug and place my sword down on top of his desk. "We just hear stories, but nothing for sure. And if someone really did contract out their assignment, they're going to keep it quiet, anyway. So who knows if they're even real. Strikers are like an urban myth—"

"Such as how I strangled my Alt with my bare hands when I was but a child of ten?"

I let my gaze slide away, uncomfortable. Though I should have known he would have heard all the talk—

He pulls out a business card from his pocket. It's creased, faded, as if he's been carrying it for a while. Hands it over to me. "They are no urban myth," he says.

There's a number on the card. "What, you want me to call this number? And ask for"—I glance down at the card again—"this person named Dire? Who is he?"

"He's . . . an old friend," Baer finally answers. "Though certain differences in perspectives have led us to . . . drift apart, I think he can help you. If you want his help."

"With what?"

"You don't qualify for weaponry right now, and if paid lessons are out of the question, then Dire might be able to give you the best kind of training there is."

A chill runs down my back as I connect the dots. "He's a striker, isn't he? Your friend. Dire."

Baer shakes his head slowly. "No, he isn't. He only hires them."

"But I always heard strikers work independently."

"They do, but they also have to get their contracts from someone."

"So, he's like a pimp."

The corner of Baer's mouth twitches. "I think Dire would prefer the term 'recruiter,' Grayer."

"Why me?" I ask him. I place the card down on a nearby desk. Suddenly it weighs too much—it weighs of decision, a fork in the road, a path to take. One that could lead to darkness from which there is no way out.

For a second, Baer doesn't answer, and I'm almost glad. It should make it easier to walk away, especially when a part of me is already curious.

"Sometimes the system isn't right, no matter what the Board tells us," Baer says. "It's not always black and white. Dire will tell you the same thing, even if he's not quite so . . . restrained with his words. We both skew what nature might have intended, though my training method's an approved one and his isn't. And as much as I might not agree with how he works, I do think there's a method to the madness. You've got skill and guts, West Grayer. If you have the chance now, does it truly matter how you get better, as long as it helps you complete your assignment?"

Slowly, I pick up the business card again. Despite the card being so worn, the number is still impossible to miss.

"But don't walk in there blind." Baer's gaze doesn't waver, confirming what I've already begun to suspect. It would be the point of no return. "It can get to you, completing assignment after assignment, even if it's not your own—perhaps *because* it's not your own. And then there's the Board. Right now, unnatural completions at the hands of strikers don't happen often enough for them to warrant much of the Board's manpower. As far as they know, at least. But that doesn't mean it's never going to happen. And if it does, and they manage to catch you . . . Well, it's not a choice to take lightly."

"Yeah, I get it." It's all I can think of to say.

With that, Baer moves to the cabinet that lines one side of the room. He pulls out a cardboard box, starts tossing weapons inside. Each is more surreal than the last—daggers, nunchucks, shurikens, some that I don't even recognize.

The clanging of the class materials is loud, but the next words out of my mouth are even louder. They can't go unnoticed. Or be taken back.

"What's that?" he asks, the new wariness on his face telling me he didn't miss what I said the first time. The box sits forgotten in his arms.

"*Is* it true that you killed your Alt with your bare hands?"

Saying it out loud again just makes it sound more idiotic than ever, and I feel the way I used to whenever one of my brothers managed to fool me into something. I mean, it's Baer I'm talking about here—a *weaponry* teacher. Not combat, not kinetics.

After a few seconds of silence, he finally answers. "Yes, it's true."

I can't hide my confusion. "But why the weapons, then? Why do you want to teach us how to use them, if you didn't even need them to complete your assignment?"

"Because as I was strangling him, I knew it didn't have to be that way," Baer says, his voice flat.

I try to picture Baer as a little kid, fighting his Alt at ten, but it's impossible. Not that it matters; he probably relives it enough in his own head.

Baer shifts the box in his arms. "About Dire. If you do contact him, he's got quite the bark, and he can bite, but his hatred doesn't lie with you."

"You mean the Board?"

Baer watches me with his cool eyes. "As I said, the system doesn't always work the way we want it to." He gives me the slightest of nods, just as he did in the library yesterday, and I know he's done. "Thank you for a rather interesting session. One year. Don't die on me before then." Then he's gone from the classroom, his footsteps moving heavily down the hall.

I'm standing in the empty classroom, my mind going a mile a minute. Trying to think back and remember everything I've ever heard about strikers. It's not much. And I have to cut through the smoke and mirrors thrown up by kids' imaginations, the spread of stories and rumors. But clearer than anything is the stark realization that I haven't actually decided against it.

"West."

The sound of my name from the doorway startles me enough to make me drop Dire's card on the ground. But I already know who it is, and I use the excuse of having to bend over to pick up the card to steady myself.

When I look back up and into Chord's face, my heart both lifts and sinks. As long as I've known him, I've never felt this way before. Anxious, awkward, a kind of sweet and painful desperation to renew something that's been lost.

Why did it have to be his Alt who drove us apart?

"What are you doing here?" he asks, his expression slightly guarded, unsure. He turns to say good-bye to someone in the hall behind him. His friend Rush, who was friends with Luc before, too. Rush, who's a complete now, as of last year.

"What are *you* doing here?" I ask in return when Chord faces me again. I'm wondering how much he heard of the conversation between Baer and me, or if he heard anything at all. Because if Chord picked up on the word *striker* even once—

"I forgot something in my locker. It's just across the hall." His eyes are nearly black, too dark to read. "I heard your voice."

I want to stuff the card into my pants pocket, but I'm worried if I draw attention to it he'll ask me about it. My hand closes into a fist, and I can feel the card crumple inward. "Um, yeah, Baer wanted to talk to me about weaponry. For next year, I mean."

"Yeah, I know. I heard you guys talking," he says.

The accusation in his voice is undeniable, and my mouth is dry. "Can I grab a ride home with you?" I blurt out, busying myself with my bag. I sling it over my shoulder, fiddle with a strap, press the card further into my palm.

"Sure, let's go," Chord finally says. But then he takes my hand—the one still awkwardly trying to hide the card—and teases my fist open. He pulls the card free, smooths it out without reading it, and offers it back to me.

"Here." His voice is low and exceedingly calm. "You might want to put this away. I don't think you want someone else finding this, if you accidentally lose it."

I shove it into my pocket. Fine. He knows. And I have absolutely no clue what to say to him.

Suddenly Chord's sitting down on a desk, pulling me to stand in front of him, his hand still holding mine. We're nearly at eye level, inches apart, and I'm no longer breathing. My heart flips in my chest, lazily, languidly.

"Tell me it's not true, West," he says. It's how I know he's really upset. The way his eyes shoot fire even as his tone stays soft. The effect, as always, is more unsettling than if he just lost it outright.

I can only shake my head. All too easily I could let him fight his way through, his plea deciding for me.

"So you're serious?" Chord's jaw goes tight. "You're actually going to call that guy up and sign on as a striker?"

"I don't know what I'm going to do," I manage. His hand is warm around mine, and it's hard to think.

"Do you know what kind of trouble you could get into with the Board if they find you? They would—I don't even want to say it."

"They would have to kill me, probably." I can't pretend there's another choice, not when there wouldn't be. "I mean, being a striker and interfering is the very opposite of what we're supposed to do, right? Let nature weed out the weak so only the strongest are left, in case the border is broken."

"The filtration system is set up to protect us," Chord says, agreeing. "Why would you fight that? Don't you think if there was another way, we would've taken it by now?"

"I'm not sure what I think," I say. "Except it wouldn't be because of that. I wouldn't be *fighting* anything."

A pause. "You know they offer free counseling down at Board headquarters in Leyton Ward, if you think that might help. There's a satellite branch somewhere here in the Grid, too."

"No, I can't." No way. No way am I talking to some stranger about stuff I can barely stand to think about, let alone begin to try to accept.

"Is it so hard to just be here, West?" Chord says quietly. "To believe that when you get your assignment, you're the one who's supposed to win?"

His words have my pulse thudding, the beat of it enveloping all my senses. "What if I'm not the one, Chord? What if it all goes wrong again?"

He finds my other hand, inches me even closer. His face is tortured. "You mean, the way mine did? Is that it? You can't stand being around here because of what happened to Luc?" *Or being around me.* His eyes asking what his words don't.

My throat aches, pushes the words out. "I know it's not your fault, but I keep seeing it in my head. It was your Alt, and his face . . . so much like yours, Chord. And if you hadn't been Luc's best friend, he would never have been anywhere near there."

Chord's eyes go hollow, his features stricken with grief. "West, I'm sorry. For accepting Luc's help and getting him killed for it. For not sitting back and just waiting for my Alt to come. But most of all—"

"I—I would *never* have wanted you not to fight," I stammer out, interrupting him. The idea of it claws at my gut. How did things get so muddled between the two of us? "I—"

"—most of all, for still asking you to want me here. Even if it does all go bad again." His gaze is on me. "Just give me a chance, all right?"

Too close. He's getting too close. If something happens to him because he thinks he needs to be there for me when I get my assignment, because of something Luc asked of him . . . if he's even just standing next to me—

I yank my hands free and take a step back.

"If you heard me and Baer talking, then you also heard what Baer said," I say to him. Cross my arms in front of me so he stays away. "That being a striker would be the best kind of training there is. And then you won't think you need to stick around or anything. I know Luc probably bugged you about it before he—before what happened."

"Screw Baer!" Chord snaps. "He should never have told you about that guy." He glares at my wrists, as if already seeing the tattooed stains spiraling around them, the permanent marks a striker takes on for life. Like manacles. And then his face goes dark—with anger, grief, something else. "You don't need to become an assassin just to save me from your Alt. And I wouldn't be saying this just for Luc, West. All right? We're friends, too."

I force myself to shrug. Look past his shoulder so I can't feel him as much anymore. "You know what, don't worry about the ride. Marsden and Thora are still here finishing a makeup test, so I'll just—"

"No, c'mon, West—"

"—walk home with them after they're done."

"—I want to." Chord sighs. "Drive you home, I mean."

I don't know what to do, sure that whatever I decide is going to be wrong. So when he stands up and says nothing, simply waits for me to make the first move, I give him a sideways glance and head out the door. He follows and soon we're getting into his car in the parking lot.

It's the longest ten minutes of my life. I spend it sitting as far from him as I can get in the passenger seat, hoping he won't ask anything else, that I won't need to come up with more answers when I'm not even sure of my reasoning myself. Hoping that he'll stay away now, for both our sakes. Telling myself it's what I want, too.

Though I never thought it would be this hard.

By the time he pulls up to my house, I'm a wired ball of nerves. I turn to him, about to force out a good-bye, when he jumps out of the car and heads for the front door.

"What—Chord, what are you doing?" I climb out and follow him. I should have known he wouldn't let me escape this easily.

I meet him at the top of the steps. My father's potted plants at our feet, their blooms long gone to seed. Luc's bike pushed up against the siding. Signs of a dead life, all around me. "What are you doing?" I ask again. "I'm busy, you know." A lie. Everyone's gone now. My time is my own.

Chord shoots me a look, not caring that I know *he* knows I just want him to go. "If you're really thinking about doing this, you owe me one thing," he bites out. "As a . . . friend."

I ignore the way my stomach drops, how my heart thuds a bit faster. "I don't owe you anything," I manage.

"I just need to know one thing, and then I'll leave you alone about this." Chord's sudden smile is fleeting, a mere flash across his lips, but I can't miss the misery there. "Who am I to tell you what to do, right?"

Just the one person I have left to keep safe, that's all. Unable to say anything to him, I punch in the key code to unlock the door.

"Wait here, okay?" he says to me before heading upstairs, reminding me that he knows this house as well as his own. We live only five houses apart. After his family moved in when he was six, either he was at our place or Luc was at his.

Until now. It hits me with a pang that this is probably the first time he's feeling less than welcome here. And it's because of me.

Chord's back within seconds, and he finds me in the kitchen, where I've gone to get something to drink just to keep myself busy. In his hand is Luc's gun. He took it from the desk in Luc's room, where he knows Luc always kept it.

My knees go weak, and I slip into the nearest chair. "What are you doing with that?" I ask him, my voice faint and way too shaky.

Chord was the one to clean it for me after Luc died. I couldn't bear to hold it for long. It somehow continued to feel sticky with Luc's blood, even after I wiped it over and over. But Chord did a good job. The matte finish is smooth, cool-looking, and most of all, has no trace of blood whatsoever.

So why can I still see it? If not directly in front of me, then in my head, where memories continue to loop? The liquid ease of the blood spreading everywhere, the blackening of it as it dried. How our fingerprints swam in the tackiness of it, whorls bright and perfect.

I shut my eyes and breathe in. Then out.

When I open them, the gun is just a gun again. Held securely in Chord's grip. Nothing more, nothing less.

Chord passes it to me, handle first. I don't have a choice but to take it. How can I think about becoming a striker if I can't even hold a gun? And Chord's watching me, searching for any sign of weakness.

It fits my palm with more ease than I would have thought likely. All those days and weeks and months spent with Luc, training and perfecting my arm, my eye, my stance—all of it seems so far away, like it wasn't even us. But I guess you really can't unlearn some things.

"So show me," Chord says, his voice hard, not his at all.

"Show you what?"

He points to the wall on the far side of the kitchen. "Shoot. I want to see how good you are."

My fingers stiffen. They don't want to curl around the trigger, and my palm is suddenly damp with sweat. My arm is trembling. "I don't need to show you. I'll be fine, okay?"

"Humor me, then. I want to see."

"What difference does it make?"

His face is like thunder. "The difference between you getting in over your head over an Alt who means nothing to you, and you getting the chance to challenge your own Alt."

"Will you promise that it'll be enough for you, then?" I ask him.

For a long minute, Chord doesn't answer. Finally, reluctantly, a soft "I'd be lying if I said yes, but I promise I'll try to pretend it is."

He takes my hand, the one still holding the gun. He squeezes his fingers around mine, until we're holding the gun together.

"Let go, Chord."

He doesn't. Instead he points the gun at the wall across from us and fires.

The sound is enormous in the enclosed space. A neat black hole mars the smooth white of the drywall.

Chord drops his hand from around mine and says, "Now aim for that same hole."

"You just blew a hole in my kitchen wall," I say quietly. Then, without saying anything else, I lift the gun and take aim. I will it to not be too far off. If I'm even the least bit rusty, Chord won't be satisfied.

But the second bullet lodges itself within an inch of the first. Two sinister eyes stare back at us.

Casually, I put the gun down on the table. I can see that my hand is shaking again, so I clasp it tightly with my other hand, forcing it steady. A part of me insists that it was dumb luck, but what does it matter now?

"There," I say, my voice flat. "Good enough?"

Chord nods, defeat written in every line of his body. His face is still set, but now at least there's some relief there, as well. It's going to have to be enough for him to not think he's failed me in some way. As though he's failing Luc all over again by not stopping me from becoming a striker.

A rush of emotion has me grabbing his hand. I know how hard guilt is. It's like a weight on your chest, suffocating you, only it goes on, with no end in sight. Thinking that it's me putting him through that is almost enough to tell him, *It's okay, I'm not going to become a striker.*

Almost.

I want to believe I can deal with my own nightmares, the ones that come out in the dark and only barely stay quiet when it's light. But it's not even just that. It's Chord, getting too close to me . . . my Alt . . . the crossfire between us. And it would rip me apart until nothing was left if I lost him, too.

That's me being selfish. Selfish enough for both of us. Becoming a striker will fill my life and keep me from going crazy. It will lend me the skills to survive.

"Chord. I'll be okay." My voice is close to shattering. "And then *you'll* stay okay."

He exhales. Crouches down so he's level with me. His dark eyes roam my face.

"You've already decided, haven't you?" he asks me. His hand is gentle around mine, somehow able to calm my own tensed grip.

I have. My decision was made as soon as the card passed into my hand and refused to be forgotten.

"Yes," I say, nodding, "and there's nothing you can say that'll make me change my mind." I can't help but touch his hair, the way it falls over his forehead, how the soft brown strands slip through my fingers. "I'm sorry."

Chord watches me for another moment, as if trying to memorize how I look before I'm changed forever. I want to tell him that I'll still be the same person, but I don't. Because I don't know if that's true.

He touches the side of my face. "I'll see you later, West," he says hoarsely. And he stands up, steps back, and walks away. I hear the sound of the front door shutting and his car taking off.

Good-bye, Chord.

Becoming a striker isn't much different from becoming active, really. We give up a little to get a lot back.

Why do I feel like I've already given up far too much?

Chapter 3

Standing in front of the building, I'm dumbfounded. All those hundreds of times we ran past it as kids, racing back and forth as we played Alt Against Alt. Or if the day was particularly restless, our mood especially wild, when we played Striker Against Alt.

I glance down at the card in my hand. Make sure I have the name right. That I've written down the address correctly.

Yes. This is it. No mistake. I tuck the card away in my bag and feel for the shape of the gun I'm carrying in my jacket. The weight alone tells me it's still there, but already I've developed the nervous habit of double-checking. It was a last-minute decision to take it with me this morning, and I still don't get why I did it. I'm in no danger here. As it is, meeting up with someone like Dire with a gun that's still more Luc's than mine is probably as effective as walking in bare-handed.

The music store looks like any of the other stores that line the block. The rippled front window is etched with faint shadows of old graffiti, the outer ledge of it dotted with lumps of putty-colored gum. Cheap interior lighting. Gray linoleum floors that clean up easily enough with a soggy mop. A steel-framed front door painted with the name: DIRE NATION.

I pull the door open, step inside, and pass from one kind of life to another.

There are customers strewn throughout the store. Most of them are at the plug-in stations, lining up music to be wired into the music players implanted in their eardrums. There are also downloading stations, for those who still carry external players. And a handful of racks, for die-hard collectors of more tangible formats. Holograms of bands cover the concrete walls:

Kamiquasi. The Finger Project. Munch.

But this is the Grid, so the stations are double-bolted to the ground and to each other. The racks are still standing but have been beaten to near death. And the holograms blink and flicker, shorting out every few seconds.

I recognize the song that's playing over the sound system. It was a favorite of Ehm's. I haven't heard it since she died, and the sound of it now is like a splinter in my chest.

"Help you with something?" a voice behind me asks.

Cool sweat breaks out along my brow, and I take a deep breath as I turn to look at him.

Pudgy, plodding, features as thick as pudding. A name tag with *Hestor* written in blue letters.

It's almost hard to believe he's even a complete, he's so soft. If he is an actual striker, he's a parody of everything we've ever imagined them to be.

"I'm trying to see if you guys have this band in your library, but the station lineups are really long," I say to him, knowing he's the one who can take me to Dire.

"Nothing to complain about, that's just good business, girlie." A snicker. "What's the name of the band?"

This is it. If I'm going to turn back, it has to be now. A vivid image of Chord flashes in my mind, like a final chance. Except he's dying. Like Luc, everyone else. And I'm holding him in my arms, feeling his life drain away.

My fault.

"Hey, you alive in there?" Hestor waves his hand in front of my face.

Doubt disintegrates. The fear of the unknown is nothing compared to what I already know—what I fear the most. "The name of the band is the Strikers," I say softly, my eyes steady on his.

· Hestor goes absolutely still. His hand stops flapping in midair, his eyes widen just a sliver before narrowing. Suddenly he doesn't seem quite so useless. "Say that again, will you," he mutters—not a request but a demand.

So I do. "I'm looking for the Strikers."

Doing what he asked only seems to make him angrier. He shakes his head, still glaring at me. "The Strikers are only suitable for a more . . . mature audience. Those over the age of twenty, when chances of assignment are nil. You gotta be a complete, you getting me?"

I stifle a wave of panic. It can't gather steam, show in my eyes or words. Panic would be a sign of weakness. "The card says nothing about that," I point out.

"Hey, it's only common sense, girlie."

"Neither did the person on the phone when I asked for Dire. The person who told me how to come find him."

"That woulda been me, and if I'd known you were a teen-ager, I woulda just shut my mouth." A loose, thick-lipped smile. "Now, this band. Their music can be a bit graphic, understand? Too much for a little chicky like you."

To have it so close—I can't let it slip away now. For a second I tasted the promise of numbness, the safety and relief of it. I was only able to get out of bed this morning because of this chance to quiet the storm in my head.

"Five minutes," I tell him. "You can give me that at least."

"Nope. Can't. Dire's a busy man. I can't be wasting no time of his by sending him some *idle*—"

"I'm not leaving until I talk to him." I growl the words be-cause I'm dangerously close to begging. And the idea of beg-ging this person, who surely can't be more than a token guard, a gatekeeper—

"Get out." Hestor's eyes flick once to the left, then to the right, aware of the other customers on the floor. Obviously this is not a conversation he wants them to overhear. "Before I make you get out."

"No, I'm not leaving," I say again. "I want to see him."

"Well, we're closed. So get your useless self outta here." He starts to put his hand on my shoulder to turn me toward the door.

It happens fast. Faster than I would have ever thought pos-sible. All those hours, days, years of practicing, and for this, at least, it's enough.

My arm swings out, knocks his hand away. Then thrusts hard at his chest. That such a thick man falls back so easily is due more to his utter shock than my strength, though.

He stares at me from the floor, his face red and squashed. And absolutely murderous. "Okay, that's it, I'm gonna—"

My hand, dropping down to the gun in my pocket, digging for it—

"Hestor." A deep riptide of a voice, like sand scraping over gravel. "What's going on out here?"

I turn to see a man who's very tall and very wide. Small eyes the color of blue jeans, hair a short scrub of dirty blond, chin covered by a goatee the same shade.

With one glance I can tell his heft doesn't come from fat like Hestor's does. It's pure muscle. And he's positioned it to hide the three of us from view from the rest of the store. Which leaves me boxed in, away from the door.

"This—this little *brat* came here to see you, Dire," Hestor sputters. "Asking about *the band*." These last two words are an indignant hiss. "But when I saw how old she was, I said no way, nothing doing. And then she goes and makes a stink about leaving."

Dire's openly assessing me. I can't get a feel for what he's thinking, and it's unnerving. Whether or not he's going to give me a chance, kick me out, or do something I haven't even let myself imagine—whatever's usually done to those who have learned too much.

"Do you always move that fast?" he asks me. The words are blunt scratches.

I don't know. "Yes. Always."

A few seconds of silence, then a curt nod. "Fine. But down-stairs. Not here." Dire eyeballs the store, seems satisfied no one has been listening. "Hestor, back to work."

Hestor is finally struggling to his feet. "Dire, this is a crazy, stupid idea. The girl is so green she might as well be a—"

"No greener than I would want." Dire turns to me, gestures. "This way."

The stairway is a skinny, dark slant of space in the back corner. Each step I take furthers my descent into a world that is suddenly all too real, no longer a game.

The same concrete walls are down here, but there's a damp-ness to them, a kind of dank earthiness. It reminds me of how a garden smells when you dig really deep, turning over soil that has never seen the sun. There are no windows, just three naked, swinging bulbs slung across the ceiling. A handful of metal chairs and a dented metal table are placed on the con-crete floor. Incongruous to it all is an assortment of sleek tablets wired to machines I can't begin to recognize.

And a woman. She's sitting at the bare table, watching me as I enter the room. She looks just as tough as Dire and about as pleasant as Hestor. Black-haired and dark-skinned, with sharp green eyes. On the table in front of her is a cardboard box.

Dire pulls out a chair across from the woman, scraping it along the floor. He holds it out. "Have a seat," he says to me.

"This is the one from Baer?" The lady's voice is soft. She continues to stare at me as I sit down. Her appraisal isn't like a mother's would be, but a snake's right before it pounces. "I didn't know we were taking them this young now."

"We're not." Dire sits down next to the woman, frowns at

me, and rubs his goatee. "What's your name and how old are you?"

"West Grayer." My words are bullets. Have to be. Being turned away is still a possibility. "I'm fifteen, and I'm not too young."

He grunts. "So you haven't completed your assignment yet?"

"No. Not yet." My hands are clenched on the table in front of me, so I pull them off the table and sit on them.

"Why would you want to become a striker when you could go active any day now? Kids your age are too busy getting ready to kill their own Alts to care much about someone else's. And rightly so. One screwup during a striker contract is just as fatal as one during your own assignment."

I nod. "I know that. I came here to get as strong as I can. And because—" I stop myself. The two faces in front of me are masks, hard and already halfway toward dismissing me, and I know my pain will mean nothing to them. It might even make them think I can't handle it. "Well, like Baer said, for the training . . ."

Dire shakes his head, his mouth a thin line. "Baer. He should have known better than to send me an idle." His blue eyes glitter like glass beneath the lights. "But this is the first time he's bothered to acknowledge I still exist—and what I do. So what does he see in you, Grayer, that would make him break his silence?"

I blink, unsure what he wants to hear. "I don't know."

The woman smiles. It makes her beautiful, and more frightening, too. "What *I* know is that you have no idea what you're getting into," she says.

"I know that you recruit strikers for Alt assassinations," I say stiffly. "I know that no one really dares to talk about you, especially the ones who actually hire strikers to kill their Alts. I also know that you've managed to avoid the Board so far, and that no strikers have ever been captured. Otherwise they would have killed you, or them, and the Board would have made sure we all knew about it."

"And yet you can't tell us about your own Alt, your own completion. What you would do when it comes down to either killing or being killed."

Except she's wrong. I know all about Alts and completions. When they're happening to everyone around you, they might as well be your own.

"See, that's what got me wondering," Dire says. "If you haven't completed, how do we know how you'll react? There's just as much chance you'll make the hit as there is of you running—or worse, leaving behind a mess that will get the Board pissed off enough to do something about it."

"I didn't know I had to pass some kind of test to become a striker, or answer a whole bunch of stupid questions." My voice turns flinty. "And I think that Baer being the one to send me here should be enough."

Baer's name has Dire's expression going dark, and it makes me wonder why they're no longer friends. Both of them oppose the Board and assignments, both give Alts their best chance of survival, even if they do take their own stance on it. Is that why they hate each other now? Baer thinks Dire goes too far, and Dire thinks Baer doesn't go far enough?

"There's no test you have to pass," Dire says finally, just as coolly. "And you don't have to tell us your reasons why. It's just because I'm curious."

"Fine. I need the money."

"You're lying," the woman says instantly.

"No, I'm not. It pays better than any job I could get right now, since I haven't completed." Two parts to this, and only one I know for sure to be true. What's fact is that idles get paid less than completes for doing the same job; what's rumor is that striking pays better than most jobs, period. *If* you're good at it.

"What would a girl like you need so much money for?" Dire asks. "Elite training? Makes no sense if you're going to be a striker."

"What difference does it make, as long as you still get the finder's fee for each client? If I have to stop when I get my assignment, it's not like I'll continue to get paid, either. And if this works the way I think it does, you'd just hand a new job off to another of your strikers."

He nods slowly. "True enough. I guess I want to be absolutely sure *you're* sure. We've never had an idle or active Alt even come in before, you know."

A few seconds of silence as we all digest his admission. The realization that I'm the first is not heady so much as unnerving.

"Baer says that you do this because you don't agree with the Board," I finally say. "That you don't think the system is always right, why one Alt is supposed to die and not the other."

"Just because an Alt doesn't think they're capable of killing someone themselves doesn't mean they don't deserve a chance to live."

"But that's how Kersh has stayed as strong as it has. By getting rid of the weak."

"It's strong in the way of soldiers and war. But what about things that make us more than machines, keep us human? Balance is good. If being weak means not being able to live with the memory of killing someone with your own hands, then maybe we should all call weakness good. Being worthy should mean more than just being able to use a gun or hold a blade."

"If you're really just trying to screw with the whole thing, so that the stronger Alt doesn't win and the weaker one does, why do you still make the weaker Alt pay?" I press him.

Dire's face goes tight, his eyes filling with derision and emptied of anything else. As if he's caught himself just in time and now has to regain his footing, step back into anger where there's no room for guilt. Who could he have lost to make him see things this way, and how bad must it have been?

"Hey, either you live or you die," he says. "Kill or be killed. Unless you want to leave behind your dead body for your family to deal with, pay up. I'll take the money every time."

Will it be the same for me? Will I end up as hard as him for using striking to fend off whatever ghosts haunt me, the way he uses his strikers to fend off his own? Will it matter, as long as I can keep going on?

"Do you understand all that, Grayer?" Dire asks, snapping me back. "Understand and accept what comes with becoming a striker?"

"Yes." I meet his gaze. "To all of it."

"They'll hate you if they find out, you know." No beating around the issue, just a factual breakdown of my life from this point on. "Not only the Board, but also idles, actives, completes—and deep down, even some of the Alts who end up hiring you themselves, simply for reminding them of what they couldn't do. Everyone who sees your marks will know you're cheating the system. That you're not killing for the greater good, but because you choose to."

"Yes." It's all I can say.

"Good. Don't screw up." And with that, it's done.

I've been accepted.

"You got the equipment ready?" Dire asks the woman.

She nods, and I can tell she's not happy with Dire's decision to sign me on. I'm a new kind of animal with a slew of unknowns, difficult to classify: a teenaged striker who has yet to complete her assignment. Am I just a waste of their time, caught up in the initial adrenaline rush of being an actual striker, only to balk at the first sign of danger? Will I go hog wild, made hungry by opportunity and a distorted sense of impunity? Will my eventual assignment handcuff me or empower me with newfound perspective?

Dire leaves the room as the woman slides the cardboard box over so it sits between us on the pitted tabletop. She lifts the lid and I peer inside, knowing what I'm going to see and bracing myself anyway.

A tattoo gun. No bullet to fire into my flesh, but something else instead: the marks of a striker. Payment, just like Dire said.

"This gun will accomplish two things," the woman says to me. "First, the laser will score your skin beneath the surface and clear out a path for the mark. Then it will flood the path with the particle ink. The ink's properties are what will allow us to keep track of you, in case the finder's fee slips your mind and we need to contact you. Our own shadowing system, if you will." The corners of her lips curl. Not to reassure me, but to let me know she's enjoying my submission, whether she agrees with it or not.

"Get on with it," I tell her.

Her smile slides off like grease from a pan. "It will hurt. Scream and I will have to gag you."

I don't scream. But tears come all the same, streaking my cheeks. Hot as flame, my first trial by fire.

When she's done, the smell of burning flesh is not just in my nose but in my clothes, my hair. I rotate my wrists and study my striker marks.

Two curling swaths of faded gray ink, the color of worn battleships. I touch one with a finger, sure it'll hurt like crazy, although she told me they would heal almost instantly. Because it's not just ink and tracking chips that she's injected into my skin, but a hefty dose of binding agent as well—supercharged particles that heal injuries from the inside out.

I frown. The sudden lack of pain is surprising, but even more surprising is that there's almost no feeling at all. The numbness has spread down to my palms, too.

I flex my hands, squeeze them into fists. I poke harder this time. Still nothing.

"Inking will do that at first," Dire says, lumbering back into the room like a bull. "You'll get most of the feeling back."

"Most? Why didn't you warn me?" A rippling coil of fear

that I'll never again be sure I'm wielding a weapon as best as I know how. That I've just wasted all the time my brothers spent training with me.

He shrugs. The motion is nearly elegant for someone who's built like a freight train. "Would it have changed your mind?"

No, it wouldn't have. I examine my marks again. The dark, thin curlicues encircling my wrists make me think of assignment numbers unspooling.

"Be careful with the marks; we never could get the ink any lighter than that, so you'll have to cover them up," Dire says tersely. "Only when you die will they no longer risk giving us away. Once the blood stops moving through your veins, it signals the tracking chips to automatically malfunction. The Board won't be able to circle back to us."

"But why the wrists?" I ask him. "Why not somewhere less visible, easier to hide?"

"Unless you chop off your most valuable assets, you're stuck with them. No chance of you going rogue on us; a striker without hands is worthless."

He pulls out his chair and sits down across from me again. "Now for the details. You will always be reachable, at all times. Unless there are special circumstances, we match up clients with whoever's available. If it's you, you'll get a text with everything you'll need—client contact info, client pic, assignment number, fresh spec sheet with Alt location. Sometimes workplace, routines, behavioral patterns, depending how long they've been tracked for. You'll then contact the client and let them know your terms of payment. Most strikers charge about what an idle makes in a month at co-op level, and it goes up from there. We take twenty-five percent off whatever you make, so make sure you wire it in. You'll have twenty-four hours to complete. However you execute a strike is up to you, but just as the Board suggests, best to keep it fast, clean, quiet." Then Dire's laughing, and the dark undertone of it points to how I've only stepped from beneath one shadow to another. "Twisted, isn't it? Us and the Board, both wanting the same thing from you."

"Yeah, I guess." I get to my feet, hoping the weakness I feel in my legs won't make me fall. I start walking away, suddenly craving light brighter than that coming from the bare bulbs in the room. "You have my cell number from when I called before." What can I say that won't sound so completely surreal? There's nothing.

Dire, still in his seat at the table, watches me walk past. "For your first contract, right?"

"What else?" My wrists and palms sting a bit now, just the slightest hum right beneath the skin.

"Grayer."

I'm at the door. "What?"

"Your first contract comes now."

My heart gallops into my throat and tastes entirely of fear. *No, not now, I'm not ready.* Slowly I turn around and make my way back to the table. "Tell me."

Dire's eyes are narrowed, cold blue flame. "None of this getting your feet wet first—we're going right for the deep end. Better hope you swim, not sink."

"Is this the test, then?" I ask, my voice a dry rasp. "Because getting my marks wasn't enough?"

"Compared to killing, your marks are child's play. So prove me wrong, and Baer right. Be sure to check your cell on the way out."

And with that I know it's begun.

Her house is in a neighborhood in Jethro's bottommost end, right before the ward gives way to Leyton in the south. On the quiet side, average income on par with the rest of Jethro's suburbs. Maybe even a touch higher, seeing how some of the worn exteriors and tired lawns have been spiffed up. Still nowhere close to white-collar territory like Leyton Ward, though.

It explains why she couldn't afford a striker. Not that money is necessarily the only reason. Principle, pride, stubbornness, confidence, apathy . . . they can all come into play. And ultimately, none of it matters. Because it doesn't change the fact that I'm here.

I slide around to the side of the house, just around the front corner, where there's a row of boxwood shrubs. They're thick and dense enough to cover me as I crouch down to hide. And watch. And wait for her to either come out or come in.

That's what I'm counting on, anyway. It's a new enough assignment—barely twenty-four hours old, according to the contract details on my cell—that unless she's broken free of the typical behavioral patterns of newly activated Alts, odds are she's still at home. Getting ready to hide, getting ready to fight. Either way, it starts here.

The spec sheet is ridiculously short. At first I wondered why Dire didn't press for more legwork from the client before forwarding the contract, but then I realized he wouldn't want to make it easy for me. Just like the Board, he wants to flush me out if I can't finish this.

I touch the gun in my jacket pocket. I can never forget what it's capable of, no matter how many times I eventually fire it. To do so would be to lose myself, become more striker than me.

In the other pocket, a blade. Another in the front right pocket of my jeans, and one more in my back pocket. Overkill, probably, but I'm nervous, and I can't say for sure how this is going to go.

And so I wait. The day passes slowly. Each second is too full, not wanting to spill over to the next. Minutes stretch, hours linger. I've never had reason to keep so still for so long before, and it's like fighting gravity, every part of my body in protest, crying out.

My eyes are so dry. They sting. My entire left leg and right foot have lost all feeling. Pins and needles like never before, spiking through and piercing everywhere.

There's hunger, too, the hollow pangs like swelling waves inside my stomach.

Sluggishly my mind rifles through past combat classes, wondering if there's anything useful there at all. Anything about the human body dealing with the mental trial of a stakeout, the torture of *not* moving.

But I come up short.

Focus, then, West—on anything else that's not you. Be numb, a striker.

How, though? Impossible when your whole being is

composed of little more than agonized muscles and quivering bones, of tautly wired nerves and hunger-induced lightheadedness.

The sun is low in the sky, the air nearing evening temperatures typical of late fall, when the front door opens. It falls shut, followed by the sound of footsteps.

I'm wide-eyed and dry-mouthed, my pulse rippling like flags in a storm.

But by the time feet near my hiding spot, I know it's not her. The gait is too loose, not fearful enough for an Alt whose status has just been changed to active.

A woman walks across the yard, heading toward the car parked at the curb. From the looks of her, she's probably my strike's mother. The resemblance to my client's picture is too strong for her to not be family.

The front door opens again. "Mom, why can't I—" The voice of a fourteen-year-old girl, wheedling and petulant, and my shoulders stiffen. It has to be her.

"Linde, shut the door and stay inside!" The woman's voice is both furious and frightened. "I told you, this is not the time to be testing my patience."

"But I'm *bored*! I don't want to stay inside all day! Why can't I—"

"Better to be bored than dead, don't you think? It hasn't even been one day since you got your assignment, and already you're fighting me on this?"

"I'm not fighting you—"

"How can I get you to see that an assignment is not

something you can just decide you'd rather not do? It's not like returning a shirt to the mall, for goodness' sake."

"I'm not *stupid*, Mom."

"Linde." A huge sigh, the sound bringing to mind my own mother, dealing with the lot of us. "I'll be right back, okay? And then we'll figure things out."

"*Fine.* But I'm still having Xave over! You can't stop me from seeing my boyfriend, you know."

"Just get inside, Linde! And lock the door!"

The door kicks shut against the frame, and the woman climbs into the car and pulls away.

I'm scrambling to my feet, gun in hand, thinking fast, wondering if I have time to get inside before the mother returns or if I should just ring the bell outright and hope she answers it without thinking, when the front door opens again.

My strike, running out of the house and sprinting across the yard, her mother already too far ahead to catch.

"Mom, wait! Wait! I forgot to—" She stops in the middle of the street, staring in the direction her mother drove, breathing heavily, hands at her hips. "This *sucks*."

Her words are surprisingly clear, even over the distance between us, and I realize just how quiet it is out here. Peaceful. Thoughts tumble through my head, and right or wrong, I decide my gun's too loud for this place, for these families in these houses on this calm night.

I pass the gun into my left hand and yank the switchblade out of my front jeans pocket. Snap it open.

And doing so slows me down. If I'd moved faster, I could

have thrown it while she was still close enough for me to not miss, and while she was still looking away. She would have died without even knowing what happened. She would have died, and I wouldn't have had to see her face.

But she's turning and heading back inside when she sees me. Her face is the same as my client's, the photo on my cell that I've memorized.

Eyes big and startled and a beautifully flecked hazel. Encoded in them are the black spirals of her assignment number. Buttery blond hair tied up in a ponytail, fashionably thick with braids and decorative feathers. She's wearing jeans and an off-the-shoulder tee. Woven friendship bracelets wind up both arms from wrist to elbow like a rainbow.

She doesn't see the blade right away, and I can see the beginnings of a question perch on her lips. But then her eyes catch on the glint of it, and fear takes over her face, draining it sickly white. Her eyes go even wider, shiny pools of spreading panic. She opens her mouth, an airless *oh!*, but the only thing I'm able to hear by then is the blood roaring in my own ears. The world has shortened to nothing more than the distance from me to her.

Then she's moving again, stumbling backward for a handful of steps in her haste to get away, before beginning to turn—

I throw. Feel the muscles of my arm flex back into life as my fingers release metal.

The blade pierces her chest. It sinks in deep and insists on staying. She wavers, stumbles, falls, a tangle of damaged flesh and blond hair and denim. The spread of blood on her front grows, seeming nearly black in the light of dusk.

I stand there, stunned. It feels surreal, being on that street in that moment, like an out-of-body experience. I've just taken down my first strike, killed my first Alt, completed my first job as a striker . . . and I feel nothing.

A man walks out from one of the houses along the street, overweight and wearing a shirt stained at the pits. A complete who's forgotten how lucky he is to be alive.

He glances down at the body at his feet, then over at me. At the gun still in my left hand. His eyes turn into slits.

"You're not her Alternate, I can tell that easily enough," he grunts out. "So what are you?" He eyes my hands more closely, and his sudden awareness stirs the ball of dread in my stomach.

Another mistake—I forgot Dire's warning to cover my marks. I try to yank my sleeves down, but it's too late. Even I know the ink is impossible to miss.

"So you're one of those strikers, then." The disgust in his voice can't be more obvious.

I shove the gun and my hands into my jacket pockets. "Yes." What else can I say?

"Well, couldn't you have done this somewhere else? This is a family area, you know. Kids live on this street."

"I'm sorry." All of a sudden, I feel like a little kid again myself, getting caught at doing something I shouldn't be doing.

He leans over the body. Takes stock. Jumps back. "Whoa, whoa, *whoa*. Hey, she's not dead."

My head snaps up. "What?" I whisper.

"She's not dead." He sounds both indignant and shocked. Like he's never heard of a striker actually failing before. "Get over here. Take a good look for yourself."

On legs as heavy as lead, I don't even have to take the few steps I do to know he's telling the truth. She's still breathing, but barely. Her breaths are shallow, far apart. The handle of the knife moves in minute flutters. Caught in her lung, then. Off by inches, again.

"Finish it." He's angry now, his voice hard.

"What?" I repeat, the word hollow. "Finish it?"

"You can't just leave her like this. I'm not going to do your job for you. I've done my part already, a long time ago, and I'm no striker, either. And I sure don't need the Board all over me if they find out I'm even talking to you."

I take another step until I'm standing over her. The last thing I want is to see her face again, but against my will my eyes meet hers.

She stares right back at me, the encoded sequence of numbers just as dark as they were before I slung the blade into her chest. There's pain and fear in her eyes now, and more than that, an awareness of her own end. There's nothing for her to do now except wait.

I take out my gun again. I make no mistake with the shot.

"Oh, *man*," the fat man says raggedly. He wipes his mouth with his hand. His face is pale, his skin shiny and clammy with a sheen of sweat. "That's *brutal*. Just brutal."

I'm at a loss for words. Whatever I come up with won't erase what he's seen. What I've done. Slowly, I begin to walk away, unable to think about retrieving the blade. Forever stained with not just blood but near failure.

The man, sputtering in protest behind me. "Wait, wait,

what about her? You're going to call clearing, or what? You're going to make me do it? Strikers, you're nothing but cheaters!"

I begin to run, trying to outrun the assassin within me. Like I can no longer stand to be in my own skin.

"You're putting all of us in danger, you know that?" His voice, finally fading. The memory of him, as far from a soldier as you can get, and my head's whirling. How does it work that such an end product is what the Board accepts, and not what Dire's methods produce? How is one better than the other?

One street blurs into another, one block into the next, until I'm no longer sure where I am. I could be anywhere, nowhere, it doesn't matter. Bright hazel eyes and hair the color of butter are all I see, mixed up with endless pavement and houses with blank faces. Only exhaustion has me stopping, and I collapse onto a curb and just sit there, gasping. I lean over and throw up whatever's in my stomach.

I don't know how long I sit there. Only when the streetlamps flicker to life do I realize how late it's getting. The sky is an ashy gray, the arched lip of the border's iron barrier curving along its horizon. Plumes of smoke from Jethro's factories rise in multiple columns. Below it all, houses sit quietly, falling farther into shadowed recesses. Branches sway in the wind. Driveways wait to be swept.

It's a nondescript neighborhood, forgettable. And I can't help but think of the first completion I ever saw. It took place in a setting just like this. Designed to fade into the background, as if to make sure the players remained vivid in my memory.

•   •   •

"West, wake up!" A hand shook my leg beneath my blanket, and I kicked it away. Way too early to get up.

"C'mon, we gotta go," Luc hissed into my ear, "before Mom and Dad wake up."

I opened my eyes, suddenly wide awake. A sick blend of anticipation and anxiety already had my stomach in knots. I'd seen portions of completions before, but never one from start to finish.

Through the pink-hued gray light of dawn, I could make out Ehm's quiet form in the bed next to me.

I looked at Luc more closely. "Why are you dressed?" I whispered loudly. "Why are you even awake? Aave said you had to stay here."

He shrugged. "Ehm's still sleeping," he pointed out. "She won't even notice we're gone. Besides, it's not like I've never seen one before."

True. Luc went through this at nine, two years ago, when our father took him to see his first. Now it was my turn since I was nearly old enough to qualify, and Aave had decided he was old enough to take me himself.

I swung my legs off the bed, already in jeans and a hooded sweatshirt. I'd slept in my clothes, knowing we had to be as quiet as possible. My parents wouldn't have wanted us to go on our own, and if we'd thought it through and really considered the danger of PKs, we might not have wanted to go, either. But as idles, we still had our childish sense of immortality. Nothing could hurt us except our Alts, and that wasn't going to happen that day.

"Fine, but don't lose it if Aave still says no," I said to Luc as we crept down the stairs.

"He won't," Luc argued. "And who knows when we'll see another one the whole way through, right? One we know about ahead of time."

"It's not supposed to be fun, Luc," I muttered, shoving my feet into my sneakers.

Even in the half light, I could see him rolling his eyes at me. "You know what I mean, West. Jeez."

I did, but I still felt bad for not being overly sad when an Alt died. It was hard to feel that way when the Alts were strangers. All of it was real without being *real*, if that makes sense. And since neither of my brothers had gotten their assignments yet, each completion they saw was only like adding on another layer of armor, another technique they could remember.

We slipped out the back door, as silent as thieves in the early-morning gloom. The way we would one day hide and move in the dark as actives with assignments.

Aave was already waiting outside. And Chord, too. Not a surprise. Chord was actually good friends with both my brothers, and tolerated me and Ehm well enough, but being the same age as Luc—and sharing the same geeky obsession for all things remotely electronic and tech related—Chord mostly hung out with Luc. The fact that he lived just down the block didn't hurt, either.

Chord pushed the hood of my sweatshirt off my head. My uncombed hair became an even bigger nest. "Good morning, princess." He drove a knuckle into the top of my head with a grin.

I swatted at him and made a face. Made a show of smoothing down my hair. "What are you doing here, Chord? Don't you ever go home?"

"I did. I'm back."

"Yay, lucky us." But I didn't mind too much. Chord was all right . . . most of the time.

Aave was frowning. At thirteen he was still a kid, but sometimes he came across as so much older. "Luc, you're supposed to be watching Ehm."

"C'mon, Aave, she's sleeping," Luc complained. "And I want to go. Besides, you're letting Chord go."

"*Someone's* got to watch Ehm. And I asked Chord to come because I was worried, in case West has a meltdown or something—"

"Hey." I elbowed Aave in the side.

"—and I'm stuck trying to get her home by myself."

"I'm not a baby, Aave!"

"Ehm's not going to be up for hours," Luc said. *"C'mon . . ."*

Aave narrowed his eyes at him, then sighed. "Fine. But I'm not taking the blame if we get caught leaving her alone, though."

Luc snickered. "Not like you would have been able to stop me, anyway."

Aave ignored him and turned to look at me. His dark brown eyes were very serious. "You ready, West?"

I nodded, tried to ignore the nervousness in my stomach. "I think so."

"Let's get moving, then." His longer legs had him pulling slightly ahead, so I fell into step with Luc and Chord instead.

"I guess your aunt doesn't know you're here?" I asked Chord.

He shook his head. "No way, she'd kill me if she found out."

"I guess Taje wasn't ready . . . ," I began. Not that Taje wasn't ready to see a completion—at eight, he would have been fine—but he might not have been ready to hang out yet. His and Chord's parents had died just that past spring, and Taje was having a hard time of it. A part of his mind kept him trapped in that car, imagining what it must have been like to have it spin out of control, over the divider, into traffic coming the other way.

"Not yet," Chord replied after a few seconds. We shared a look. "Soon, I think."

Luc kicked a green bin back to the curb. The loud scrape of it made me shiver, and I glanced around furtively, feeling guilty for some reason. Whatever it was—the slow-lifting light, the chilled and damp air—it suddenly seemed like the most morbid of treasure hunts, the group of us hunting in the still mostly dreaming streets of Jethro that morning.

Luc must have seen me shiver. "Don't tell me you're getting scared, West," he teased. "I'll let you stand behind me."

"I'm not scared," I said. "I was just thinking."

"About what?" Chord asked.

"Well, it's just . . ." I stuffed my hands into my front pockets, tried to think how best to put it. "When there's a completion, do you think of it more as an Alt having to die or an Alt getting to live?"

"I don't get it," Luc said, shrugging. "It's the same thing."

"But it's not."

"Yeah, it is. One makes it, one doesn't. That's it."

"You mean how there's two different ways of looking at it," Chord said. "Glass half full, right?"

I reached up to grab a low branch from a maple tree. Shook it so dying red, orange, and yellow leaves rained down on us. "Yeah, I guess. But I can't decide if one's more right than the other."

"Maybe it's something in between," Luc said. He yawned. "I don't know. This is hurting my brain. It's way too early to have to think so hard."

Chord reached over, plucked a leaf from my hair. Crunched it up so bits of it fell back onto me. "Maybe we're just supposed to try our best, whatever that is," he said, "and hope whatever happens is meant to happen."

I waved him away and pulled my hood back on. "I think Luc's right. It's too early."

Luc huddled farther into his jacket. "Whatever. All I know is I'm freezing my butt off out here."

Just then, an outer ward train blasted by us, blowing my hood right back off and stirring Luc's and Chord's dark hair. The sudden rush of air had me blinking rapidly and taking notice of how far we'd actually walked.

We were there.

Aave was already at the train stop. Bolted to one side of the metal frame arching over the long bench was a worn plate: REMEMBER ALL ACTIVE ALTS ARE EXPECTED TO ENGAGE AND COMPLETE ASSIGNMENTS IN A DISCREET, RESPECTFUL, AND RESPONSIBLE MANNER THANK YOU THE BOARD.

The three of us stepped up to stand next to Aave.

"Is Hoult sure?" Chord asked him. "About the time and everything?"

I'd heard the name before. Hoult was a classmate of Aave's—had been, anyway, before he'd gotten his assignment a few weeks earlier.

Aave nodded. "He's been tracking him. Says his Alt takes the outer ward train at this time each weekend, switching between Saturday and Sunday. He wasn't here yesterday, so it's gotta be today."

They kept their voices low because we weren't alone at the stop. Even on a Sunday there was a morning train rush for the early shifts.

A man in a suit with a briefcase and a cell pressed to his ear.

A woman in a server uniform.

Another woman dressed in a lab coat and carrying a duffel bag.

"Why would his Alt keep taking the same train at the same time if he has an assignment?" Luc asked Aave. "No one's that stupid. He's got to know Hoult's out here somewhere, looking for him."

"Hoult says his Alt's got the IQ of a june bug. He's already fallen behind two years. Him switching between Saturdays and Sundays *is* his idea of not being stupid."

Luc shook his head. "Wow, Hoult really lucked out, didn't he?"

"All right," Aave said, "so it sounds like we're good to go." He looked over at me. "Don't forget, West. It's about what to do, but also what *not* to do, got it?"

"Got it." I stood next to Luc and Chord as we all pretended

to be waiting for the train, there alongside the man and the two women.

Within minutes, Aave was saying quietly between his teeth, "Okay, there he is."

From the far end of the street, a tall teenaged boy approached. He was thick in the waist, with light brown hair the color of milk chocolate, glasses, jeans, a gray jacket, and a book in his hands. He was actually reading it as he walked. His mouth moved along with the words.

"Whoa," Aave said in disbelief. "What an idiot. He deserves it. This is going to be a cakewalk for Hoult."

I looked over at Chord, who looked over at me, and we both looked over at Luc. He stared back at us, and what Aave said echoed in our heads. I knew we were all thinking the same thing. If there was only room for either him or Hoult, the weaker had to go.

The Alt kept reading as he walked, not looking up even once to see if Hoult could be nearby.

I felt sick. To know that he was about to die, that it made sense for him to die and not Hoult. Sick because he still looked very much like a little kid, too wrapped up in the world he held in his hands to remember the dangers of this one, the real one, the only one that mattered in the end.

Watch what to do, what not *to do.*

A movement on the other side of the street, directly opposite where Hoult's Alt stood on the sidewalk, caught my attention. A rumbling in the bushes, a shaking of evergreen leaves and spindly brown branches.

Hoult burst out, hair wild, eyes wilder. I'd never seen him before in my life, but I knew it was Hoult because his face was exactly the same as his Alt's. He even wore glasses, though the frames were thinner. And Hoult's thickness had a different kind of density, bulky muscle rather than lumpy fat. Proof of how environment and habits could make you veer just slightly off course from your Alt. Hoult exercised regularly; his Alt didn't.

Hoult was holding a gun. Small and efficient, nearly swallowed up by his hand.

My breath was caught in my throat, trapped like a bug in a cupped fist, wings vibrating in dread.

One of the ladies on the bench, the server, uttered a short squawk of surprise. Immediately covering her mouth as dismay crossed her face. She dropped to a half crouch. FDFO.

That got Hoult's Alt's attention. He glanced up from his book and toward the train stop, his mouth hanging open, a blank expression on his face. I watched his lips start to form a word, though I couldn't actually hear him from where I was standing.

Wha—

Hoult fired. The sound of the gun was bright and loud. It made me think of smoke and fire.

At thirty feet, most active Alts with even the minimal amount of training probably had a good chance of at least nicking their target. Hoult had no more than twenty to cover. And he had trained.

His Alt fell, a punctured balloon. His book flew through

the air, pages fluttering in the wind. His glasses shattered into shiny shards that sprinkled on the pavement. His head cracked like a dropped pumpkin.

I watched, breath finally coming, but shallowly, making me light-headed, as Hoult crouched over his Alt's body. Double-checked for death before leaping away, finally safe, finally a complete.

"Let's go," Aave said firmly. "Before clearing gets out here."

Luc looked at him. "Don't you want to go congratulate him or something?"

Aave shook his head. Flicked a glance in my direction. "No, not right now. I'll see him soon enough."

We all turned from the scene and began moving away from the train stop. None of us had much to say; it was strange to have everyone so quiet. But words came hard when your head was still replaying what happened over and over.

At one point the siren of a clearing truck began to blare, getting louder as it got closer to the scene. It sounded like crying, the wailing of someone mourning, and I thought of the lady sitting on the bench. The look on her face made me wonder if she knew the Board offered counseling to bystanders, too, not just survivors of incompletes. I felt odd inside, like the world had been shaken and set back down, no longer quite the same as it had been. Somehow messier, less coherent.

"You okay, West?" Chord asked. The worry in his eyes was obvious. "Maybe it was too soon for—"

I shook my head. Tried to blink away a sudden wave of heat in my eyes. "No, I had to see one start to finish sooner or later, right?"

"And Hoult's safe now, just like we wanted," Luc said. "His Alt didn't really stand a chance, so I guess it was meant to be."

"He'll probably be back at school tomorrow," Aave said. But his voice wasn't quite right, as though he was speaking just for the sake of saying something.

"You're happy for him, right, Aave?" I grabbed his arm, needing to hear Hoult living meant more than just his Alt dying. "Since he was your friend?"

Aave nodded. He seemed relieved, but sad, too. Maybe he was thinking about Hoult's Alt's glasses on the ground, shattered. Had the shards looked like tears to him, too? "Yeah, I'm glad it was him. It was always supposed to be him."

I kept walking, my head down, my eyes still burning. Aave was so sure. From what I'd seen, I was sure, too. So why did my stomach feel so queasy?

Chord moved closer, gently pulled my hood down over my head, and let me lean against him as we headed home.

A ball whizzes by my feet, startling me out of my memories. My eyes chase it until it disappears into the shadows of a nearby lawn.

A boy runs over to pick the ball up. Farther down I hear someone yell at him to be careful. The voice is young, so maybe a brother, or a friend. Then a third chimes in, a girl's voice this time.

We used to play just like this, when we were kids. When the world was bathed in dusk, its stars just blinking on, the ever-present barrier looming at its edges. After we were done training for the day, the four of us would run up and down the streets and across neighbors' yards, playing whatever came to mind beneath the yellow glow of streetlamps as drivers swore at us from their cars.

The girl I was that day, when I saw my first completion . . . she was horrified by what was only natural, an Alt killing his Alt. How would she react to what I just did? What would that West think of me now?

I have to believe that with each strike, I won't be killing someone so much as I'll be letting someone else live. That I'll be saving someone else's life.

It's fully dark by the time I get up and start walking again. But the stars still haven't come out, and I'm left to navigate my way home without them.

Chapter 4

The doorbell rings. I barely hear it over the sound of running water.

Who could it be? Not Chord; I told him weeks ago I wanted to walk to school from now on. By myself.

He went quiet, and from the look in his eye I knew he was as upset as he was angry. But he didn't argue. As much as he understood that it was hard for me to see him because of what happened to Luc, he was also still struggling with the fact that I was a striker. That right or wrong, whatever I needed couldn't be found with him. Which made it hard for him to see me, too.

My eyes dart over to the clock above the stove. Nearly nine. I finish washing the specks of blood from my hands and turn off the water. Glance at the switchblade on the counter I was in the middle of cleaning.

It must be something important. I don't think Chord would come by otherwise. Not after how we left each other last time, when I refused to get into his car for school.

I kick my open bag out of the way as I run from the kitchen, reminding myself that I still need to throw something in there for lunch. At the same time, I yank my sleeves down over my wrists, poking my thumbs through the holes I've cut out. The motion is almost second nature now. At school, and around Chord especially, I'm always sure to hide my marks.

Doorbell again.

And when I open the door, it's not Chord standing there after all, but an Operator from the Board.

The way he's dressed tells me instantly he's a Level 3— standard assignment policy. Still rising in the ranks, they're the ones sent out to deliver the news to idles that they're now actives. Clad in dark gray from head to toe, from the cuffs of his trousers to the tweed epaulets on the shoulders of his jacket. A slip of silk in the left front chest pocket is the lone splash of color. The bright red of poppies and pomegranates and fresh blood, it's the signature color of this particular Level within the Board.

So numb. Still, I take in every detail.

The morning sun hits his scalp, bare from the required daily shave. Nails trimmed to the very quick and buffed to a mild shine. No jewelry of any kind, of course—that would speak of some individuality. And his eyes are intentionally and carefully blank, just as they have been trained to be.

The tips of his gray shoes are slightly scuffed.

How is it possible the Board missed that when they sent him out? I wonder dazedly. Even for a Level 3, it's important to maintain the uniform to the most exacting, demanding degree. It has to be all the legwork, I tell myself. As early as it is, I'm probably not the first assignment he's had to deliver today.

"West Grayer?" the Operator asks. His voice is bland, stuck in neutral, without an inkling of personality.

I've been told that when it finally happens, it's like watching the whole world go dim, all lights extinguished with one swift snuff. That suddenly I won't be able to breathe, as though I am already dying. That most of me will freeze up, not wanting to deal—neither charging nor hiding but just trying to make the inevitable go away.

That's what they said it would be like. But they were wrong.

It's Chord's face in my mind. A horrible, bone-deep surety that I will never get to know more of him than what I already know. And it's far from enough.

It's anguish over my lost family, cutting through me like a blade. So unfair, that they all died first. What could I have done to have it be so unfair?

It's the face of my Alt staring back at me. My own face.

I am going to die.

"West Grayer?"

I jerk my head in a nod. Blink myself back and stare at him. "Yes. I'm her. I'm West."

He holds his cell to my face at eye level, and a flash of light blinds me for a few seconds, followed by a searing flash of heat across my pupils. Then activation software in the device beeps to signal that my assignment number has been properly triggered.

My eyes, now spiraled with a sequence of numbers that I share with my Alt. Wherever she is at this moment, I know her own Level 3 Operator is right there with her.

"Cell, please," the Operator says.

My hand slowly pulls my cell from my pocket and passes it over. I can see the blood still staining the beds of my fingernails, crescents of evidence of last night's strike. I ended up having to use one of my blades—up close, not over a distance, the idea of throwing still too raw for me to try again—which always leaves more of a mess than the gun does. Getting home super-late meant having to clean up this morning. I put away the gun and the two blades I didn't use last night.

He holds my cell up to his own so it can receive my assignment details. "You'll find everything you need in the file," he says. Another beep. Passes my cell back to me. "As per Board rules, please be sure to read it in full."

Somehow I make myself nod.

The Operator punches something into his cell to close the document and relay to the Board a successful assignment delivery. He neatly tucks his cell away.

"West Grayer, as of this moment, you have exactly thirty-one days to complete your assignment. If at thirty-two days it has not been completed by either you or your Alt, your Alternate code will self-detonate."

I nod again. All I can do.

"Be the one, be worthy."

With that, he's gone, a gray phantom. Only the one dab of blood over his heart remains vivid enough in my mind for me to know he was real.

So that's it. I have my assignment. It's the last thing I would imagine to be possible: that at fifteen, I'd be both an active Alt and a striker.

Though only one is by choice.

I stumble away from the door, heading somewhere else, anywhere else. My eyes dully take in the sight of my bag, still in the middle of the floor, still waiting for a lunch, on a day that is not going to happen as planned.

Get moving, West. You know you have to leave if you want a chance. It's my voice in my head . . . except there are traces of Luc, too . . . all my family, Baer . . . Chord.

I know all the stats, the numbers, the odds. As a striker, especially. But I'm suffocating now, and none of that seems so important anymore. Safety was being in an assassin's world, staying in the dark, memories gone mute, when it was never me but some other Alt about to die.

I return to the kitchen, study the switchblade I was cleaning just before. There's still blood where the blade meets the handle, deep in the joint. I wonder if I can scrub it away if I try hard enough, long enough. Try to make it disappear before it seeps too far inward.

I turn the water back on, hold the switchblade beneath the flow.

There's a loud banging at the front door before it crashes open. Chord's rushing toward me, his dark eyes meeting mine, and I know what he sees. As good as I might be at denial, it's impossible in the face of his reaction.

"You shouldn't be here, West," he whispers roughly. "Why are you still here?"

I shudder at the sound of his voice. If feelings alone could save a life, neither of us would ever be in danger.

"West, what are you doing?" He takes in the running water, the sink, the blade. "I just saw an Operator leaving your house!" He turns the tap off with a hard twist of his hand.

I breathe out and dry the switchblade with the tail of my shirt before folding it up and tucking it into the front pocket of my jeans. There it is again—that same mix of pain and pleasure at having him so close. "You're going to be late for school, Chord," I say to him.

"Don't mess around, West!" he says, nearly yelling. "What's wrong with you?"

"Nothing." There is no real thought behind my answer. Just rote movements of lips, tongue, air. His hair is wild, his mouth a harsh, savage line. "I'll be fine."

He walks over to my bag and upends it onto the floor.

My mouth drops open. "Hey, Chord, wait. . . ."

But he's already halfway up the stairs, empty bag in hand. The last time he was here, he demanded I shoot for him before he would leave. What does he want from me this time before he's safe and free of me?

Chord is still moving, and as I scuttle after him I pass my parents' bedroom. An image of the remainder of my father's sleeping pills, the bottle still in the medicine cabinet, flashes in my mind. The pills he intentionally took all the way to his death, already more than halfway there after my mother died as a PK. For her to survive to be a complete, only to be killed anyway, was too much for him to wrap his head around.

But then Chord's in my bedroom, and all thoughts of the pills dissipate.

I walk in to see that he's tossed the bag on top of my bed

before ripping open the door to my closet. I close my eyes at the clink of cheap wire hangers being moved around, the shuffle of stuff falling off the shelves and hitting the floor. Each sound is a testament to Chord's frustration, his fear.

Sweaters, jackets, jeans, all landing on my bed to create a small mountain. He throws a pair of shoes across the room. Another pair lands on my desk, sending a pile of sketch pads flying. They tip over one of the pails I use to hold pens and brushes and tubes of paint. More than a few of these roll off and hit the ground.

"What are you doing?" I say to his back. Though I know exactly what he's doing. It's what I should have already done.

He turns around and glares at me. "What do you think I'm doing?"

"Get out of my closet, Chord," I say, my voice mechanical even to my own ears. "Stop messing around with my stuff."

"I can't even look at you right now," he says, his disgust too great to hide. "Here." He pushes the bag at me. "Pack it. Take what you think you'll need. I'll give you as much cash as I have with me, to buy whatever else later. Just pack it and get away from here." I crush the bag with my hands before letting it fall to my feet.

"I don't need your money," I tell him through numb lips. "I've been working, remember?"

The reminder of my striker status only upsets him further. "I know you're too smart to touch whatever you've got, if you've been putting it away. Not unless you want it to show up on the Alt log."

He's right, of course. The Alt log is the Board's database for an active's movements. Once an assignment goes live in the system, all transactions require an Alt's eyes to be scanned. The information—assignment number, location, time—gets fed right into the Alt log. Active Alts can then access this data from the terminal station, Kersh's checkpoint during assignments.

I'm live as of this morning. Bank transactions of any kind will need an eye scan now. And that would give my Alt her first clue . . . to where I've been, where I'm going, where I might be.

I can be Dire's highest-paid striker, and it won't make a bit of difference. Apart from the handful of bills I stashed in my dresser after last night's strike, I'm cleaned out. So wrong and stupid to think I was even *close* to being ready—

Chord grabs the bag from where it's still lying at my feet. He starts shoving in fistfuls of clothes. "West, *move*! What are you waiting for? *Her?* You want a personal introduction or something?"

I can only shake my head. My own anger is starting to simmer, kindled by Chord's rage. "No, I—"

"I have no idea what's going on, why you're still here. Why we're even discussing this. But you're running out of time. Did you even bother to read the assignment details on your cell?"

"Yes." The weight of the cell in my pocket seems to double, heavy with the lie.

Chord's eyes narrow, and he grimaces. "You haven't, have you? You don't know how far away she is—or how close. For all you know, she could be here any minute, if she's managed to do what you haven't."

"You know they never decide that fast. They always—"

"*We* did, West. Remember? We decided right away to find my Alt."

And Luc died, didn't he?

"What we did wasn't typical," I insist, pushing away the memory of that day, that room. "Most new actives take a while to decide—"

"West, you really want to talk numbers now?" Chord looks down, sees the slim bulk of my cell in my jeans pocket. He drops the half-filled bag, holds out his hand. "Let me read it, if you won't," he says roughly. "You can't wait any longer."

I don't move. My nerves sing and thrum, beating back more panic. A flashback to us in that restaurant in the Grid, me reading his assignment, me forcing him to bend, me being the one who let his Alt get the first shot.

"West, pass me your cell," he says, his voice grim. "Don't make me beg."

"If you leave, I'll do it, I promise," I say to him. I don't let myself think about whether I mean it. Anything to get him away from me . . . from her.

His face darkens, goes tight. Quick as I've ever seen him move, he reaches for me.

"Chord, don't!" I shove him away, his determination to help me.

He steps back, runs his hands through his hair. Black fire in his eyes. "None of it is going to mean anything if she gets here first. So move!"

"I said I'll do it!" I yell back at him.

He grabs me by the arm, harder than he probably knows,

swearing under his breath. "I was beyond scared the day I got mine. I started thinking that it maybe *wasn't* supposed to be me, that I wasn't meant to win. And it was you who made us go down there to find my Alt. Not me, not Luc—*you,* West. I miss that person." He drops his hand, and it squeezes into a fist at his side. "That's who you have to be again."

Chord's words cut through me, an echo of what I already know. But in whatever way I might have saved his life, I also ended Luc's.

"It's okay, Chord," I say to him, calm again. "I'll do it on my own . . . when I'm ready. I told you, I don't want you here, remember? I don't need you." *Hurt him so he'll want to leave.*

"West—"

I push him. *"Go!"* My voice breaks, and I can't say anything else.

Silence in the room, thick with our breathing. Then he's gone.

I stand there, frozen by the need to keep time from moving forward. To stop the beginning of the end. But I can feel it anyway. I'm being drawn closer to my Alt and her to me. Only three outcomes possible: my end, or hers—or both.

A shiver racks me, even with the light shining in. The morning sun is much higher now, the day crawling closer toward afternoon. Then it'll be evening, then night, and it'll start all over again, thirty more times.

I can no more stop what has to happen than I can keep the earth from spinning.

And I have less than seven hours before it's dark.

I dump the freshly packed contents of my bag back onto the bed.

Chord has picked all the wrong things, of course. He never feels the cold like I do. I need layers, not bulk. The test comes in a few weeks, closer to winter, when the temperatures drop steeply at night.

If I make it that long.

I stuff thermals into my bag. A thicker fleece pullover to double as a jacket. A lightweight shell for rain. A pair of jeans, because although denim's heavy, it's also warm and sturdy. Socks and underwear, enough to last me for a few days, so I won't have to wash or steal more right away.

I bend over, pick up the pens and brushes and tubes of paint that fell from my desk, and tuck them back into the pail I set upright. Pile up my sketch pads again.

Then I get down on my hands and knees, and from underneath the bed I pull out my old jewelry box. Ehm gleefully claimed it as her own years ago, but after she died, I took it back, a part of her mine again.

Carefully, I lift the lid and move aside the old shirt I tossed in there to hide the real treasure.

Inside is Luc's gun—*my* gun—cleaned and ready for the next job. Beside it is Aave's old knife roll, what I now use to hold my own collection of blades. They're nothing fancy, but more than adequate.

I'm still not as good with a blade as they were—Aave, especially, who was at the top of his class. But I'm getting better, stronger. No longer does my blade catch when slashing. No longer does my wrist seize up with the quick motion. Years of training with my brothers, coupled with my work as a striker, all to prepare for something that will last no more than seconds.

Only with my aim am I less than I should be. My weak spot, what nature's decided to make me work for, forcing me to go against the tide just to keep up.

The knife roll—minus the one blade still in my jeans pocket and the other that I slip into my jacket pocket—goes into my bag. The gun I put into my jacket's other pocket. Together, they'll be what keeps me alive. Not food, not clothes, not money. What will any of that amount to when I finally see her? When she sees me?

It's habit that has me going through the rest of the house, turning off lights, pulling down blinds, and locking all the windows and the back door. In the garage I drape drop cloths over the largest of my father's factory belt servicing tools, his off-site building components, his programming tablet. After securing the heavy metal door to the driveway, I return to the kitchen and wipe out the sink and throw away the milk I find in the back of the fridge. Little things like that. Normal things.

And that's it. I'm done saying good-bye to my home . . . and it didn't break me. I guess it really is just a house now. A case made of concrete and wood and drywall. I've been living here, but it's been long empty in every way that counts. From Aave's death onward, life has seeped from the walls like blood from a wound, refusing to stop until there's no more blood to bleed. It's finally dry. *I'm* dry.

I open the front door and step outside. Lock the door behind me by punching in the key code.

He's sitting on the bottom step, and I've been moving without really seeing for so long that I nearly fall over him. At the sight of him an ache shoots through me from head to toe.

Maybe it's because I truly thought he'd left, but the depth of it catches me off guard, leaves me winded.

"Chord." I go down the stairs to stand next to him, my eyes locked on his face. "What are you still doing here?"

He gets to his feet. "Thought I'd stay until I knew you were ready to go. Safe."

I shift the shoulder straps of the bag. Already it feels too heavy on my back. I packed too much. "What made you think I was going to leave anytime soon? I never said I was ready. You might have ended up waiting all day."

A quick flash of a grin that's loving and bleak and desperately unhappy, and I know the sight of it is going to haunt me for a long time. "You've always been ready for this, West," he says. "You just forgot for a bit there, that's all."

I can't think of anything to say, but somehow it's okay. The silence between us isn't awkward or tense, but almost trembling and fragile, a haunting kind of vulnerability where we're just happy to be together and not wanting to think about anything else.

A few seconds, and then it has to be over. "Chord, I have to go—"

"Take this," he says abruptly. He holds out his hand. I can see a bunch of bills there, a cell. And a flimsy black strip I don't recognize, about the length of my hand.

"I don't need your money," I tell him, shaking my head.

"You will. C'mon, don't be stupid. Take what you can get. Being stubborn's not going to help you anymore."

"You should keep it, Chord. You don't know what you might need it for."

"I need it for this. Will you quit finding reasons to argue with me and just take it?" He lifts my hand and forces the money, cell, and strip into my palm. He says nothing about the sleeve I've got pulled over it, even though he knows what it's hiding.

"What's with the cell?" I ask him. "It's not yours."

"No, it's just an extra one I had lying around. I was just . . . messing with it. You know how you always bug me about having all that tech stuff in the house."

"Well, your room *does* look like a parts shop."

He smiles. "Anyway, keep it on you as a backup, in case something happens to yours. It's bare bones, but it should work well enough for texting and calling."

I hold up the black strip. The material is more mesh than solid, a fine web of the thinnest black wire I've ever seen. "And this?"

"It's a key code disrupter."

"That doesn't really tell me much, Chord."

"It's for bypassing locks," he says. "For when you need to get inside somewhere. Or if you just need to get out of sight . . . hide."

"How does it—"

"Hold it between your wrist and the lock faceplate. It'll read the chips in your marks, scramble them, and temporarily mess up the lock's key code. The broken signals will unlock the door. Quieter and faster than having to force your way in."

"Oh. Thanks for thinking of that."

"I didn't really have a choice."

I don't know how else to ease his worry, so I carefully zip

it into one of the outer pockets on the side of my bag for easy access. I tuck the cell into the main compartment, the money into my jeans pocket. Just by feel I can tell it's too much, but still not enough.

Suddenly I'm unable to look away from him. When will I see him next? Whenever it is, it will be too soon. I don't want him near me at all. Not while I'm a walking target.

"So let's go, then," he says.

I go cold all over. "What are you talking about?"

His eyes are hard now. Gleaming against the sunlight as they scan my face. "I'm going with you."

I laugh, though there's no humor in it at all. "No way."

"Why wouldn't I? There's no reason for me to stay here."

"School." I'm scrambling, grasping. "They would notice if you just stopped showing up."

Chord shrugs. "I'm over fifteen," he says simply. "I can just tell admin I'm opting out to work somewhere." He takes a deep breath. "And Luc would have wanted—"

"Luc again? Chord, I told you, you don't need to do this for him. *I* don't need you to do this." Even as the words leave my mouth, Luc's request echoes in my head. How he wanted me to promise him I wouldn't keep Chord in the dark, that I wouldn't shut myself off from him.

I press a hand to my chest. There's a pain that comes with the memory of his voice. And, worse, with the realization that I'm not going to be able to keep my promise to him, after all.

I'm sorry, Luc. But you're already gone, and Chord's not.

"He wouldn't have wanted you to go it alone," Chord says. "Not if you didn't have to. And, West . . . I told him, you know?" His voice is husky, full of the same memory that's in my head, full of purpose. "As he was dying, I told him I would. How can I fail him now? I can't screw up again. So I'm coming with you."

I know that voice . . . and I know I have to hurt him some more. Because as hardheaded as Chord is, his stubbornness is nothing compared to mine. And I've become a very good liar these past few months.

"Fine." I make sure to sound ungrateful about it. It's what he would expect, and I can't afford to have him thinking anything else is up. "Keep an eye out while I run in and grab a bag for you. No way you're making me carry all this by myself if you're coming with me."

"Time." Chord's watch instantly processes his order, spits out the numbers in a modulated burst. Nearly eleven in the morning. I think of Luc's watch, carefully strapped around my own wrist.

He frowns, knowing I've already lost a couple of hours, and says to me, "Okay, but be quick, all right? We want to get a good head start."

I don't let myself look at him, as much as I want to. It would be written all over my face. What he doesn't know, what he can't know—that for me, this has to be good-bye.

I run back into the house and keep going straight through until I'm leaving again, this time out the back door at the other end. If I stop for even a second, I will go back, hold on to Chord, and not let go until someone is dead: my Alt, me, or Chord, somehow caught in the middle.

I step out onto the porch, lock the door behind me, and silently cross the length of the yard until I'm at the back fence.

Three boards over from the left. I can hardly dare to believe that I still remember.

I count them with my fingers. One, two, three. The third cedar slat wiggles slightly; it has more give than the others, just as it always has. I slide it over until there's a gap in the fence. It's no more than a foot and a half wide, but I know I can squeeze through. There is no choice but to squeeze through.

For one horrible second, I'm stuck, the sheer bulk of my bag catching on the sides. But I work it free and replace the loose board so the fence looks whole again.

I'm moving fast across the neighbor's yard now—past the large sugar maple cradling the old tree house in the back, along the side of the main house, through the tangle of bushes at the front—to come out on another street altogether. Chord's in a hurry. He'll be heading inside any second to see what's taking me so long. And I can't risk his seeing me.

My eyes burn as I run down the street, and soon I'm blinded with tears. Throat on fire from a withheld scream, chest tight with agony.

I'm sorry, Chord. Stay safe. Stay away from me.

CHAPTER 5

Ten days left.

The thin, keening whistle of a fighter jet wakes me up. It's far away, deep in the Surround, probably miles from the border. Merely routine, not nearly loud or close enough to have Kersh be at the ready.

When I open my eyes, the sky is already light—the dull, sinister gray of winter mornings, but still light.

I've slept for too long.

I sit up slowly, my legs stiff from both the cold air and having been awkwardly positioned all night. Given the amount of supplies in the cab of the truck, there wasn't much room left for me to stretch out.

But it was safe enough, and cheap. It didn't take a lot to convince the warehouse owner, and I knew it wasn't the first time he'd taken money to let an active crash in one of the delivery trucks in his back lot.

Getting ready to climb out, I automatically run my hand over my jacket pocket, feeling for the shape of my gun; then the other pocket, for my blade. Pat my jeans pocket to make sure that blade's still there, too. When I reach for my bag, my hand hits a little taped package placed on top. It wasn't there when I fell asleep.

I swear at Chord silently through clenched teeth, like I always do when he does this. Not so much for following me, but because he's able to do it so easily. How *is* he doing it?

It'd be a mistake to discount Chord's tech background. He has to be using those skills somehow, even though he didn't exaggerate about the cells being bare bones. There's no software that even resembles a shadowing system, as far as I can tell. If he's really able to track me down without any other means, then it could prove to be that easy for *her,* too.

I push away the thought before it has the chance to dig in. Make cold fear become irritation again because it's easier. Chord and his little care packages. I'm grateful for his thoughtfulness, but I hate it at the same time, knowing he's in danger because he refuses to stay away. Wondering if he's observing from a safe distance even now, I tear open the package.

Inside are the usual two items: cash and a fresh, fully charged cell. His timing, as always, is eerily perfect: the old cell is practically dead. It takes me only a few seconds to transfer all my data from one to the other. Once the old cell is wiped clean, I toss it into one of the outer pockets of my bag for recycling later—the new one goes securely inside. The cash I split up: half on me, half in my bag. I can't care that it's Chord's. After a few weeks on the run, I'm past that now. It'll buy me whatever I need—food, clothes—when my own money can't.

I ask for the time, and when my watch beeps out that it's a quarter past eight, I realize just how close I'm cutting it. The specs of the strike I accepted last night tell me I have to go now if I'm going to find my strike where I want to find him.

Shoving the mess of my hair farther into my hood so I look somewhat passable, I climb out of the truck, reach back in for my bag, and sling the straps over my shoulders. I weave my way through the dark and intense hustle of the Grid's morning rush, the surging bodies that have places to go, places to be.

I stop and take note of where I am, making sure I have the address right.

One block over, then one down. If I've got my timing right, the shop is about to open. And I'd better have it right—I'll only have about a minute before the window I've allowed myself closes. That's how long it'll take for him to get from his car to the back door of his family's store. I've read my client's spec sheet on his Alt enough times that I can almost recite it by heart, in my sleep. Particularly the part about his Alt's routine.

> *He's (we're) eighteen and finishing his co-op term at Lear & York Barristers in Calden Ward. Also works at Tweed's Stationery on Mathers Street in Jethro in the mornings. Getting it from both ends right now—Lear & York wants to know his career plans if he ends up completing; his father wants him to commit to running Tweed's full-time because he wants early retirement with the wife.*
>
> *Been tracking him for four days now. He's too tired to care about leaving a pattern.*
>
> *His car is a black Verve hatch, plate #C4D9P7X7.*
>
> *His weapon of choice is a gun.*

I cross the street with the lights, and over the sea of bobbing heads I see it.

Tweed's Stationery is a storefront combined with a vintage paper press in the back that still produces specialty items, according to the tagline on the front window etched below the store name. It's old-fashioned and charming and one of those places I could have easily spent hours in, lost in crisp textiles and clean lines and the smell of glazes and ink.

No longer possible now. Another life, another time.

I enter the alley that runs behind the block of stores and see right away how tight it's going to be, how little room there is to move. Unauthorized, small-scale dumping grounds are pretty common throughout this part of the Grid, and the ward will sometimes go for months before finally getting around to clearing them out. This particular alley is choking with dying cars, the sides of it lined with them, a crooked, broken train of vehicles that runs the length of the whole block. Some are already starting to go orange with rust, urban sunsets in a concrete jungle.

The smell of decay is sharp in my nose as I crouch down between two cars. Positioned here, across the alley from the back lot of the stationery store, I have the best sight line to where my strike is going to be.

"Time," I ask as I tighten the straps of my bag over my shoulders.

08:42. Eighteen minutes left to go until he shows up, since the doors open at nine.

But then a huge tow truck is coming through, slow and rumbling. Another behind that, and then a third, a fourth.

They keep moving, only cutting their engines after they're practically right in front of me. No way of seeing Tweed's from here now; instead I watch, stunned, as four guys climb out of the tow trucks and noisily start hooking up the abandoned cars for removal.

I don't know if a striker's ever had to pull back because of something going wrong at the last moment, but I don't want to be the first. If I can't think around this . . . if my Alt were to catch me off guard somehow and I couldn't find a way to recover—

"Time." I scramble to my feet, scan my surroundings again, turning around once, twice. The sight lines at eye level are no longer workable, so I scan higher—the roofline of the buildings around me.

08:47.

Thirteen minutes left and I'm getting desperate, my throat going tight, looking for anything now—when I see it.

The fire escape on the side of the four-story building diagonally across from Tweed's back lot. Portions of it are swinging free from its attachments, whether by neglect or force I don't know, but it's still intact enough to spiral its way up to the roof.

I head over, cutting my way through the tight maze of creaking steel. There's enough commotion that I slip by unnoticed. I jump onto the top of the nearest car and step onto the bottom platform of the stairs. Start climbing.

"Time," I huff out as the ground recedes farther and farther. My throat's still tight, too—no longer from panic but from knowing I've never done a strike cold like this before. Such little preparation, groundwork unlaid, perspective unknown.

08:51.

As soon as my feet hit the roof—a flat plain of dark gray, slightly dipped in the middle and still damp from last night's rain—I run to the edge and peer down. The distance is close to forty, possibly fifty feet, and another twenty feet on top of that to the store. Farther than I'm used to, but not enough that it should be an issue.

The workers down below are still at work, slowly loading the tow trucks.

And a Verve hatch, black and dusty, weaves its way down the alley. By the time it drives past me and pulls into Tweed's back lot, I've already pulled my gun free and have it aimed.

Plate number *C4D9P7X7*. A match.

The person climbing out of the car looks the same as the picture of my client. He seems older than eighteen, broken sleep still etched in lines on his face, his wispy brown hair nearly as thin as his frame. Black pants, gray shirt, navy bomber jacket.

His gun is cradled in a holster that hangs too loosely around his hips. It swings as he turns in my direction, and knocks back against his body as he starts walking toward the trunk of the car. His head is exposed and vulnerable.

When the sharp, cold lick of wind comes, freeing long strands of hair from beneath my hood so they whip the side of my face and slap against my lips, I don't think anything of it.

My bullet is a roar. It blisters through the air like a rocket burning through fuel. It thrums a minute vibrato as it shears along the outside of his head. He screams, stumbling to his knees with a hand pressed to the wound, his other already feeling for his gun.

I should have remembered the distance between him and me, farther than I'm used to. How a bullet riding along such lengths of space can be set adrift by a breeze. How a bullet riding along such lengths is still very much subject to gravity.

But I didn't remember. I missed. Only by a couple of inches, maybe even one, but it's enough to fall short of the mark.

My gut's twisted into knots as I shoot again, and again. Finally he lies still.

For a long moment, everything's perfectly silent, and I can almost pretend the strike hasn't taken place yet. That there's still the chance to plan better, aim better, be better.

The yells of the workers down below bring me back, and I tuck my gun into my pocket and climb down the fire escape. No matter how botched a job, it must be completed. Death must be confirmed.

Walking across the alley, I feel the eyes of the workers on me. I hear the words *striker* and *assignment* and *cheater* even as they go back to hooking up steel skeletons. From around the corner come the loud honks of thick traffic, the clatter of heeled boots on pavement. The day goes on. Life continues.

I move close to the body, avoiding his blood as much as I can as I check for a pulse. When I feel nothing, I pry open one eyelid. His pupil is clean, his assignment number gone.

A text to my client with instructions for the rest of my payment only takes seconds. As does reminding him to contact ward clearing.

As I turn away, I can feel the heat coming off the still-cooling engine of his car. I can't help but hold my fingers to the warmth. It's bliss against the chill in the air . . . the chill inside me.

Go, get moving.

The sight of Chord across the alley startles me into nearly tripping over my own feet.

He's watching me walk away. The tired backdrop of the old building behind him, dulled with layers of industrial exhaust and smog, only makes him more vivid. I don't know how long he's been there . . . or how much he's seen.

The idea of him seeing me work makes me uncomfortable, uneasy—a sensation way too close to guilt. I don't like how it feels, like a greasy weight that wants to cling, and I shake it off resentfully. I have to stop caring what he thinks about my being a striker. Stop caring about him altogether.

I hunch into my jacket as I walk and refuse to look at him. I'm about to pass him, and when it becomes obvious that I'm planning on ignoring him, Chord moves close enough to block my path.

"Stay away from me, Chord," I say to him. I move around him, out toward the street.

He follows. "You know I can't." He pauses. "Can we talk for five minutes?"

"No, I don't think—"

He grabs my arm, surprisingly gentle despite his insistence. "Good, I'm glad you're thinking for once. Talk to me, but not here. Clearing is going to be here soon."

So he saw me kill, then. The knowledge that he can't possibly see me as he used to, that I've fallen to new, unspeakable depths, twists in my chest.

We're lost in the crowd already, caught in the flow as we walk up the block. I look around, wary, wondering if we're as anonymous as I hope we are.

Thinking fast, needing to put distance between us, I say stiffly, "Luc's dead. He won't know if you stay away."

Chord sighs, slips his hand down so it's closer to my own. "Give it up, West. I've heard that way too many times to let it bother me anymore."

I try again. "I'm serious. You need to quit following me. What if you get sloppy and slip and get *her* on me?"

Chord shakes his head. "Even if she sees me, so what? She has no reason to wonder who I am." He looks down at me, pulls me closer, his hand tensing. "I saw her," he says. "This morning, early."

My stomach clenches. Pure ice inside me. "How do you know it wasn't me you saw?" I ask. My voice sounds faint, even to my ears, barely audible over the other conversations floating around us.

"I can tell." It's all he says.

"We're exactly the same." I shake his hand off. He's too close again. I wrap my arms around myself. "Or similar enough that you could make that mistake."

"Her eyes . . ." He grins, the smile a poor imitation of his real one. "Believe it or not, they're even colder than yours. Even with the way you're looking at me now."

I scowl. "Thanks. I think."

"She's practically on top of you, West. You need to get out of the Grid. You shouldn't be in Jethro at all—not until you figure out how you're going to hunt her down."

We're passing a lingerie shop, and I grab the opportunity and duck inside. I know Chord's going to follow me—he's too stubborn not to—but I'm hoping he'll feel too awkward to want to stay long. I'm hoping he'll cut our five minutes short all by himself.

"So, is that what you wanted to tell me?" I lean over to examine a rack of filmy black bras. I can see our reflections in the long mirror that lines the room. I can almost believe we're just another couple hanging out. "Was there something else?"

Chord keeps his eyes fixed on me. To my frustration, there's no sign of embarrassment on his face. Or he's too good at hiding it. "You just found out your Alt is right here in the Grid. I thought it seemed pretty important."

"Well, thanks for letting me know." I hold the sheer material up to my chest. "If there's nothing else you need to tell me—"

"How about why you're still taking striker contracts now that you're an active?" he says. He doesn't even sound angry. Just confused, almost hurt. "It can't be the money. No way you're getting paid in straight cash instead of direct cell deposits— even *I* know strikers don't make personal contact with their clients. Besides, if you ever needed more, you know you can ask—"

"I don't need your money, so stop giving it to me." Aware of the other shoppers and the sales clerks roaming around, I hold the bra up higher for him to inspect.

Chord swats it away irritably. "You need food, don't you?"

"That's not your problem." Then I hesitate, thinking of all the actives forced to eat from Board-endorsed kiosks, where an eye scan buys not only discounted food but also an automatic

Alt log entry. I think of myself buying food from friendlier places, where an extra bill of Chord's money helps grease the wheels, where my eyes are conveniently overlooked. "But you're right. I do need it. So, thank you, okay?"

A pause, then he asks, "What about the cells? Any problems using them?"

I shake my head. There's tension in his voice, and I'm assuming it's because he knows I've been mostly using the cells to make contact with Dire and striker clients. Anyone other than him. "No, they've been fine," I tell him. I hold up something that is especially flimsy, deliberately swinging it through the air.

I don't think he even notices; he's too intent on watching my face. "So, can you tell me why you're still taking contracts, then? I thought once you got your assignment . . . once you were able to deal with what happened to Luc . . . you'd feel differently about being a striker."

I take a couple of steps away from him and make a show of going through a stack of lacy and completely impractical panties. My hands are shaking, thick and clumsy in clouds of diaphanous fabric. "It's exactly what Baer said, that's all. This is the best kind of training I could ever ask for. Why would I turn it away now?"

"C'mon, West," he retorts. "It's been long enough; you've *learned* enough. It's your own Alt you need to kill now, so stop running!"

"I'm not running; I'm just trying to keep going!"

"How does being an assassin keep you going?" The sound of his voice has me finally meeting his eyes.

The look in them is heartbreaking, a mix of utter bewilderment, anger, hurt. It gnaws at me to know that I'm the one who's put all that there—that both of us have made such a thing possible. Like everything that's happened since Luc's death has forced us to meet each other for the first time again, strangers starting completely from scratch.

"Because I don't want to think about anything else," I whisper. There's a dull roar in my head. My hands are fists, too rough for the delicate fabric. "You know, if I'd become a striker earlier, I could have handled them all. Your Alt, too. Then Luc wouldn't have died that way."

Chord untangles my hands and takes them in his own. He glances down at my sleeves, pulled low over my wrists, my thumbs sticking out from the holes I've poked out with the tip of a blade.

"It's you now," he says quietly, "not them, and not me. You always said that when it was your turn, you wouldn't run or hide. I would have thought that of anyone—with you doing what you do—you'd know that you're almost out of time." He tilts his head down as he lifts my chin up. "Ten days, West. That's all."

It doesn't surprise me that he's been counting, too.

"Won't you be able to deal with me for just ten days?" Chord asks. Low and soft, weakening me.

Then my eyes are drawn to the mirror against the far wall, and I can see my face staring back at me, as well as Chord's head, his wide shoulders, the slope of his back. In a single blink, I'm not me anymore but my Alt . . . so close to him, close enough to hurt, to kill.

I can't make that mistake again.

I pull away. "I—I've gotta go," I stammer.

Frustration tightens his jaw. "West—"

"I can't." My hands shoot out to ward him off as I back away. I don't want him touching me. I'm glass right now. I can feel myself starting to break. "I've gotta go," I say again. "Good-bye, Chord."

I stumble out the door and down the street, instantly dissolving into the crowd and trying to not hear the echo of his voice in my head, pulling me back. Not that the next little while will be any less difficult. The empty hours of waiting between strikes are the loudest, the most likely to wake the memories lurking just beneath the surface.

And if what Chord says is right, then I've already been in the same spot for far too long. It's time to disappear again, to no longer be West Grayer but someone else.

You need to get out of the Grid.

A sudden spurt of anger at Chord, building with each step I take until I'm walking blindly, not entirely paying attention to where I'm going. I don't want to know that my Alt is here. I've already left home once, and now he's telling me I have to leave it again. The Grid is what I know—for her to chase me out could be the end of me.

When I finally realize where I am, it's too late to avoid it. It looms in front of me, a building as large as a whole city block, wanting to draw me in.

Kersh's terminal station. The brainchild of some old Level 1 Operators, it's supposed to be a safe house for active Alts. Food, beds, shelter. But because you can't get in without an eye scan, the building itself can be a death trap. It offers sight lines and collision points, potential meeting areas. The danger of running into your Alt skyrockets when inside the terminal; nearly half of all assignments are completed within its walls.

Alts of two extremes come here. Those who finally break and accept they're going to die, no matter what they do. And those who know nothing but confidence—being worthy is a given. A small part of me is sure that if my Alt *has* been at the terminal—or even is there right now, as I'm standing across the street from it—it is because she is one of these. One without doubt and without fear.

Since the activation of my assignment, this is the closest I've dared to come to the terminal.

For a few minutes more, I linger. It's interesting in a morbid kind of way, the same way a car accident can be interesting. Many active Alts—made just as obvious by their furtive steps and haunted, backward glances as by their encoded eyes—scuttle past the terminal's front doors. Only a handful go inside.

My stomach growls, and I find a sandwich bar two blocks from the main street. I sit down in a booth that faces out so I can see the street, the sight wavering just enough that I don't forget I'm sitting behind bulletproof glass for a reason. I wash my lunch down with tea that's both bitter and weak, stretched through oversteeping. Making a silent, grudging toast to Chord with each sip, I try not to imagine him sitting with me.

At one point, a group of students from the university art campus comes in. They sit at a table right behind the large glass window and eat without a care in the world.

It's always these kinds of completes—the ones who aren't

that much older than me—who have the power to make me jealous. I drink them in, a life just beyond my reach. The way they sit there with their leather bags from the campus store hanging over their chairs, filled with textbooks and novels and flexi-readers with neat lines of knowledge. The way they smell of another world altogether—of being complete and finally allowed to start living, of never again having to look over their shoulders for their own murderous faces bearing down on them.

My leather bag would be brown, a soft camel. It would always be full. Not just with art and technique books and assigned novels that just happen to be by my favorite authors, but with thick tablets of painter's paper. Tins of soft pastel sticks, tubes of bright pigment and paint. The lingering sharpness of thinner throughout. No knife bundle. No balls of soiled clothing kept just in case. No cell with assignment specs. No gun. No scent of desperation, spent smoke, dried blood.

It never takes long anymore for envy to become laced with hate—for them, for myself. Even if I survive and become a complete, it won't erase my striker marks. It can't undo my choice.

When I'm done eating, I can't avoid the fact that it's time to go on a supply run. The store is three blocks down, around the corner, then one block over. I need more bullets.

The glass sign overhead is only half-lit. Most of its letters are shattered into near nothingness, with just enough remaining to still be legible. Barely. But I know it just the same. Dire directed me to it—not only for what they sell, but for what they let slide. I slipped once, accidentally revealing my marks, and when no one seemed to care, I knew that at least in this store, I could move freely.

Except this time, I'm going in not just as a striker, but as an active as well.

It's just as dreary inside as I remember. Like the air's been sucked away, and most of the light, too. It takes a special type of store to cater to those who require guns, I think, one with a certain kind of brutality, because there is no denying the purpose its goods serve.

The worker is the same old man. I can't tell for sure if he recognizes me, but I think he does, just as the best dealers come to know their junkies when they return for more. And it's almost unheard of for a striker to be as young as I am.

Without meeting his eyes, I point to the wall behind him. "Two boxes. Those: two rows in, three down." Saying nothing, he turns, wiggles the boxes of bullets free, and places them on the counter between us.

When he's done, I finally look him in the eye and reveal my active status.

A single flicker in there. That's all. When he doesn't do or say anything else, I slowly hand over two bills—one that covers the cost of the items, and a bigger one that I saved for this.

He takes the cash, pushes the boxes toward me. Still doesn't say a word.

My hand is shaking as I push the door open.

Thinking to the night ahead, I realize I still need to figure out where I'm going to sleep. With my Alt now in the Grid, I grit my teeth and hop on an inner ward train bound for Jethro's suburbs. I pay the full fare, ignoring the free bypass for actives that's offered in exchange for an eye scan. I want to think it's Chord who's making me leave, not my Alt, but I can't hide that it's my fear, too. I'm being chased, when I should be chasing.

Getting off the train is like stepping into a paler, less vibrant world. The noise out here in the suburbs is muffled, quiet, a whisper compared to the constant shout that is the Grid. There's more space to move, space to breathe in air that's not someone else's still-warm exhalation.

I haven't returned since the day I first got my assignment. When I ran from home, from Chord. Now that I'm back, I feel almost like a stranger . . . and more vulnerable here in the open than I ever have in the mad chaos that is the Grid.

Roaming, watching the sun slowly sink, I come to a ravine along one of the back roads. I make my way down; it's deeper than it appears, evergreens still fragrant. I'm far from the first to discover this hidden spot—strewn along the path are snapped branches, flattened flora, and bits of litter—but for now I'm alone.

Down at the bottom the canopy is thickest—the perfect place to wait for the cover of darkness.

I open my bag and pull out my knife roll. Select a switchblade. Shake out my wrist.

Even from the beginning of my training, Aave could tell I didn't have a natural skill for throwing. Both he and Luc did their best to make me better. And it worked . . . somewhat.

An image of my very first strike, that girl running from me, flashes in my head. I was off with my blade; those few inches were the difference between a fast, clean death and her neighbor having to tell me that I didn't do what I was supposed to do, that I wasn't worthy.

I've only dared to use a blade for close-contact kills since then. Unless I get near enough each time, I know it's going to fail me. *I'm* going to fail me.

So I throw, one after the other. Soon the face of the tree trunk I've chosen as my target can barely hold the blade, it's so soft and shredded, and my fingers are sore from twisting the metal free over and over again.

The repetitive thwack of steel against a target and the squeak of the blade being removed bring me back.

"C'mon, West!" Aave wiggled the switchblade free and passed it to me, handle out. "What do you call that? Do it again, all right? And maybe you could, you know, *aim* this time."

I swore at him. Kicked an empty beer bottle across the concrete and sent it careening down the alley. It kept rolling, out onto a street in the Grid. "Shut up, Aave. I *did* aim."

"Someone's got to bug you about it. If it were up to you, it'd be all about the gun. But learning how to use a blade is important, too. Blades won't ever run out of bullets on you."

"I *know* that." I fingered the blade, careful not to slice myself. I did know Aave was right—not that it made it any easier to hear from him how much I sucked. But Aave was so good with a blade that sometimes I just felt like I was wasting his time. And mine. And hitting the same bull's-eye over and over again—taped to a compost bag this time, just one of many that towered along the back wall of the restaurant—was harder than it looked. Some days were better than others. Today was not a good day.

Stupid bull's-eye. Usually it wasn't so hard to see it, to feel it out. Today it might as well have been miles away, a sly bird fleeting through the trees. I wanted to blame the traitorous turn of the blade on a gust of wind, a hateful speck of dirt in my eye, a twitch of my muscles at the wrong moment.

But none of that would be true.

I hissed through my teeth. I was four for nine on this round. Major suckage. One last shot to go.

Curling my right arm back and over, I waited until it was in direct line with the target before letting the blade go. Pulled back just in time so I wouldn't do any damage to my arm muscles by overextending. Made sure not to let my wrist snap, the telltale sign I've held on to the blade one millisecond too long and was about to send it wheeling out of control.

The blade spun from my fingers, a whirl of silver.

It missed by more than a hand span. Five inches, at least. More than wide enough to miss anything vital, which would be what I was aiming for.

I strode up and pulled the blade free before Aave could do it. Next time I would be better—because I had to be.

Snapping the blade shut, I tossed it to Luc. "Here—you're up. I'll take Ehm now."

She was hunched over in the far corner of the lot, oblivious to us as she dissolved her chalk into colored dust on the concrete ground. This was her least favorite part, waiting for us to take turns at the row of targets Aave and Luc set up. She liked it best when we were on the move, exploring the nooks of the old, dank buildings and uncovering new, hidden spaces.

Luc put me to shame. Eight for ten.

"Suck-up," I murmured under my breath.

Luc grinned as he came to sit next to me, and I almost managed to trip him with a well-placed foot. "I'm kicking your butt next time," I said to him.

"Sure, sure."

"Hey, Ehm," Aave called out as he moved the fast-disintegrating target to a fresh spot on the bag. "Come on over. It's your turn."

She sighed before heading over. Her sticks of chalk were bunched in her fists, a bouquet of pinks and yellows and greens that stood out in the grayness of our surroundings: the old cement walls of the buildings, the damp pavement beneath our shoes, the drizzly afternoon air of a Kersh spring.

"Pick your poison, kid," Aave said to her. He held out his oldest practice switchblades so they splayed from his fist, his own startling bouquet. Though the blades didn't seem like much, I knew firsthand they were well made. Sturdy and reliable, wrought from strong base metals. They had to be, to last this long through each of us.

Three for ten. Not much better than any of her previous attempts. Not that Ehm cared too much. At seven, the reality of her assignment was light-years away.

Aave shrugged. "She'll be okay," he said to us. "Luc, you sucked pretty bad in the beginning, too. And West, you're still not very good."

Luc sat up. "Hey!"

I said nothing, just made a face at Aave as he turned to help Ehm get set up again.

"Three years left," Luc said to me. "She's got time on her side, I guess. But still . . . what if all this isn't enough?"

I shook my head. No point in wishing for what wasn't possible. "You know we can't afford any outside training. Mom and Dad don't have the money for that."

He sighed, resigned. "I know. I guess it's just waiting, then. Kinetics, combat, then weaponry."

"It's not that far off, Luc."

"Far enough," he muttered.

"What's with the sucky attitude today?"

"Yeah, sorry, I'll shut up now. Let's just get on with it so we can get out of here." Luc opened Aave's knife roll and ran his fingers over the blades, neatly lined up like soldiers at attention. He slipped one free from its slot and passed me the roll. "First mark wins, two-minute cap."

"You're on," I told him, picking out a blade for myself. First one to break skin before time was up would have to do the other's chores until next week, when we'd be back at this all over again.

"I'll give you a handicap, because you're a girl," Luc said, grinning. He put his right arm behind his back, held his blade with his weaker left arm.

I snorted and flicked the switchblade open. The drizzle had turned into a steady patter, and raindrops danced off the polished surface of the edge. I had to be careful not to cut him too badly again. The last time he'd come within millimeters of needing stitches. My own fault, for getting carried away. That was something else I needed to work on, besides my aim with a blade—reining in my immediate instinct to lash out. "Whatever. I don't need a handicap. I just hope I don't make you cry again."

He laughed. "Just watch the jabbing. Try slashing—it won't go as deep."

And then we were off, one on one, dodging and weaving, circling each other as hunter and hunted. That was how the four of us spent that Sunday afternoon—and many others. In a back alley where the ground was hard and gray beneath our feet, the sky above just as unforgiving . . . playing, fighting, surviving.

Overhead a crow's shrill caw pierces the air, making me look up even as I'm switching blades. The sky has turned from a cool, burnished steel to a near black.

It's time to get moving.

I creep back up into civilization and with a practiced eye start my nightly search.

I used to hate trespassing. Even though Chord's key code disrupter means not having to break any windows or work around a lock to get inside, it still felt wrong to be there. Like I was walking onto some sort of sacred ground, a place still breathing from the newly dead. But coming across an empty—a house freshly claimed by clearing after the death of its occupant, to be inherited by family or passed on to an agent to sell—kills all hesitation easily enough. Already difficult in the Grid with its honeycomb density of Alts living on their own, drawn to cheap rentals and entry-level shift jobs. Here in the suburbs, where most Alts who die leave behind families still living in their houses, discovering an empty is like striking oil.

Countless blocks of lit houses later, I'm cursing Chord again for driving me out here. For making me fully taste my own fear as I keep running from her, unable to even think about seeing her, let alone how I'm going to fight her.

The white tag sways gently from the front doorknob, calling to me.

If the bushy boxwood on the landing had been moved over just another few inches, I would have missed it altogether. As it is, I know immediately it's a claim tag from Jethro's clearing division—and an empty house. The end unit of a row of town houses, the place is tall and skinny. Windows all dark, both upstairs and downstairs. One of the lightbulbs on the porch is burnt out.

I run across the street, climb the short, steep flight of stairs that takes me to the front door. I yank off the tag—stamped with the words PROPERTY OF JETHRO WARD CLEARING DIV. DO NOT REMOVE. Now the house gives nothing away. And it's late enough to know I'll be undisturbed here for the night—by family or an agent or anyone else.

Holding Chord's disrupter around my wrist, I press the thin black strip against the faceplate of the lock. A series of tumbles and clicks, the lock gives, and I open the door and step inside.

In the few moments it takes for my eyes to adjust to the darkness, I hold still, breathing through my mouth so that I make absolutely no sound. When I can finally see the room, empty and silent, furniture like black humped animals in a jungle of gray, I dare to blink again. I hang the tag on the inside of the door so I won't forget to put it back tomorrow before leaving. I flip the latch of the secondary lock—it's flimsy, for backup purposes only—but without the key code to engage the primary lock, it will have to do.

It's almost as cold indoors as it is out. I guess the heat's been turned off, and I wonder how long the Alt has been dead. I walk across the front room. Run my finger along the surface of the coffee table—no sign of dust.

So it hasn't been long, then. A few days at the most.

I grab a crystal vase off the fireplace mantel: the taller and more top-heavy the better, I've learned. Then spot another, short and fat. In the slatted moonlight, my eyes skim past a framed photo sitting alongside the vase, telling me the story. In it are a very old man and woman, standing next to a teen-aged girl. Her grandparents, maybe; she might've been sent to live with them after her parents died, some kind of accident like Chord's parents'. Then *they* die, leaving her behind with a house. And then she receives her assignment, draws the ultimate short straw, and now the house is an empty once and for all.

Would be, if it weren't for this one intrusion.

Don't worry, you won't even know I was here.

Returning to the front door, I stand the skinny vase flush up against the metal, then balance the fat one precariously on top. If anyone tries to come in, the sound of crystal falling onto hardwood should be loud enough to wake me from any sleep.

In the kitchen, I flip the light switch, ever hopeful. The room remains dark. I flip it again a few more times, even though I know it's pointless. It's the rare occasion when the power still works. But sometimes I'm lucky and clearing gets bogged down, and I catch an empty where they haven't finished shut-down yet.

In the pantry, I toss the most nutritious of what I find into my bag. Vacuum-packed slips of tuna, salmon, chili. I stuff trek bars into my pockets. Everything I pick is protein-heavy, calorie-dense. I have to be careful what I take. The weight has to be worth it. I'm okay with going a bit overboard this time, though, since a lot of the stuff is completes-only, final remnants of the grandparents' last few trips to the grocery store.

I twist open a large jar of orange segments and use my fingers to eat them. My body shudders at the sudden spurt of sweetness—it's been a while since I've tasted sugar, with most of Kersh's supply being reserved for completes. Then I open a package of what Aave used to call squirrel crackers, so heavy with grains and seeds that they get stuck in my teeth as I crunch through them. A handful of multivitamins. A tin of salty ham washed down with tap water that tastes like rust. The uneven thump of the water splashing into my hand reminds me that it can't be long before Gaslight—the ward in charge of Kersh's water distribution—halts the supply to the house.

When I'm finally full, I head out of the kitchen, toward the stairs.

And stop.

There's a draft coming down from upstairs. It washes over my cheeks and plays with strands of my hair.

Two thoughts burst into life in my head, quick as birds taking flight: First, someone must have left a window open— one of the clearing guys, an agent doing a quick appraisal, a family member looking for something—*someone* who had good reason to be here. Second, I'm not alone. Odds are it's not my Alt, because it wouldn't make sense for her to be here first. Someone else.

My hand falls to my jacket pocket, feeling for my gun. I start up the stairs, not bothering to stay quiet. If there's someone on the second floor, she would have heard me in the kitchen.

In fact—

I point the gun to the side and fire a single shot into the wall. There. Now it's obvious I'm armed. The question is whether she is.

It's close to freezing up here. A shiver rolls down my back, and I don't want to admit—even to myself—that it's not entirely from the drop in temperature.

Two bedrooms. The draft is billowing out from the one on the left, spreading its way across the floor and down the stairs. I edge closer and peer inside the same way I would peer into a cave—braced for something to fly out at me.

A boy is straddling the sill of the open window. The outlines of thick tree branches behind him make it obvious that he climbed inside. A bag has been thrown over his shoulders, and his body is tensed as he gets ready to climb out. His eyes are wide and terrified, his assignment number black spirals against the lightness of his pupils. His cheeks puff in and out like a wheezing accordion.

I exhale and tuck my gun back into my jacket pocket.

If anyone's got all the signs of being a new active, it's this kid. The armor vest beneath his clothes is overly heavy and too bulky to move in easily. The bag over his shoulders is bursting at the seams. He's not yet thin enough in the face to have been on the run long.

Before he faints and falls out the window, I say quickly,

"Don't worry, it's okay. I'm just an active. Like you." Is this what it's like talking someone off the ledge? I would have thought I'd feel like a hero, but instead I feel more than just a little guilty. Knowing I scared him as much as if I really were his Alt: the ominous sounds coming from below, the creaking of the stairs, the shot of the gun.

He can't be any more than eleven, possibly twelve. Not much older than Ehm would have been today, had she completed.

My shoulders slump. Now that I know I'm in no danger, adrenaline leaves and exhaustion stays behind, swamping my head so it's hard to think clearly. All I want is to find a bed and sleep.

"I'm not going to hurt you," I say, and start backing away to show him. "Is it okay if I share this empty with you?" It won't be the first time I've shared one with another active, and it won't be the last. It can't be as hard as sharing a ten-foot-by-ten-foot apartment with a thirteen-year-old active who wept the entire night, clutching a gun too big for her small hands. I slept on the floor, in the opposite direction from where the shaking barrel was pointed.

"So?" I stop in the doorway. "We're okay?"

A slow nod, the still-wide eyes. This one's not a talker. A part of me wonders if it's because somehow he *knows*, even if he can't see the marks hidden by my sleeves and the dark. He senses my striker status the way med dogs sniff out disease in the dying.

If it were Ehm in this boy's position, in an empty with some other active, I'd want to think she had no reason to be afraid of him or her. Not when her own Alt would have been enough.

"Next time, if you don't want to share with another active,

take the clearing tag off the door," I say to him. "We all look for that, okay?"

Another nod. This time he carefully swings his leg back inside, and I'm relieved. At least *his* death won't be on my conscience.

"One more thing." I point at the windowsill, where he's left the tool he used to pry open the window. "Pack that up now so you don't leave it behind if you have to run."

Without waiting for a response, I turn around and walk into the other bedroom. The large oak tree outside the window is perfect. The branches are thick enough, more than able to hold my weight if it comes to having to run.

I shut the bedroom door behind me and lock it, slip the straps of my bag off my shoulders, and lay the bag next to the pillow on the bed. Still fully clothed, I slide beneath the covers, not caring about the unwashed state of the sheets. What's filth when I'm already filthy? I hate showering in the dark, anyway. I'll do it in the morning, early. Then I'll decide where to go next, see where my next strike is going to take me.

Except I can't sleep.

I get up from the bed, already knowing what's gnawing at me, what won't go quiet until it's done. I grab my bag with one hand and open the bedroom door with the other.

The door to the other bedroom's shut, so I knock on it.

A shuffle of sound from inside and then the boy's standing in the doorway, looking up at me. From the stiff set of his shoulders, I can tell he's still a bit scared of me, and the guilt I tried to ignore enough to fall asleep is back in full force.

"You shouldn't have opened the door," I tell him, trying my best to keep my voice light.

He blinks. "Huh?"

"You should've said I could enter and then waited for me to come in. Let me be the one to not know what to expect."

"Oh, I guess." The boy reaches up, scratches his head. Smiles timidly at me. "I'll remember for next time?"

Ehm would have said the same, I bet. But whether she actually would have done so, I'm not sure. Just like I'm not sure if this boy is going to actually remember.

Awkwardly, I hold up my bag. "Up for some throwing practice?"

"Uh, what do you mean?"

"Your blades?" I give my bag a shake. "In your bag?"

"Well, I only have one. But I guess I could—"

"You're kidding me, right?" I ask him. *Don't freak him out, West. Don't make it sound like a big deal.*

But it is. Blades, especially—they get snapped, bent, lost. You don't want to be caught without a backup, ever. Even two are bare bones, the minimum. Back up your backup, if at all possible. I feel naked with less than three.

"I've got a gun," he says. Not defensively, not smugly, just stating a fact. That he thinks it'll be enough.

"Is that your weapon of choice, then?" I ask him.

He shrugs. *Yeah, of course.*

"I didn't see you holding it earlier when I surprised you."

Now he does look defensive, and he shrugs again. Scowls. "I didn't get a chance to take it out of my bag before you came in. Otherwise, I would have been."

It's really not very fair of me to judge him so harshly. He's not old enough to be in the Alt Skills program yet, so whatever he does know, whatever skills he does have, at least it's better than the nothing it could have been.

But like it or not, he's an active. And his Alt would be more than happy to catch him off guard again.

I shake my head and try for a smile, a real one this time. He managed to do so for me, in spite of his fear. And he's just a kid, nearly as young as they come, and without even a fraction of whatever experience I have.

"C'mon," I say to him. "Let's go downstairs and find something we can destroy. And I have a couple of extra switchblades you can borrow."

"I . . . okay, sure."

"But take off that armor vest, will you? It doesn't fit, which means it'll hurt you before it'll help you."

"No, you're putting too much of your arm into it," I tell him. "You're going to pull something."

"But last time you said I was letting go of the blade too *early*, West."

"You were." Sitting on the floor of the front room, I look over the switchblades laid out between us, trying to decide which one I want for my next turn. Because the power supply's been cut, only the streetlamps from outside let us see what we're doing. I'm relieved there's little light, though. I don't want Dess to see the striker marks on my wrists.

Dess sighs. "I'm never going to get the hang of this," he moans. He walks up to the wall, yanks his blades free. He missed the bull's-eye—an impromptu one drawn on the wall with a thick black marker we found in the junk drawer in the kitchen—by a little more than a hand span with each of his three throws. But on his previous round, he was off by a much larger margin, closer to three hand spans with each throw. Not bad for a newbie . . . but not great for an active with an assignment nearly a week old. He needs to keep practicing.

And so do I. Because his aim isn't much worse than my own, even though I've got years of practice on Dess.

A very familiar dread starts to collect itself in my stomach, the kind that never fails to appear whenever I'm faced with the possibility that I might never get any better. That I've reached my maximum potential with my aim, that this is as much as I'm ever going to know of this special relationship between arm and wrist, eye and blade. I remember how very good Aave was, how his ability to connect blade with target seemed nearly supernatural. The marked difference between him and me— and even Luc, though not to the same extent—made it clear he must have inherited that talent from his other parents. The ones he shared with his Alt, not the ones he shared with me or Luc or Ehm.

"West? You want to take a turn, or should I go again?"

I hastily pick three blades and get to my feet. "No, I'll go. My arm's looser now, so I shouldn't be so off this time." If I say it out loud, it'll make it true. Not something so hard to beat, after all.

"Yeah, maybe," Dess says, sitting down to watch me with eager eyes, ready to soak up whatever advice I can give him, whatever trick I can show him. "I hope so. I bet you're really good most of the time." There's a note of pure admiration in his voice, and it makes me feel both embarrassed and ashamed.

Who am I to let him believe a bit of practice can make someone invincible? Can create an Alt who's too skilled to die, too worthy to waste?

When each of my throws goes even wider than any from my previous rounds, his disappointment is obvious. But it's nothing compared to my own distress. I almost feel like I'm going backward. Becoming less every day. The memory of my first strike vivid in my head, a sore that keeps flaring up.

"Well, that's okay," Dess says, clearly trying to make me not feel bad, "just go again. That was just bad luck."

It wasn't. "How about we quit for the night? It's nearly eleven and I'm getting tired. I swear we've been throwing for hours."

"It doesn't feel like it. A little longer?"

"No, sorry." I know when to stop pushing what can't be pushed.

"Aw, really? That's it? That sucks." His expression turns so depressed it's almost comical.

It's probably the idea of being alone again. It's hard enough for older actives to go a month with almost no company. I can't imagine what it's like for someone Dess's age. So much less time to prepare all around, in all aspects.

"Hold on, Dess. One more thing. Pass me the switchblades."

He separates his own from the two he borrowed from my knife roll. Hands them to me. "Here you go."

Sitting down again, I lay them out on the floor in front of him. Place next to them the three I just finished using, as well as the remaining two from the roll. I take a second to snap the blades open. "You can't go around any longer with just one switchblade, okay, Dess? So take two of mine."

His eyes go wide, and he looks much too young to be here, learning how to kill. "Really?"

I nod. "Yeah, I'm serious. It's okay, I'll still have enough."

"Wow, okay, thanks!" Dess stares down at the blades, taking their measure as well as he can, considering he's only used them for a little bit. Blades are funny that way. They almost seem to develop personalities of their own, the longer you use them. How one might tend to veer one way, another works best with a certain kind of hold.

"Um, this one . . . and . . . this one?" He holds the two in question out to me, making sure I'm not going to change my mind or anything.

"They're yours. Remember to practice as much as you can, all right?"

"For sure. Thanks, West!" He drags his bag over and places them inside, and I know this time that he's not going to forget to keep them safe, and close.

I get to my feet. "Help me put the painting back up."

We each grab a side of the heavy framed canvas, lift it off the floor where it was resting this whole while, and hang it back on the hook on the wall. The painting of the couple dancing covers up the slashes and dents perfectly.

"Okay, we really should crash," I say to Dess, both of us walking upstairs to our rooms. "I don't want to leave too late tomorrow."

Standing outside his door, Dess can't hide the fact that he's not looking forward to me saying good-bye. Another scowl on his face, this one to keep him from crying. His eyes are way too shiny. "Okay, I guess. I have to go, too. My Alt . . . he lives over in Gaslight, so I should head over there. Scope out some places where he might be."

Dess mentioning his Alt brings me back to reality. And reality is not us flinging knives at a wall in an empty house in Jethro. It's the fact that Dess might very well not live for much longer.

I nearly say the words out loud—offer to kill his Alt for him—but I catch myself just in time. I don't want Dess to see me as more than just another active. To know that strikers really do exist, that we do break the rules—for him to maybe protest that we don't really help Alts, we only help Alts *cheat*.

Because there's something new about him, too. Most of it's realizing he's not as helpless as he might have thought, and while some of it might be my giving him those blades, there's a sharpened drive to complete now, to *want* to prove he's the one.

"Hey, Dess, where's your cell?" I ask.

He pulls it out from his pants pocket. "Right here, why?"

I take it from him and input the data with a flurry of taps of my finger. "I just gave you my cell number. I want you to call me when you complete your assignment, all right?" Probably a bad idea to not just say good-bye right now—definitely a bad idea, actually. But the need to know that he's completed suddenly trumps all that.

He takes the cell back. "What if I don't—"

"Just think when, not if."

His eyes are outright wet now. "But what about you, West? How am I ever going to know? Will you call me?"

Slowly, I shake my head. "The only way you'll know is when

you complete. Because when you call, either I'll be there—or I won't be."

"Hey, that's not fair!"

"I know." I can't tell him why. That I don't think I could handle calling his number and reaching a dead line. Better to always wonder if he just forgot, or couldn't be bothered. If that makes me a coward, then it does. "I'm sorry."

"It's okay, I guess. I know you're only trying to help."

In the childish openness of his face, I swear I see much of Ehm, traces of Luc, hints of Aave, and I blink fast, trying not to tear up, too. "Go to sleep, Dess."

He only nods.

"And stop keeping your gun in your bag, all right? That's what pockets are for."

He nods again, kicks at the floor with his foot.

So that's it. Two actives saying good-bye, good luck, be the one, be worthy.

Back in my bedroom, surrounded by a stranger's life, I finally sleep . . . but not really. Too many dreams, where everything in my head is always louder than I allow it to be during the day, coming out of hiding when I'm most vulnerable. Memories of my family. Chord. The need to stay ahead of my Alt, always.

I crash into wakefulness, my eyes springing open, my heart already racing, my mouth dry. My stiff fingers fall from the gun that I haven't let go of all night, and automatically I reach for my bag next to the pillow. Still there.

It's my cell, a new text coming in. The specs for a new strike, mine if I want it. I accept it nearly without thinking, let relief surface and lap over. A new focus, keeping me busy calculating how I'm going to do it, how I'm going to attack—

Cell still in hand, I sit up, remembering Dess and his own assignment, how he's going to track down his Alt on his own. Then Chord's words running through my head: *It's you now, so stop running!*

I tuck my cell away. It's done. Contract accepted.

And it's dawn. Gray light filters in through the thin cloth drapes, and I'm freezing despite the blankets I've pulled on top of myself. Winter is finally here.

I have eight days left.

Shower first. Then it's time to leave. It's one of the few rules I don't allow myself to break, ever: Never sleep in the same place twice, no matter how much easier it is, how practical it might be. The comfort wouldn't be worth hearing the footsteps of your Alt finally close in on you because you got too lazy to keep moving.

Even before I open my bedroom door, I can tell Dess has already left. The air in the house is too flat and still for someone else to be here.

Sadness creeps in along with satisfaction as I leave the room. Good. He's learned he needs to keep moving. That keeping still is begging to become one more incomplete. *Go, Dess.*

There's a piece of paper stuck onto his bedroom door, a note for me. I yank it down, unable to keep from smiling at the wad of gum he used for tape.

West, here's my cell number. I know you didn't want
it, but just in case you change your mind. Also, I
was going to slip it under your door, but I was
worried you'd hear the sound and shoot at me.
Your friend, Dess

Right below his name is his number, written in large, clear print. Easy enough to toss the note and simply stay in the dark. Instead I carefully fold it up and go to tuck it into my bag.

I'm still shivering from my cold shower by the time I'm back in the kitchen. I stab at the microwave again, just because I can. Thinking of the ever-shrinking pile of Chord's cash, I eat a row of a package of cookies. Even half-stale they beat any idle-branded ones, hands down. More canned fruit, this time peaches. I toss back another fistful of vitamins. It's too much, but I'm not worried about being killed that way.

I replace the vases on the mantel. After straightening the painting over the marked-up wall just the slightest, I hang the white tag back on the outside of the door on my way out. I'd lock up if I could, to do what I can to return an empty to how it was—undisturbed and whole, not overly violated. I need to believe it's possible to keep going the way I am and not change too much, not leave too much of myself behind.

CHAPTER 6

I've just finished my strike, and am slithering from the second-floor bathroom window of a bookstore back down to the ground, when I get my first glimpse of her.

I thought it would be like looking into a mirror and seeing myself, but that's not it. Not exactly. The difference is as small as how you see your own reflection, and how you really appear to everyone else—like the two halves of your face are reversed so neither view is quite right. When I see her, I think: *So that's how others see me.*

A nose with a slight tilting up at the tip. Angled brown eyes, just a shade removed from black. Same color skin as mine, mixed undertones and all. Her hair's the same color, too, only much longer. Black as ink, straight as a heavy waterfall, and skimming over her eye like a crow's wing.

Facing my Alt is something I'll never get used to. It's like witnessing everything you both hate and fear about yourself, all of it coming to life at the same time. You can no more change the fact of their existence than they can yours. Flashes of Ehm, of Luc, of what happened with Chord's Alt . . . they spin memories behind my eyes like the worst sort of nightmare.

I duck my head low and slowly step away from the side of the fruit stands where I was eyeing the last of the fall apples, wondering if I could slip below the radar of the harried workers. I sidle the few feet over to the coffee stall next door and take in the customers waiting in line. To the left is a display rack of paper-bagged coffee, fresh off the truck from Calden Ward; to the right, a throng of customers perch at the counter, tapping their cells with short, energetic bursts.

So crowded. I move again, this time behind the rack of coffee. I hook my thumbs into the straps of my bag, tightening them out of habit. I touch the front and back pockets of my jeans to make sure the blades are still inside, then the pocket of my jacket for my third blade. I wrap my hand around my gun in my jacket's other pocket. I keep it there, hidden, as I lean into the rack and also try to hide from view.

My heart is pounding; I feel each beat as a measured bellow in my ears. Electrified nerves, alive and charged in a moment that has me as close to death as I've ever been. Cold, thin sweat along my hairline. Tension coils in my arm as an acute clarity pierces all my senses. Everything else falls to the wayside: there is nothing but this—*her.*

I have to believe the gun will be enough. Though the blade is more than adequate as backup—*if* I can get close enough. Throwing is not a possibility right now.

I peer around the stand to see my Alt.

She's making her way down the sidewalk, her face turning left, then right. Then left again. She's not hiding the fact that she's searching for someone. There is no doubt at all in my mind that it's me.

As she nears, I'm caught on a horrible threshold. Stay and finish it, one way or another? Or turn and run and stay alive a while longer? Indecision wrapped in panic has my hand around the gun going slick, trembling.

Sixty feet away.

Forty-five.

Thirty.

Fifteen.

I can see the precision of her movements. No wasted energy. No useless overswing of the arms. No sloppy looseness of the gait. Chord was right. Her eyes are very, very cold. Determined, the will to survive absolutely breathtaking and devastating— the look I should have in my eyes.

Ten feet away.

She's got her hand tucked under her arm, as if she's holding something that needs to be at the ready. In my pocket, my own hand twitches. It's more a muscle spasm than a controlled action, and it makes the fear in my heart bloom. It cuts me down.

I can't.

I can't.

I can't.

I drop into a spineless crouch. The sudden whiff of coffee is overwhelming. My breath, trickling loose from my throat in silent shudders, and it's all I can do to try to stay still. The world wavers and becomes distorted in the face of my failure.

My Alt passes by. *My Alt.* And I let her go. I'm frozen and terrified and feeling like a child again. The confidence I knew before Luc left me continues to remain hidden. I'm floundering.

A rough hand lands on my arm, making me jump. My index finger flexes on the trigger of my gun.

"Hey, you can't hide here." It's one of the workers from the coffee stall. His tag says *Market Strip Brew.* Below that, his name—*Otto.* His eyes are as hard and unfeeling as flint.

"Take it somewhere else," he grunts out. "Assignments going down here are bad for business, and I don't need that kind of stuff happening in my store."

"I'm not— I'm sor—"

"Just get out of here, fast."

I run down the street, in the opposite direction from the one she took. I don't know where I'm going, but I need to keep moving. If I move fast enough, maybe I won't be able to hear my thoughts anymore. My one chance, and I failed miserably— not just myself, but my family, all those who've ever mattered. Who still matter.

I glare at my choices on the shelf in the drugstore, wondering if it's possible to be any more at a loss.

I never thought I'd let it get so far. Or that blond came in more than three shades.

I hiss out a sigh and grab a box that promises to turn my hair a shade called Cinderella. And with my hair so dark, I know I'm going to have to strip it first. So I snag a tube of hair bleach, too. Scissors, of course.

Impossible to miss is the sign hanging along the bottom of the shelf: REMEMBER IDLE AND ACTIVE ALTS ARE FORBIDDEN

FROM UNDERGOING PROCEDURES INVOLVING TEMPORARY OR PERMANENT COSMETIC MODIFICATIONS PLEASE CONTACT US FOR FURTHER DETAILS THANK YOU THE BOARD.

Until you're a complete, facial work is off-limits: bone grafts, muscle implants, tattoos anywhere above the neck. And for actives, the temporary stuff is out, too: sunglasses, contacts, piercings.

Painting your nails is okay, as is nonopaque makeup that doesn't alter the skin tone. Haircuts and hair dye are also permitted, since the Board decided these don't change an Alt's face enough to make it unrecognizable.

I'm hoping they're wrong. I need to become someone who doesn't look like us.

Not much cash left. And I refuse to call Chord over something that's only going to prove he's right—that I *am* still running.

A cold finger dances up my spine at the memory of seeing her this morning. How close she was . . . how I fooled myself into thinking I was ready.

After I'm done cashing out, I slip my purchases into my bag. All of it, bought time until I can regain even a bit of what I was.

It doesn't take me long to get over to a nearby inner ward train station. I take the stairs that lead below ground level, where the public washrooms are.

The women's room is dingy and the trains running overhead make it vibrate violently every few minutes, but it'll do for the job. All I need is running water and a sink.

As I cut off handfuls of my near-black hair, a blend of my parents' mixed backgrounds and what might have migrated over from my Alt's parents, curious eyes take turns watching me.

Teenaged girls—both idles and actives—and working women on their way home. I refuse to look anyone in the eye, and I'm rewarded when no one says anything to me.

I sit in a stall, door shut, while I wait for the bleach to do its work before the dye. Every so often the whole place shakes, the flimsy handles and locks of all the stall doors rattling like loose teeth in a dirty mouth. I count the minutes in my head, the length of time it takes to become someone else.

Afterward, when the dye's done as much as it can possibly do, I stick my head under the tap and wash out the last of the chemicals. Seeing the water slowly run clear fills me with a strange sense of sad purpose. Like I'm saying good-bye to a West Grayer that I at least understood, if not entirely liked, and am being forced to meet a new one I know for sure I won't like but have no choice but to accept.

I stare into the mirror, fascinated. Not a stranger, but not myself, either.

No longer a skein of black but a blond cap of hair that looks like straw and feels about the same. Dry, crisp, brittle to the touch. And shorter than I've ever had it. It washes out my face, making it completely unremarkable. Forgettable.

It's perfect.

Another ward train rolls by overhead, and it's only after the sound of quickening steel blasts away that I hear the crying. A muffled kind of sobbing from the other half of the bathroom, separated from where I am by the line of sinks and mirrors.

A murmur of a woman's voice echoes softly against the tiles and concrete. "I know, but it's not over yet; she still has until nearly midnight."

"No, it's too late." The words broken up by crying. "There's not enough time to make up for what she's already wasted. Running all this while."

"Tell her she can still try." The first woman's voice sounds unsure even to my ears. "You're her mother. You need to talk to her."

"She won't listen," the crying mother moans. "Tell me what I should say, won't you? Tell me what you told yours when it was their turn!"

A pause. "Just that being worthy is the only way out. No matter how she has to make it happen."

"She says her Alt would make the better Kersh soldier." The sobs are quieter now, resigned. "Because if she really deserves to win, she wouldn't be this scared."

I don't want to hear any more. The grief in the mother's voice is too close to mourning; she knows her daughter is about to self-detonate, that thirty-one days of denial cannot possibly be erased by a final few hours of desperate flailing.

One last glance in the mirror, and I toss my bag over my shoulder and run out of the washroom, pushing my way through a fresh wave of people coming in off the latest train. Once my feet hit the sidewalk I start walking fast, trying to put those voices behind me. I try not to imagine what *my* mother would say to me if she were here today. If she'd talk again about what it was like to meet the parents of my Alt.

It happened sixteen years ago, the day my parents went to the Board's labs to draw up my gene map, the new baby they wanted to create. The next couple who also wanted a baby were, of course, my Alt's parents.

"It shouldn't have ever happened, us meeting," my mother told me. We'd been clothes shopping, getting me ready for a new school year, and had stopped for lunch at a café in the Grid. I remember how she let me sneak bits of food off her plate, the way she always did, since we had to order from different menus.

"Why not, though?" I asked.

"The lab had had an . . . incident, with one mother attacking the other, trying to keep the other baby from being. Not that it would have mattered; the next set of parents coming in would have been the ones to have her baby's Alt, then.

"It was the receptionist's first day, and she was flustered and rushed, and . . . well, we all ended up being assigned to the same room. Me, your father, them. And they were . . . normal. Normal and nice and not like monsters at all. You have her nose, West. That slight tilting up at the tip no one else in the family has. Your chin, too, more rounded than any of ours. And you have his high cheekbones."

My hand went up, touched my nose, chin, cheeks, all shapes and angles I'd known my entire life. I remember how they suddenly felt like a stranger's, not mine, not the real me.

And then my mother's face went hard. "I smiled and nodded, the four of us talking about the weather, the excellent and clean lab conditions. But the whole time, it was all I could do to not reach over and gouge her eyes out with my nails, beat him as hard as I could. Stuck in that room with those people who would give birth to and raise one of our greatest enemies, someone who could cause us to feel the greatest pain imaginable? I understood all too well how that other mother could react the way she did."

She never talked about it again, and I didn't, either. Not only was she not one to question out loud the Board's filtration system, she also felt that same sense of duty all residents of Kersh did. As for me, I didn't want to relive that sensation. The feeling that I was made up of those I didn't know as much as of those I did.

The first raindrops hit the top of my newly bleached head, where my scalp still feels sensitive. The electric ozone smell of rain meeting pavement fills my nose. I tilt my face up to the sky.

It's wholly dark now, the end of another day. The clouds are thick and endless, and I know I'm not going to be able to wait out this storm. Time to find a place to sleep for the night, when the arrival of morning means it's no longer eight but seven days left . . .

I dart across the street, to where the library sits. Chord's warning about getting away from the Grid is quickly extinguished, a spark of unwanted memory in my head. I tell myself I would have listened if I hadn't seen my Alt today. But I'm here now, and the idea of wandering for cover in the rain is far from appealing. As long as I make sure she's not here, it should be safe enough. For this night, at least.

I pull open the front door to the library and step inside, my eyes already darting back and forth in a wide sweep. It's always these first few minutes, this short-lived window when all things are possible, when she could actually be here, that have my senses running on overdrive and my heart and pulse going at too fast a clip.

I've been here a few times since becoming active, but only for an hour or two, my visits carefully spread out so I don't become familiar. It's a gray area, knowing how far to push my routine and still stay safe—how to stay faceless, to be nothing more than just another Alt coming in from the cold and rain.

About two dozen students are seated at the tables, flexi-readers and tablets in front of them and cells in their hands. A handful of older people. Of the study capsules I can see, only a few are occupied. I take in the shapes of all the backs, the lines of all the shoulders, looking for any hint of danger.

There is nothing.

But the rest of the room is a mystery to me. The stacks reach nearly to the ceiling, and if she's hidden within them she will stay that way until I start checking them to see if they're clear.

My hands return to my jacket pockets, a motion I now make in my dreams. One grabs hold of my gun, the other my switchblade. Prepared, always.

I walk down the open aisle, passing the stacks with bated breath. Each one falling behind me expands my safety zone. My steps are silent—measured and deliberate. All the juices in my mind and gut feel supercharged, and it's like I'm moving a few seconds ahead of myself. I can see before I even turn my head all the way; I can conclude even before I take it all in.

First row, to my left: a mom with three giggling girls. She hushes them with a finger to her lips.

Third row, my right: an old man with a cane. He uses it to hook a book free from the top shelf.

Three rows farther, to my left again: a teenager, cap pulled low over his face.

I keep walking until I reach the far wall.

A quick trip to the bathroom finishes the check of this floor. Then it's upstairs, where the computers and tablets and print collections are kept. All clear. I feel my shoulders drop, my hands relaxing just the slightest inside my pockets.

It takes me seconds to walk over to the right section. Only a couple of months have passed, but what's happened between then and now makes it feel longer. Reference stacks, fifth row, left-hand side. My fingers run along the soft, faded spines. *Alternates: The Complete History. Alts at War.* They fill the shelves around me.

I pull a book out. It's thin and blue and ancient, and the whiff of just how old its words are hits me with the force of a punch. I trace the faded ink of the title on the front cover with my finger. *Beyond the Board.*

What was it again? *Complete and utter garbage.* A dark smile curls my lips. I can still hear the cool disdain in Baer's tone, the words clipped and dismissive. To Baer, to Dire, the Board no longer just holds our lives in their hands—it also fails to see the blood on its hands.

I look down at my hands and picture the marks on my wrists, beneath my pulled-down sleeves. The marks are like cuffs, chaining me to my striker status . . . and to the Board. Because if the Board's guilty of so much death, aren't I as well? Aren't I altering things just as much as they are?

I don't want to think that. I want to think that being a striker is simply doing what I can to win. That I'm running because I haven't had enough strikes yet, haven't learned enough, gotten hard enough. And that it has nothing to do with being *afraid*.

"Such a lie," I seethe out loud to no one. I viciously wiggle the book back into its slot.

Baer is right in this one thing, at least. This book—all of these books—offers me nothing but a blanket of false security. Nothing in them will help me get the first shot off or the first stab in when my Alt finally finds me.

A hand taps me on the shoulder and instantly I'm whirling around. But there's too little control and too much panic. Blind on the adrenaline already coursing through me, I reach into my pocket—

I'm not ready, not ready, not ready!

—and fumble clumsily for my gun.

"Whoa! Wait! Hold on!" The terror in the man's voice chases away everything until I can see again.

It's the librarian. Short, gangly, harmless. His badge swings jauntily from the lanyard around his neck. His arms are raised up high in surrender. His name is Saul, and he's as white as milk.

It wasn't as close as it could have been. If I'd been prepared, if I hadn't slipped away from the here and now—I've been so careful not to all this time . . . I unclench my jaw and slowly pull my hands away from my body. I need to show him I'm holding nothing. His eyes are screaming this at me.

"Sorry, you just . . . surprised me." I can feel my mouth attempt a smile. It feels horrid. Saul blinks at me, blinks even more rapidly as he takes in the sight of my eyes. "We're about to close." His voice is strained and thin as he speaks through the shaking. "Ten minutes."

Of course. I forgot how late it already was when I got here.

"I'm really sorry," I apologize again. "I lost track of time. I'm leaving now."

A stilted nod and Saul's gone, his discomfort spelled out in the hurried stiffness of his walk. It'd almost be humorous if I didn't feel so bad about scaring him like that. To kill someone by accident, through carelessness, someone who's not a strike, or my Alt—my stomach rolls with nausea at the thought of it.

Never. I could never live with myself.

The bang of a door somewhere in the building startles me. No more time. I have to get going.

In seconds, I'm back down on the main floor. But instead of keeping straight and heading for the front entrance, I make a sharp right at the bottom of the stairs and continue walking. I slow down just enough to deftly pull a random book from a nearby shelf before I slip out the side exit door.

The door is the kind that self-locks from the inside. I wedge my toe so it doesn't shut on me. From the book I carefully rip out a single page. Not from the middle, but from the back, one of the blank ones, so I don't take away any words. Paper books are limited as it is. I fold the page in half, then again.

With one hand I hold the folded paper over the hole along the doorjamb, right where the door bolt slides home. With my other hand, I twist the knob until the bolt recedes back into the door. Only then do I slowly pull my foot free, until the door shuts, flush with the jamb again. I let the knob gently untwist back into position.

For a second, I think the paper isn't going to hold—that it's too flimsy and the bolt's going to either push it out of place or break right through it. But it doesn't. It's fine. It holds.

I chose this side door because the one straight out back exits to the library's parking lot, and the door on the left side leads to an alley that opens quickly onto the main street. Either one would make sense for the library's employees to take as a fast way out. But no one would be using my exit, the only one facing an office building, quickly emptying for the night.

I press my ear right against the cold metal of the library door and wait it out. The rise and fall of voices. Assorted shuffles, clicks, bangs. The sound of a vacuum. The unmistakable thump of doors being opened and shut. Being locked for the night.

For the next ten minutes there is nothing but thick, utter silence from inside the library. Finally I lean back from the door and ease it open, twisting the knob carefully so the bolt doesn't suddenly spring out and catch. The folded paper falls to the ground, and I pick it up and tuck it into the back pocket of my jeans. No use returning the page—that won't undo the damage.

Stepping back inside, I'm met with darkness that smells more strongly of aged damp than ever, the scent amplified to make up for what I can't see. My breathing is the only sound. It's both neat and creepy, to be alone in such a large, empty space. But whatever ghosts are here seem content enough to share it.

After waiting a minute for my eyes to adjust, I slide the book back onto the shelf from where I first grabbed it and choose a study capsule close to the fire door so I can leave easily if I have to.

After eating the contents of a dented tin of tuna and a smushed-up trek bar that I fish out from the bottom of my bag, I place my head down on the desk, crossing my arms beneath my cheek to create a makeshift pillow. One hand stays hooked through the straps of my bag sitting on the desk next to me. Slatted metal bars cut into the back of my knees, against my ribs. I don't mind too much—the sensations remind me that I'm still alive.

Rain slaps the tiny window carved into the fire door, and the plinking sound of it eventually lulls me to sleep. How deeply I go under, I'm not sure. But I know I dream of a face that is too much like my own, of those two mothers in the train station bathroom, of Chord's face when I left him. When the rain finally peters out around the brink of dawn, it's the return to quiet that jars me awake.

I wait, still groggy, still tired despite having slept, as the room lightens by degrees, coming back to life. Only when I hear the sound of the back door being unlocked do I get up, toss my bag over my shoulders, and leave through the same side exit I used earlier.

It's cold out. And the rain is already starting again, a miserable gray drizzle that has me longing for firelit rooms and food so hot it burns my tongue. Hunching my shoulders, I pull my hood farther over my head and tuck my hands into my jacket pockets. The feel of steel in both is my only comfort as I lose myself on streets blackened with the wet of winter.

Seven days left.

By the afternoon, there is still no sign of her. I've watched the terminal from every vantage point, from as many angles as possible, and nothing. She's not going in or coming out.

I chew my lip, study the people passing by. Rain bounces off their hunched bodies, and I wonder if I'm just wasting my time, even though a part of me simply believes that she should be here. Not as the kind of Alt who's given in, who seeks refuge, but the kind of Alt who stands firm, who seeks a fight.

The only way I can find out if she's living here is to go in myself. I take a deep breath, pushing past the curdling fear that's settled into my gut, and approach the front entrance.

The lobby is wide and clean and well lit. A central core elevator that leads to the different floors: Alt log stations and wireless access points; food and drink dispensers; hygiene and sleeping quarters. It looks exactly the same as the last time I was here, two years ago on a school field trip during my year one. How long ago that seems now; how funny to think back and realize just how innocent we all still were then, me and my friends and the rest of our classmates. That we didn't see that the next time we came back, it'd be under threat of death.

I squint in the light. It's *too* well lit in here; good for seeing who's around you, bad if you're simply trying to stay in the dark.

The attendant behind the counter glances up at me from her computer. "Yes, can I help you?"

"Can I just have a minute with the Alt log? I'll be fast."

She holds up the eye-scan gun. "Please come forward for admittance procedures."

I take an instinctive step back. "I don't . . . can I just skip the eye scan this one time? All I need is one minute."

The attendant shakes her head. "Sorry. You know I can't do that." She sounds bored, and I don't blame her. How many times has she heard the same plea, from how many Alts trying to sneak through here?

"One minute, that's all." I'm begging, desperate and hating it. "Please."

"No, can't do it, sorry." The attendant goes back to her screen.

"Would you be able to take a look for me, then?" I think of the last few bills I have in my pocket, wondering if it's worth the risk to show them to her, but the fact that she's employed by the Board makes me hesitate.

She cracks her gum. Stale mint wafts out at me. "Sorry." Then she frowns. "Besides, weren't you just here this morning?"

I shake my head. "No, I—"

"You should know how it works by now. No in and out privileges without a scan."

It hits me then. A ripple of adrenaline cuts right through me. "Thank you," I say on a blip of a breath, trying and most likely failing to sound remotely normal. My Alt. She's talking about my Alt.

"The weather's turning," the attendant goes on. "So if you want a bed, better be on time. Eighteen hundred is when they open." Her smile is bland. But her eyes give away a slight gleam, and I read it for what it is. She can't help but let me know *she* knows she's helped me.

So it wasn't a slip of the tongue, then. Do I remind her of someone she once knew? Why would she tell me this?

As if she can read my thoughts, she waves a hand carelessly, already tired of me, just another active coming through the terminal. "Well, you need all the help you can get." Another snap of her gum. "Your eyes, they're nothing like hers. Good luck, you're going to need it."

I leave the terminal on shaky legs. The cold is wet and biting, but I'm too busy coming to grips with what just happened to really feel it. Knowing that my Alt has been staying here, I hope she'll keep coming back again. Otherwise, she might be anywhere in the Grid, anywhere within the borders of Kersh.

When I see a girl coming down the sidewalk, the idea clicks into place. Exactly how I'm going to try to peek into my Alt's head, know what she's thinking, planning.

Slightly younger than me, maybe thirteen or fourteen. Her face is open, a fresh active's, not hardened the way I know it will be in another week or two, if she makes it that long. She's got too much expectation in her eyes and not enough fear. But I can't be too sympathetic—it's that very weakness I'll have to use to my advantage.

Quickly I assess her clothing, the state of her skin and hair. Her clothes are still relatively clean, but inadequate for this point in the winter. She didn't prepare for how cold it gets at night. She's pale, her hair limp and unwashed. And she looks hungry.

Yes.

As she passes me, I fall into step with her. "Hey, do you have a few minutes?" I ask in a low voice so only she can hear.

She stops walking and nervously shifts her bag over her shoulders. It's too large for her frame, and I bet anything it's very heavy. She glances around before her eyes settle on mine. The spiraled numbers are very dark.

"What is it?" she asks.

"Are you going inside the terminal?"

"Maybe, I was still thinking about it. Why?"

"I need a favor."

"Well, what is it?"

It's all or nothing. "Can you check something for me on the Alt log?" From my pocket I pull out the page I ripped from the library book last night. Scrawled on it is my assignment number, a sequence of digits I see in my sleep: 574206918344. "Punch this in and see what comes up?"

The barest flicker of understanding in her eyes. "You need to know if your Alt's been here."

"Yeah," I reply, even though I already know she has. Now I need to know more: when, how often, patterns and habits. Any sign of weakness.

She looks at me, obviously confused. "You're allowed to read the Alt log whenever you want, and the terminal is open to all actives. Can't you just do it yourself?"

"The attendant tonight, that lady in there?" I point in the general direction of the terminal lobby. Careful to keep my voice level, to not give away how much I need her to believe me. If she clues in that it's the eye scan I'm trying to avoid, my reluctance might scare her off before I get what I need. "She's still annoyed with me for jamming the system last night, even though I totally didn't mean to. So I thought it'd be a good idea to let her cool off before she sees me again."

The girl's still unsure, but I'm prepared. It's rare for an active to do anything for free. I flash the rest of Chord's money in my hand. "Here, look," I say to her. "It's yours. You can get something to eat if you do this for me."

Her eyes go wide as she considers. Hunger clings to her like a smell, coming off in waves. But still she hesitates, and I know it's because she's suddenly realized who has the upper hand here. "That won't buy me much . . ." She deliberately lets her voice trail off. What else needs to be said?

Not nearly as gullible as I thought. My stomach hollows out, and I can't even really blame her for asking—not when I would do the exact same thing.

After a long minute, I slowly work Luc's watch off my wrist. Only the knowledge that he would kick my butt for *not* doing it lets me speak. "This, too, okay?" I say stiffly as I hand it to her. There's a sharp hitch in my chest, and I breathe it away. "There's a place you can hock it around the corner. It's not worth much, but better than nothing."

She stuffs it into a pocket. "Okay, I'll do it." Her voice is almost surprised, as if she didn't expect to get more, didn't even know she was capable of asking for it. "Wait here, I'll be right back."

I rub the newly exposed skin on my wrist as I watch her enter the terminal. It's wonderful and horrible all at the same time because her risk is my gain. It seems Chord was mistaken when he said I wasn't cold, after all. She might have gone in on her own, yes . . . but she might not have, either.

The girl's back within minutes. She thrusts a printout at me. On it is a series of dates and times, and even though I'm reading it all too fast, I can feel my heart start to race.

Yes.

My Alt's been at the terminal, off and on, over this past week. My eyes fall to the most recent entries at the bottom half of the page, where a pattern begins to take shape.

From three days ago:

```
Morning (Bag Ct. 1) Sign Out 0853
Bed Claim (Bag Ct. 1) Sign In 1817
Sign Out 1856
Sign In 2033
Sign Out 2149
Sign In 2213
```

Two days ago:

```
Morning (Bag Ct. 1) Sign Out 0927
Sign In 1335
Sign Out 1351
Bed Claim (Bag Ct. 1) Sign In 1849
Sign Out 1916
Sign In 2054
```

One day ago:

```
Morning (Bag Ct. 1) Sign Out 0843
Bed Claim (Bag Ct. 1) Sign In 1802
```

```
Sign Out 1912
Sign In 2235
```

Then just this earlier today:

```
Morning (Bag Ct. 1) Sign Out 0803
```

She's been crashing here for the past three nights. Maybe nothing definitive, but it's *something*. Since my life's been winnowed down to less than 168 hours, it could be *everything*.

The girl startles me when she speaks. I forgot her in my growing excitement. "Um, you were going to pay me?"

I stuff the printout into my bag before handing over the last of my bills. Only loose change left now, rolling around in the bottom of my bag. It's pretty stupid of me not to have kept more for myself, but I have to do this. Part of it is guilt for using the girl and her naïveté, despite my happiness at her awakening survival instincts. The rest of it is grim acceptance that I've stepped over some invisible line.

Her fingers are careful not to touch mine as they take my money. Her nails have been gnawed to the quick. There are still crescent moons of candy apple polish on them.

"Cool. Thanks." She folds the money into her jeans pocket. Starts to turn around to leave, then stops, takes a deep breath, and holds something out to me. "Here. I think you need it more than I do."

Stunned, I slowly take Luc's watch from her hand. "Are you sure?" I ask through numb lips. That hitch in my chest is back.

"I *know* you need it more than I do, actually."

So what if I do? "I think you're wrong," I say quietly as I put the watch back on and feel armored again. Just a watch, metal and plastic and micro bits. But, logical or not, so much more.

The girl shrugs. The look in her eyes is of pity, close enough to what I was feeling for her, and it makes me uneasy. "It's okay, I'll manage," she says. With that she disappears into the rushing crowd, leaving me to stare after her.

She reminds me a bit of Ehm, if only because she has a bit of the childish innocence that Ehm had, that Dess still had in spades before he left. But whatever I sense of that in this girl is already dying, mostly gone. It has to. It has to give way to whatever cruel steel she can find within her if she wants to live any longer than Ehm did, to eventually complete her assignment.

That's why I want to think she reminds me a bit of myself, too.

Except that I wouldn't have given the watch back.

I turn around and start walking again, getting ready for the best chance to kill my Alt yet. There's hope now . . . though it hinges on little more than numbers and letters on a piece of paper, a sample size so minuscule it should mean nothing. *Would* mean nothing if it weren't for my desperation making its importance grow by the minute, hour, day.

CHAPTER 7

More rain.

The wetness combines with the chill in the air to penetrate through my jacket and sweater and undershirt and right into my skin. Hours of waiting, and I've never felt so cold before.

Nearly eleven at night, and my Alt is not doing what she's supposed to be doing. A break in her pattern.

Sitting beneath the awning of a cell repair shop across the street from the terminal, I shiver and sink farther into my jacket. People walk by without a second glance, a continuous wave of human traffic that hasn't yet shown signs of letting up, despite the hour or the darkness. Gritty from exhaustion, my eyes begin searching for what could be my bed tonight. It has to be close by. I can't risk missing her. Not for something as insignificant as sleep.

Not the alleyway beside me. Though the location is ideal, with a clear view of the terminal entrance, it's simply too open. Someone else might consider staying there alongside me.

None of the store entrances, either. They go deep enough

so I wouldn't be on the sidewalk, but are way too vulnerable to anyone passing—

My train of thought stops dead, and the next second has my breath catching in my throat. My eyes narrow into slits, and I draw farther back beneath the sodden droop of my hood.

I see her.

My Alt's path is unwavering as she cuts through the tightly packed sidewalk. Her profile—so familiar to me—is carved out against the light of the terminal. I watch as she makes her way inside.

Through the window I can see the front counter. Seated behind it is the same attendant I talked to that morning. I watch her face as my Alt speaks to her, as she holds out the eye scanner. There is nothing odd about her expression, no indication that anything is off. If anything, she comes across as even more tired and bored than the last time I saw her. Is it possible she doesn't remember our conversation? Who was I but another Alt with a desperate request and even more desperate eyes?

They talk for a moment longer, and as it goes on, I can feel myself starting to flail.

What do I want to do? What do I want *her* to do? Am I ready for this? Or do I just want her to stay inside so I can have more time, just a little bit more time? *Then I swear I will be ready, more than ready to kill her and complete my assignment.*

She's turning in her bag to the attendant to be checked, and pushing the front doors open again, and I have no more time to not be ready.

My Alt's leaving the terminal. And she's headed straight toward me.

Before my heart can beat normally again, she abruptly stops walking and says something out loud to herself, probably checking the time. Then her cell is in her hand, and she is speaking into it as she spins on her heel and turns down the street, away from me.

I take a deep breath, brace myself for the pain, and bite down hard enough on my tongue to draw blood. Fully awake now, the taste of old pennies and human weakness filling my mouth. I never want to know the feeling again.

So I follow her.

Both my hands are sunk deep in my jacket pockets. In my left, my switchblade; in my right, my gun, the tip of it digging reassuringly into my stomach.

She keeps going straight for another four blocks, then turns right for another three. Left again for another five or six. Who is my Alt talking to all this time? But I push the question aside, extinguish it into nothing. It can't make any difference to me, and as much as the idea of this person hearing her die over the phone is horrible, it wouldn't be enough to stop me.

Minutes later she's finished talking and her cell disappears from view, leaving us truly alone in the crowd. Jostling bodies surround us, and I have to be careful I don't let them drive us apart.

We've cut west straight through Jethro and are in Gaslight now, the most run-down of Kersh's four wards. It houses the city's water processing plants, and we walk past multiple lots of glassed-in solar distillation centers. Rainwater harvesting operations cover most roofs, from businesses to residential. Dotting the western edge of Gaslight is the sheen of desalination factory domes, where seawater from the Pacific is continuously piped in.

My Alt's pace slows to a lope. Whether it's because she's unfamiliar with these surroundings or because she senses me in some way, I have no way to tell. I have no choice but to pull back on my speed a bit and put more distance between us, despite everything in my gut screaming at me to stay close. Here within this congested crowd, she should be more difficult to track. But somehow she isn't. Her stride, the way her hair swings and sways with each step . . . I can't help but know it deeply.

I wouldn't have thought it possible, but the sky darkens even further, becoming a true solid black. The hissing steam grates that line Gaslight's sidewalks fight for attention with the bright neon lights strung above doorways and windows. They illuminate the faces of the passersby, the lights' gaudiness flashing off the half sheets of galvanized metal rolled down to protect the worn storefronts along the street. Most businesses here can't afford even the poorest grade of bulletproof glass.

Here is the Quad. If places could have Alts, this would be the Grid's. As the Grid centers Jethro Ward, the Quad does the same for Gaslight. A mixture of residential homes and family-run businesses, the Quad was originally carved out by immigrants from four distinct nationalities, now long forgotten. All these years later, the lines between those groups have melted away, leaving a blurred mosaic of all shades and tones. What was once a few small blocks is now nearly half a square mile in size.

The Quad runs on its own unique pulse—not one of

constrained violence and hard-edged desires, but of age-old traditions and sprawling, multigenerational families that make up the heart of the neighborhood. When we were little, my brothers and I explored the Quad almost as much as the Grid. Buying flimsy toys that we kept in our desks at school, ready for a trade or a bribe: splintery finger puzzles; rolls of plastic poker chips; stink powder and fart bombs. We'd stuff ourselves with cheap street food—from the vendors who sold to idles, anyway—buns and pastries, fried bits of shellfish scavenged from the beach, right where the iron barrier runs alongside the ocean in Gaslight Ward.

None of this is new to me, but I can see that my Alt is fascinated. Her pace is even slower now; she's distracted by the calls of vendors, the electric lanterns strung everywhere. A few times something fully catches my Alt's attention, and when she turns her head to look, the familiarity of her profile is both fitting and strange.

Space is at a premium here, too, and people have to walk single file to fit between the vendor stalls and the parked cars on the road. It's the ultimate bottleneck, and it makes me nervous. I'm naked without the cover of the crowd, both sides of me open and vulnerable. But I have no other choice except to stay with her. All I can hope is that she doesn't turn around to look back. I'm more than aware that *I'm* the one who stands out here. My cheaply dyed blond hair poking out from beneath my hood is like a weed in a garden of dark orchids. I reach up to push back a strand that's tickling my cheek. I still haven't gotten used to how it looks. It's so short now. Yet another way in which I feel naked.

I'm about ninety feet behind her when she stops at one of the open food stalls. From the sight of the bamboo baskets, I know she's buying something to eat. My stomach growls, and I press into it with the tip of my gun to shut it up.

Move. Now.

While her back is turned to me, I dart across the street and duck into the narrow alley that intersects a multilevel office building. It's past office hours, all the windows shuttered and without movement.

I slide into the empty quiet of the alley's darkness, dropping immediately into a crouch. For cover, it's more than adequate.

My Alt is directly across from me. I can see the black silk of her hair, the compact build of her shoulders above the line of parked cars on the street behind her. It's not much, but it'll do. I've hit my mark with less of a target before.

To have gotten this far, it seems almost anticlimactic. Has it all come down to this, then? To finally extricate her from my life like yanking out a nagging thorn? I think back to when I first saw her—when the sight of her froze me in my tracks and reduced me to nothing more than useless, second-best, unworthy.

I breathe in, exhale deeply, roughly. It's not going to happen again. I won't let it.

Slowly, I ease the gun from my pocket. It's nearly weightless in my hand now, as though it's always been mine. I raise it with an arm that is rock steady and true. My pulse is a steady thrum along my wrists, down the front of my neck and into my chest.

The target on her back calls to me. My eyes zero in so that it's the only thing I see.

I aim, and my finger starts to squeeze down on the trigger, curling, flexing, and then—

A flurry of movement.

My Alt is pulling out her cell again. She's speaking into it, and this time she seems almost annoyed, agitated as she glances from side to side. Her movements are all over the place, and I swear to myself in frustration. A nonstatic target, no matter how steady the shooter's arm, is a risk to those around it—especially in an area this clogged, this packed, where not everyone's going to do an FDFO. I want to think I'm steady enough that I won't hit anyone else. But I'd be lying.

My hand trembles, the gun wavering. I can feel a drop of sweat dribble down my hairline and come to rest along my jaw. It's cold, even colder than the air around me.

She's staring at something to her left, still speaking urgently into her cell.

Suddenly things are in motion, so quick and frantic they tumble over each other like crazed, rabid animals trying to tear one another apart.

The cell slips from my Alt's hand and hits the ground. I watch, unable to move, as my Alt—in one smooth gesture that has her hair swirling around her in a perfect pirouette—swivels her head and stares right at me.

Our eyes meet. Her surprise borders on innocence, of someone younger than she actually is . . . and I see Ehm in her features. My hand jerks to the side even as my finger clenches. The bullet explodes from my gun.

And I know it's going to be off.

It grazes her cheek, slicing it open, before smashing into

the tower of bamboo baskets behind her. Steam and bread and meat fly in every direction, and for too long I lose sight of her.

I've missed.

Some people are running, a few scream. There's even a mocking cheer. Some of the younger idles actually do an FDFO. But most barely blink an eye in their need to just keep going. They've seen all this before.

A soft whistle streaks past me.

Trapped breath. No time to think. I know that sound all too well.

Reflex has me falling flat to the ground to avoid the next bullet. As I go down, I'm stunned by what I see—my Alt, still staring at me. But there's a feeling other than surprise in her eyes now, written all over her face as though she can't even begin to contain it. Satisfaction, relief, elation.

And she's not holding a gun.

What the—

Utter confusion overtakes me. *If it's not her, who's shooting at me? I can't—*

Another shot: this one hits near my leg. I pull it in automatically, making my body smaller even as my brain stretches in all directions to find an answer.

Only one makes sense.

She's got a striker on *me*.

The thought barely exists before the sound of gunfire comes again. This time the bullet hits home, driving into my left shoulder, obliterating flesh and muscle and tendon in its searing path. The pain is hot, terrible.

I don't make a sound, because that would be the beginning

of the end. My control is beginning to slip, and that scares me most of all. I can't die here. Not this way, on the ground and as helpless as a snared rabbit in the woods. Only a dim kind of awareness keeps my gun from slipping out of my right hand and onto the gravel. A shallow pocket of sanity beneath the welling pain.

I'm supposed to stop the bleeding. I know that. It's instinctive, an ancient drive for survival, the first thing to do. Instead I press my shoulder hard into the wall of the building next to me.

Thick, fresh waves of agony radiate down my arm. But it works; it gets me moving; it clears my head. I'm on my hands and knees, backing up farther into the alley. Then I'm on my feet, breathing heavily, chugging air like it's impossible to get enough. The front of my jacket is stained with blood and mud and rain. My bag perches precariously on my one good shoulder; blood flows too fast, too hot from the bad one.

I see the mark my bullet has left on her face, a thick slash of red that's black as ink in the electric-lit night. It's going to scar. *Good.*

My right hand lifts off my wound, moves to aim my gun again. I don't want to see how my arm is shaking like a junkie gone cold turkey or how slow I'm moving, thrown off balance by my damage, blood loss, the huge shock to the system. My finger squeezes, dissolving the space between trigger and gun until there's nothing left but my wanting her gone.

It doesn't happen.

Someone comes to stand next to her. A boy, about the same age as me, as her. His face is an eerie moon beneath the neon lights—blondish hair, light eyes, a strong nose and cleft chin—and he's pointing a gun right back at me. The black eye of it is huge and yawning.

But then—

Something down the street has my Alt turning to look. Her face flickers in panic, and she turns to the boy, yelling at him, pulling at him to move, *move!*

And they're gone, weaving into the hustling crowd like sylphs into thin air.

It takes me a whole minute to fully realize this. Or maybe it just feels that long. Maybe it's really only seconds. Time blurs in and out, distorted and off-kilter. And beneath the haze of it my complete bewilderment . . . why they took off . . . what saved me . . . why I feel relief as well as disappointment.

I stumble back even farther into the alley. The gun dangles from my fingers before slipping. I don't even hear the sound of it hitting the ground. Suddenly dizzy, I know I need to sit down somewhere, anywhere. Just for a few seconds. Then I'll find a place for the night and fix up my shoulder with whatever supplies I can find. A hospital is not an option. They would scan my eyes, and I can't let that happen.

My back and shoulders hit the chain-link fence. It's a dead end. There's nowhere else to go except up the steel mesh, and I know I can't climb with my arm the way it is. Maybe if I just rest it for a bit. Maybe then I'll be able to do it.

I slide down until I'm sitting on the dusty gravel. Leaning

over to rest my face against the side of the building, I let my eyes fall shut. Just for a few minutes, I tell myself. That's all I need.

When a hand gently probes my shoulder, I swear under my breath and make a motion to push it away. It hurts so bad and I've only just closed my eyes. It hasn't been long enough. Not nearly.

I hear a low, ragged oath full of worry.

This time when the hand returns, I let it stay. Because I know it can only be one person.

Slowly I open my eyes. They feel swollen and entirely too heavy, but I struggle to not go under again.

Crouched in front of me is Chord. In the shadowed darkness of the alley, I recognize his familiar figure immediately.

"At least it's not my shooting arm, right?" I croak out. I can't deny the fact that I'm happy to see him.

For a minute, he doesn't even speak. Then softly, "You really think this is funny, West?"

I inhale. Exhale. "No. I know it's not funny. But I don't feel so hot, and even less like arguing with you again."

"I'm not the one doing the arguing," he says. "What happened?"

I begin to shrug, but wince at the pain. "Um, I got shot?"

"Yeah, I figured that part out myself." His hand is still on the wound. As hot as the injury is, his skin is even hotter. I can feel it through my clothes, through the chilled air that swirls around us.

"Chord, it wasn't her." The words are out before I know it. "My Alt, I mean."

A pause. "I know."

"What do you mean, you know?" I ask slowly.

"I saw him, West. Just as clearly as I'm seeing you now." In the dark his eyes go flat. "The striker she has on you."

I shake my head, getting rid of the last of the cobwebs. Something is not right.

"But she wasn't even searching for me when I found her," I tell him. "I caught her totally off guard. Why would she even know to have her striker ready? Why was she even with him? Strikers aren't supposed to meet their clients. It gets messy." I frown, considering, weighing, thinking out loud. "But she was on her cell almost the whole time. Maybe she was telling him where she was. . . ."

Now Chord's shaking his head. "I don't know. What I do know is that he was trying to kill you, and he was with your Alt. Unless you've got a whole bunch of people wanting you dead that you never told me about, it only makes sense. They ran off together, you know—when I came after them."

"So it was you who scared them off." I should have known. "How did you . . . know? To be there?" *That I needed you?*

Chord looks away for a long second, as if debating something, before meeting my eyes. Blunt stubbornness there, without a sign of regret. "You know the cells I've been leaving for you?" he asks quietly.

I nod, a new kind of knot in my stomach. "Yeah, what about them?"

"They're chipped. Connected to my computer at home. To my own cell, too."

I suck in my breath. "You've been tracking me!"

"Yeah, I have," he says, his voice rough. His eyes are as dark as onyx, brilliant even with the lack of light, and beneath the anger I see pain. "And I would do it all over again if it keeps you alive, West."

Just like that, I'm deflated. Defeated. Because if it were him on the run, I would have done the same.

"Why does it seem like I'm always thanking you, when you're always driving me crazy?" I mutter. "How were you doing it, anyway? I never found a shadowing system in any of the cells."

"They were wiped clean by the time me and Luc got our hands on them. Not that I had time to load a system on the first cell I gave you. When I realized you'd probably think of that, I went with a chip instead."

"Well, it worked. I never thought you'd go old-school."

"Sometimes simpler is better." He shrugs, then smiles. "And you don't have to thank me. Just . . . know that I'm here, okay?"

I nod. Unsure how far I can let this go before I have to start lying.

"Maybe the next time you run into her, you could just ask her about her new friend," Chord says lightly.

I smile. It feels misshapen on my face. "Maybe. But not today. I'm not really up for seeing her again so soon."

My eyes are used to the darkness now, and I can make him out clearly. His face with the high cheekbones and sharply defined jaw, the large, dark eyes framed by slashing brows, suddenly softening as he touches a lock of my newly blond hair. "Can I be honest and say I like your old hair better?"

I'm startled enough to laugh outright, and it leaves me wincing. I grab his hand, the one covering the bullet wound. "Help me up, okay? I need to get inside somewhere, clean off this mess before it gets worse."

Careful to not press down on my shoulder, Chord pulls me to my feet with his arm around my waist.

The world sways, and my teeth start to chatter from the freezing air. Maybe also from something creeping at the edges of a different kind of fear—the first twinges of fever, spreading inward from my shoulder. He tightens his arm around me to keep me steady.

"I'm coming with you," Chord tells me, "and don't bother saying no. You can barely stand, let alone walk."

I'm too tired to argue. And he's warm, and whole, and I think I can let myself be weak this one time. "Fine. Just until I get inside somewhere. I wouldn't want to shake up your routine or anything. I mean, how are you going to follow me if I'm already with you, right?"

"You just don't stop, do you, West?" he murmurs. But there's relief in his voice, not annoyance.

We start walking down the street, his arm around my waist as support.

The Quad is crowded, but the sidewalks are thinning out, traffic slowing, people starting to head home for the night. The sensation of having actual room around us is almost sinister. Like we're being left out in the open, with no bodies to swallow us up.

"We've got to hurry and get inside," I tell him, my voice low and uneven. "It's too late to be out here." I'm moving as fast as I can, feeling like I'm walking on stilts, clumsy and in danger of falling. I'm being stupid, asking for even more damage by trying to push myself. But panic mode's kicked in for me, and the voice inside my head is urging me to hurry.

Suddenly Chord's arms sweep me up. He shifts my weight until I'm settled against his chest.

"Chord, let go." I cross my arms in front of me, both flustered and mortified. "Seriously."

"It's faster this way, admit it. So *you* let go for once." Chord's voice is surprisingly serious, and I frown. I don't really know what to say, not quite sure what I want. Still unsure, I force myself to relax a fraction.

We're both quiet. Only the sound of our breathing can be heard, and the cadence of it is soothing. Before long, my eyes are begging to close, my head is jerking forward, and my arms are wrapped around his neck. The pain in my shoulder and along my arm has become a dull, steady burn.

"It's okay, West. Sleep, if you need to. We'll be there soon." His voice lulls me to rest my head against his chest, and his clean scent fills my nose and my mind.

It's the first time in a long time that I fall asleep without feeling alone.

The half moon winks at us through the window, revealing the misery of our surroundings. The dirt and age of the tiny studio apartment, the sagging of the bed in the middle of it. On which we're both sitting now, simply because with the power supply cut, it's where the light is strongest. We're going to need as much light as we can get, if we're going to do what needs doing.

I've never felt more embarrassed and nervous in my life. The fact that Chord has gone strangely quiet tells me he might be feeling the same way, too.

At least I've got the benefit of a hefty dose of painkillers coursing through my system—already I can feel them starting to kick in. There was a bottle in the med kit Chord found beneath the bathroom sink, and I was happy enough to take a bunch in preparation for having the bullet removed from my shoulder. If it makes me feel groggy and say something really stupid, I'll have no qualms laying blame.

Chord clears his throat. "I can just tear off the sleeve. If you want, I mean."

"You can't," I murmur. An odd sense of lightness, the painkillers really taking effect now. "I don't have another shirt."

Many seconds of silence between the two of us, alive and electric. "Lie down on the bed, then." Chord's voice, low in the half dark. "It'll be faster if I do it."

So I lie on my back and I can't breathe as he unbuttons the front of my shirt. His hands feel warm, even through the fabric. My eyes don't leave his face as he works, and from the set of his jaw, I don't think he can breathe, either.

When he's done, he carefully slips one half of the shirt over my shoulder and down my arm, just enough so he can see the bullet wound. Self-consciously I try to cover what I can of my bra with the other half of my shirt. Why does it have to be one of my more sheer ones, the kind that only just hides my skin? My face is as hot as fire, and Chord's careful to keep his eyes averted as he messes around in the med kit beside him on the bed.

"You ready, West?" he asks, finally facing me. There's something shiny and silver in his hand. Tweezers. And they look sharp.

"Yeah," I lie. "This is going to hurt, isn't it, even with the painkillers?"

"Probably. I hope not. I'm sorry."

I shake my head. "Not your fault. It's fine."

A few minutes of biting back my whimpers pass before one particular jab has me unable to keep quiet any longer. I gasp. "Are you sure you can do this?"

"Yeah, I am."

I hiss at the pain and clench my teeth against the feeling of having my shoulder turned inside out. I want more painkillers, but I've already taken as much as I can and not overdose. Another long minute passes. "Where did you say you learned how to do this?" I ask him.

A low grunt of concentration. "I didn't."

"Are you kidding me? Please tell me you're kidding me."

"Relax, West. I saw a SIM of this once."

"A *what*?"

"A SIM. You know, a simulation, a mock-up. I used to play this RPG all the time with Luc—"

"An RPG?"

"Role-playing game, West. How can you not know—"

"*Chord.*"

"Well, one of my main characters was an extreme surgeon. Trust me, this is nothing."

"I guess whoever said video games were a waste of time was wrong," I say mildly.

Chord laughs, but softly, so as to not jar his hand or my shoulder. "Yeah, I guess."

I think of how he and Luc spent hours taking unnameable components apart, then putting them back together in different ways, their fingers deft and sure as they handled diminutive tools, chips, bits of material. The way they slung strange words back and forth, a dialect I couldn't be bothered to learn. Parallax drives. Clover cables. Syntactic boards.

"But I don't know if using tweezers to play around with gears and wires and whatever else is quite the same thing," I say to him.

"I'm the best you got." He takes a second to grin at me. "Though I don't doubt you could do better, if you weren't so messed up already."

"So long as we're clear on that," I say.

"Good. Now quit complaining."

"You're digging a bullet out of my shoulder," I remind him. "I'd better be allowed to complain."

"Not to me," he says. "I don't want to hear it. And quit moving, too."

"I'm *not* moving."

Another soft laugh. I let a few seconds go by before telling him.

"By the way, thanks. For doing this, I mean."

"Don't thank me yet. Though we're almost there."

A final shooting wave of agony, rising above my soothing cloud of painkiller-induced numbness, has my entire arm
convulsing in reaction. I utter a low moan and fight the urge
to curl over onto my side, to shield my shoulder from further
damage.

Chord exhales loudly. The release of his tension is palpable.

"Okay, I got it." He holds up the tweezers to the moon in
the window. Pinched between its tips is a small slab of silver.
The bullet would be nice and shiny if it weren't still coated
with my blood.

I take it from him, this minute ball of mortality. Rolling it
between my fingers, I feel grateful, relieved, and disgusted that
I even let it happen.

I drop the bullet on the dirty carpet. It makes no sound as
it disappears into the cheap plastic fibers.

"Finish, Chord," I say to him quietly. "Please."

The rest goes much faster. The med kit is surprisingly well
stocked. Along with the painkillers, there's rubbing alcohol,
packaged swabs of antibiotic cream, a roll of gauze. A bottle
of expired penicillin from which I swallow a couple of pills.
Nothing for the stitches Chord thinks I need, so he makes do
with a lot of gauze and butterfly bandages.

"West, if these don't hold it together . . ." He doesn't finish
the thought as he positions the last of the sticky, H-shaped
coverings over my shoulder. But I know what he's thinking. *If
these don't hold it together, we might have to go in.*

No hospitals. No records of how much she's hurt me, of
maybe being put under to be worked on—and having her track

me down, find me defenseless. "They'll hold, it'll be fine," I tell him.

He says nothing, in reluctant understanding of my fear. Gently he helps me pull the shirt back onto my shoulder, not looking at anything other than my chin as he buttons it up.

The last button done, Chord smooths back my awful hair with heated eyes and a low sigh. Still saying nothing, he starts to clean up around me. I stay on the bed, my shoulder pounding despite the medication, and let my eyes roam the room in an effort to distract myself.

There really isn't much to see. We found the ground-level apartment on the west side of Gaslight. A cold breeze kicked in as we went by, and the white tag on the knob on the front door beckoned us like a flag of surrender. Though I knew Chord didn't want to stay so close to where she last saw us, it was obvious I was in no shape to search farther out.

So here we are. The studio is older than old, the layout cramped and outdated. A main room cluttered with cheap knickknacks and stacks of yellowed, dog-eared books. A closet of a bathroom, a kitchenette with too little room to move, let alone cook. The previous owner has been gone for a while, and the air is stagnant with disuse. I don't think it was an active Alt, though—the contents of the studio don't fit the profile of a new co-op or a young student. I think it was just a person who lived and died alone, and while his body was cleared quickly enough, his apartment fell by the wayside. Gaslight's clearing division must be either backlogged or massively understaffed.

My stomach is aching with hunger. It growls.

Chord walks over to me. "I'm going to run out and get you some food. You'll sleep better if you eat something."

"Where are you going to go?" Whether it's from hunger or anxiety at being left alone or just from him leaving, I can't tell, but my insides suddenly clench up.

"There's a twenty-four-seven down the street. They'll have something hot, even if it's only something from the warmer. Maybe some coffee would be good?"

I look at him, and I think I'm more stunned than he is when his face goes blurry. I'm crying, but I can't be bothered to wipe the tears away. I don't know why exactly, except that it seems foolish to attempt to hide them from Chord.

"What is it?" he asks in a low voice. I can tell he's at a loss. He's not used to dealing with tears of any kind. I don't think his brother, Taje, was one for crying, especially after their parents' accident, when he shut down and refused to feel much of anything.

I have to tell him. He'll know soon enough. But it's so hard—knowing how bad I screwed up, no matter what the excuse. "Chord, I lost the gun."

"The gun."

"Luc's gun. Mine, I mean." I can still feel it, how he pressed it into my hand. "I left it behind. In the alley, after seeing her. Him. Both of them." My words come in a purging rush, leaving me hollow. "I think I was in shock, from the blood and everything. I don't even remember how I . . . I can't believe I would ever—"

Luc, I'm sorry. You died thinking it would keep me safe.

Chord sits down on the bed next to me. He's awkward now, all angles and limbs and clumsy movements. It reminds me of when he was younger, before he grew into himself. These days he is tall, lithe, still lanky but muscular at the same time, with a kind of tensile strength that he didn't have back then.

He reaches behind him, yanks at something caught underneath his jacket. He pulls it out and places it in my hand.

For a second, the weapon feels almost strange, almost out of place. But then just as quickly the sensation is gone, and the gun has settled into its groove again. It's nestled perfectly across my palm between fingers and thumb.

At least I wasn't shot in my right arm. It'd be useless, then. *I'd* be useless.

"Thank you." I put the gun down on the bed next to me. I still can't quite believe my eyes. I was so sure it was lost for good. "*Again.* I owe you big-time."

Chord shakes his head. "You don't owe me, West," he says, sounding almost angry. He turns away, to see anything other than me. "I made a promise, but that's not the only reason why—"

"You don't need to do this," I blurt out. It shakes me, to see how his promise weighs on him. Why do I let it tear at me so much? "I don't need you." A lie, way too huge for either of us to believe anymore.

One side of his mouth twists, and when he turns to me, his expression is furious and full of frustration. Want. "You do, but you don't want to, and that's what's killing me! Do you know what my first thought was when I saw that you dropped that gun?" Chord's voice is low, soft and dangerous. "I wanted to leave it. I wanted to throw it into the ocean, or into the Surround. I wanted to bury it so deep even Luc couldn't tell you where it was. I wanted it anywhere else except in your hands. Somewhere so far away you would never find it again."

I'm barely able to think. "Why would you—"

"Because maybe then you'd let me help you. Maybe then you'd want me to stay." He gives a tremulous, drawn-out sigh, then he turns away from my frozen stare, looks down at the ground, and runs his hands through his hair. When he says my name, it is rough and agonized. "West."

I'm breaking apart from the inside out. "So why did you take the gun back with you, then?"

"Because." His face is haunted, too old. "What if it all went wrong on me? You wouldn't have it to protect yourself . . . and you still wouldn't want to see me."

"I do want to see you," I whisper.

Chord doesn't say anything. I guess he's trying to figure out if it's more lies or the truth this time. It's both.

"I wasn't that far behind you, you know," he says carefully, his emotions in check again. "And when I saw that you'd found her, I started watching her instead. Not because I wasn't worried about you, but because I was wondering what she would do if she actually saw you."

"Maybe I was just following her. Not to attack, but to see where she was heading."

He laughs, harsh and grim. "No way. I know you. You had the advantage of surprise. It wouldn't be like you to not use it."

"And I stand by what I said earlier," Chord continues. "About her being so different from you, even though you look the same." A frown on his face, and his brows crease with the memory. "When she was standing there with him, her striker—*your* striker, I mean—and we looked at each other . . . I don't think I've ever seen someone so . . ."

"Cold," I finish for him. "I remember you saying that. Before."

"It wasn't that she was just cold, though. It was that there was nothing else there. Seeing that emptiness on her face, how it was so much like *yours*—" He breaks off abruptly, then continues. "Even when I saw you kill—when I saw you *strike* that one time—you couldn't ever be like that."

"But I *should* be like that," I say before I can stop myself.

He blinks at me. "What do you mean?"

"That's how *I* should be, Chord." Just saying it out loud makes it more real. That she can beat me in will alone. "It wasn't emptiness you saw in her face—it was determination. To kill me before I kill her. She doesn't doubt that she can do it."

"Wait—"

"Chord, if I mess this up, it's like I'm failing my family, somehow. I'm the last one left. What if my best isn't good enough? What if her will to stay alive is just . . . stronger than mine?" I swallow and force the words out. "What if she really is the one who deserves to win, and I'm the weak one after all?"

In the thin moonlight, his eyes burn. "You're not weak, West. You've always been a fighter, for as long as I've known you. Since we were little kids. You're like . . . I don't know . . . a bulldog refusing to let go."

"A bulldog."

"Well, yeah. You've always been so stubborn. Even now I

worry all the time, thinking it's that streak in you that's going to get you hurt."

Or you, if you get in the way, if you get any closer. My chest goes tight.

"Here." I thrust the gun at him, grip first. "Take this with you when you go. Strictly self-defense. She might be out there. Or the striker she's hired, if that's who he is. Even if you can't shoot that well."

"I don't need it." He gestures to his jacket pocket. "I have my own."

I'm stunned. Chord's a complete. He doesn't need . . . "You're carrying it with you? Why?"

"I started to carry again when I began tracking you." He smiles crookedly. "Even if I'm 'the worst shot in Kersh' as Luc used to say, it was good enough to scare her off. When some maniac starts running down the street with a gun in his hand, and he's coming right for you, instinct says you should probably leave. Even if your Alt is right in front of you."

I lift one eyebrow, my eyes scanning his features, trying to imagine what his face must have looked like to scare her off so badly.

Chord's brown eyes, closer to amber in certain lights. His mouth generous, as easy to laugh as it is to tighten with emotion. Square chin, angled jaw, dark hair that's always messed up. I know his face so well. And it's his alone, no one else's. Nothing about it could ever truly scare me.

My stomach sounds again, breaking the moment. "Don't be gone long, okay?" I say to him.

For a full minute he just looks at me. Then he gets to his feet and moves toward the door.

"Spit it out, Chord." I can tell something is on his mind, something bothering him enough that he wants to tell me but wonders if he should.

He stops at the door, staring at it as if it's going to tell him what to do, before eventually turning back to me.

"You know what you said about her being more determined than you?" he says slowly. "That if she wants it more than you, then she deserves to complete?"

I nod stiffly, uneasily.

"It's not true, West. I've always thought of you as one of the strongest people I know. But here's the thing: the difference between you and her is that it's not *just* determination you feel—you feel too much of everything, too much of the time. I don't think you know how *not* to. Like being pissed off at me so much of the time. All the worry. Guilt." A slight pause as his eyes go a shade darker. "Love, even."

My good hand twists in the thin bedsheet.

I need him to go now, before he breaks me down completely. It scares me that it might already be too late, that I may be trying to shut him out when he's already broken past my last defense. Even worse is that part of me that doesn't seem to want to fight it anymore.

But it's the other part that terrifies me. The idea of not being alone anymore, and everything coming back to life. Everything hurting again.

Without looking at him, I say quietly, "When you get back,

can you not wake me? My arm's feeling better now, so you won't have to stay."

A long, long pause. "West, I—"

"I'll see you around, Chord." I blink rapidly against the warning of heat in my eyes. I breathe through the ache in my lungs.

"What did I—"

"You didn't say anything, okay? It's me. It always is. You should know that by now."

He says nothing. Seconds later I hear the soft snick of the door shutting behind him.

I collapse inward until I'm curled up on top of the bed. The tears don't come. Instead they fester inside me, like a punishment.

CHAPTER 8

I fall asleep before Chord returns and wake up after he's already left.

The cramped apartment is almost spacious now that he's gone. And too quiet. The only sounds are the starts and stops of traffic outside and the heavy migration of footsteps on concrete. They come in through the thin walls like a rude wake-up call. The day is already in full swing.

Annoyed with myself, I inspect the food he's left behind for me. Of course it's all stone cold by now, but I don't mind because it's also from the complete section of the store. Pizza with real tomatoes and cheese. A chocolate chip muffin that has actual chocolate chips. A banana that's still unbruised. Real orange juice. I say a silent, heartfelt thank-you to Chord for abusing the privileges of his status to feed me.

As I'm cleaning up my mess, I also find myself checking to see if he's left a note for me somewhere. Just in case there was something else he wanted to tell me. Like when I would see him next.

There's nothing.

I dump the crumpled wrappers into the trash with irritation. I don't even know why I'm angry. It's not his style to leave a note, especially since he knows the odds of my even reading it.

Well, I might have now. Despite how we left things last night, talking with him made me realize just how much I missed—

Enough. Get on with it.

I sigh. Put the thought aside for now. I will have time later to dissect it all, what it means for both of us. Most likely at night, when I'm alone in the dark, trying to sleep and not think of him.

I inspect my bandages. Chord did a good job. Better than I ever could, anyway. I apply another layer of tape just in case and gingerly move my arm to test the shoulder. At least it missed the bone.

I wince at the intense soreness, though it doesn't surprise me. A bullet is like a sharp ax shearing through a newly planted forest. Saplings splinter, crack, fall. I can imagine all too well the damage inflicted by this bullet, the fraying of muscles and smashing of other living parts. But I deserve no less. For failing to kill my Alt when I had the chance. For not finishing the job. Unworthy.

It's raining again. I need to grab a proper rain jacket from somewhere. What I'm wearing now is still sodden from last night. Actually, I need to get more clothes, period. I don't have another spare set. My fingers skim over the front of my shirt, over the buttons Chord touched, before falling away. He's gone now, which is exactly what I wanted.

My cell buzzes with an incoming text, lifting me from my bleak thoughts. I pull it out to read it.

It's a new striker job. As the details come through, a bright flare of doubt lights within me. I hesitate to accept the contract, hearing Chord's words again in my head, from when we were in that tacky lingerie shop back in the Grid and he asked me point-blank why I was still a hired assassin. His plea at the very beginning, in Baer's weaponry classroom, when I first decided to become one.

Is it so hard to just be here, West? To believe that when you get your assignment, you're the one who's supposed to win?

It was difficult to put it into words. How each Alt I killed made everyone who left me less vivid, softening their faces, quieting their voices. How filling my mind with nothing more than the details of the next job helped numb my guilt over Luc's death, helped me forget Chord's part in it. How going through the motions passed the hours and made it all almost easy.

Almost.

Because she's never too far away. I only have to catch a glimpse of my face in a window, a reflection in a mirror, for it to come roaring back at me. My Alt is still out there, and Chord is more involved now than I ever wanted.

Six days left.

I punch in my acceptance of the strike without much feeling, though my shoulder is throbbing enough to remind me that I can't fall short again. The specs arrive within seconds, and I read them, digest them, already working through them.

It's time to go. I've slept past dawn, and the sight of my

surroundings in daylight has me feeling restless and out of sorts. But before I leave, there's one more thing. Now that I know what I'm looking for, it shouldn't be too hard.

I use the tip of my finest blade to open the back of my cell. Then I flick out a minuscule silver chip and let it drop to the carpet. Like the bullet from last night, it disappears without a sound. I replace the cover and tuck everything away.

I've only just gotten to Leyton Ward and already I'm itching to escape. I stick out like a sore thumb, with my cheap, wild hair, my stained, sketchy clothes, my wary eyes that see shadows everywhere.

Standing on the sidewalk, I can feel the movement of the crowd around me, smooth and controlled. The crowd here is different from the one back home. Less thick. Less chaotic and rough, driven not so much by the simple need to survive as it is by the need to keep things the same. I take in the minimalist street décor, the clean, sterile lines of the buildings, the storefronts built from welded steel, brushed aluminum, shiny bronze. The windows are perfectly transparent, thin as a sliver and without a ripple in sight—only premium-grade bulletproof glass for the businesses here.

Leyton is Kersh's wealthiest ward. While Jethro fulfills the city's industrial demands—as Gaslight does for hydro and Calden for agricultural—Leyton produces nothing of its own. Its contribution to Kersh is strictly white-collar, its businesses largely finance- and tech-based. And money has its own demands. Food gets trucked here before making its way to the rest of the city's wards. Mandatory rolling blackouts are shorter. Water seems to flow fresher; heat burns hotter; light shines brighter.

"Hold up, coming through, sorry." The voice cuts into my thoughts, and I narrowly miss tripping over an active cutting in front of me to cross the street.

He's moving in a hurry, but not so fast I don't get a good look at him. Everything about him reminds me how Leyton's money is obvious in more ways than one. His sure, quick movements speak of well-trained muscles. His clothing is made from the latest advanced fabric, disguised to look like typical cloth, thin enough to breathe yet strong enough to deter the point of a blade. And the gun peeking out from his jacket is one I'll never be able to lay my hands on: a genuine Ronin, the same kind carried by the Board's Level 2 Operators, the ones who specialize in field ops and tactical duties. Hocking it would probably bring in enough money to keep someone on the run for a good year, let alone one measly month.

I watch him disappear around the corner, knowing that he'll most likely beat his Alt. The odds are good for Leyton kids. They can afford what's considered elite training, which goes beyond the Alt Skills program offered by the public school system. It means being able to hire the most skilled completes as private instructors, or enrolling in courses that use only top-of-the-line, cutting-edge weapons as classroom material.

In this way, the Board is no different from us strikers. Just as we take money to kill the poor, they let class and wealth play into which Alt wins. Both of us let money become a factor, whether it's fair or not. Wealth counters those things that simply can't be bought: an innate sense of how to home in on a target, an instinct to chase and not be chased, an attraction to violence, even.

Stats pop up in my head, long-memorized numbers that reveal Leyton's advantage. On average, Alts from here complete 69 percent of the time. This rate changes depending on which ward their Alt is from. Against Calden, for example, the rate drops down to 63 percent; Gaslight sends it rocketing up to 74 percent. For Alts from wards other than Leyton who are pitted against each other, it's a much more level playing field—close to fifty-fifty odds.

The real kicker is that it's not just money or information or technology that drives this ward, but the fact that the Board calls Leyton home. Of all Kersh's four wards, this is where the Board's presence and power are felt the strongest.

I only have to look to the horizon to see the central tower of the Board's headquarters rising above the sprawling structure of the main building. It's sleek and silver and makes me think of bullets and blades and the tinny taste of blood. On top of the roof is the Board's symbol, the profiles of two identical teenagers facing each other. It's elegant, almost delicate, but still strong, like a spiderweb. Wrought from the same black iron used for the barrier, it's all curves and bends and twists, no straight lines anywhere. Black spirals for the eyes, and only when you get close can you see that they're long chains of iron numbers. All of it perching there like a figurehead on the prow of a ship, guiding the course of the Board's filtration system.

I'm supposed to feel safe, seeing this symbol. Instead I feel vulnerable. Hunted.

The blaring of a clearing vehicle down the street has me asking for the time.

Half past four in the afternoon.

My client is a co-op. He's supposed to be in his cubicle for another thirty minutes, which is when his Alt would be waiting for him to leave. Which is where I'll be waiting for *him*—my client's Alt. I'm the little bird that has to eat the spider that wants to swallow the fly.

But I need to change first. I can't get anywhere near Leyton's business core, let alone my strike, looking the way I do. The dried blood on my shirt and jacket is a visible remnant of my bullet wound, already making more than a few heads turn.

Slip in and out. Leave no memory. Leave no footprint.

The weight of the fresh cash Chord slipped into my bag, back in that cramped apartment in Gaslight, pulls at me. It wouldn't be too difficult to stroll into a shop and buy a new outfit with it. But I'm reluctant to spend it right now. Six days left. Too long, too short.

On the corner there's a boutique selling clothing. Not the kind of place you would find along the Market Strip in the Grid, but prettied up with slick displays and fancy labels. Frosted glass interior walls and a dizzying maze of silver wheeled racks help conceal me as I stuff a knit sweater, a pair of dark jeans, and a thin jacket into my bag. The security tags are attached with thin coils of wire—no match against deft flicks of my switchblade.

There's a District Grill restaurant across the street, and I head over to it. The outside is entirely too clean, the lights blazing, and the leather booths inside are smooth and unmarked. The contrast of this location with the District Grill back in the Grid is jarring.

Inside the bathroom, I slip on the new clothing, careful to transfer my gun and blades as well. I don't recognize the brand, but I can tell just by feel that it's better quality than anything I've ever had. I wish I'd thought to grab an extra pair of shoes, but there's nothing I can do about it now. I chuck my old clothes into the garbage. More pieces of my past, gone. I linger for a second over my shirt, the memory of Chord's fingers, before letting it go as well. No looking back.

The door swings open and a bunch of girls file in. They're all about the same age as me. They don't even look up as they take over the long mirror, plumping and primping.

Their faces are fascinating, almost too smooth to be real. Their hair is too glossy, too healthy, their clothes too clean and tailored. And while they're nothing like my friends back in Jethro, I'm reminded of them all the same. That sense of place with a friend, within a group, of belonging somewhere. Suddenly I feel a very real pang of loneliness. For that life again, the sheer normalcy of being nonactive.

Over their shoulders I catch a glimpse of myself in the mirror.

I look dirty and sick in comparison. Broken, almost. My skin is pale where it isn't scratched or bruised. My hair is a nightmare, and I can see that a touch-up dye job will be needed within the next few days.

As they continue to speak in spurts of high-pitched squeals and shrill giggles, I decide they can't all be completes. It just isn't likely, given their ages and that there are four—no, five—of them. Which means that some of them are idles. But I can't tell the two apart. They're all behaving without fear, doubt, worry.

Is the ability to hire strikers their secret? Do they think their years of elite training will make them ready at all times? Are they being overly optimistic, or is it just fact? That it really is easier for them, simpler?

In the end, it still comes down to only one bullet, one slash. Skill, luck . . . in death, there isn't much difference.

I double-check that I have everything. I pat my bag down, then my pockets, feeling for the comforting shapes of my weapons. The sounds of the girls' voices fade as I step into the lobby, where I'm soon enveloped in the heavy scent of grease. It clings to my skin like a film. It makes my hunger come out of hiding.

I should eat.

I order a combo off the idle menu: burger and fries and syrup water. All of it is bland, filling without actually satisfying. It makes me wonder why I'm trying so hard to stay alive if I just end up eating total junk. Still, I stuff it down, trained against wasting anything. As I eat, I can't miss the printed blurb on the tray liner: REMEMBER NOTIFYING WARD CLEARING STAFF AFTER COMPLETION IS REQUIRED THANK YOU THE BOARD.

When I'm done, I dump everything off my tray, liner and all.

My client's workplace is only five blocks down, three blocks over. I'm there within minutes.

Forester Finance is just one of the many businesses housed in the tall building in front of me. One glance tells me there's at least thirty floors. Normally I would worry about having to go too high, because the higher I go, the longer it takes me to get back down and out. But going inside is not a factor—not this time, with this strike.

The assignment's already ten days old. That's how long my client tracked his Alt before deciding he couldn't complete on his own. Not that the time has been wasted; he's included enough details on the spec sheet to help me hunt down a hunter. The contents unspool in my mind like a well-read book, but it's his notes from the last five days that are most significant.

> *He's been making daily rounds of all the places I used to go to regularly: Forester Finance on Graden Street; the Boomerang Café across the street where I'd go for lunch; the Freshery a block over on Sees, where I'd buy groceries on the way home; the inner ward train station on Fortis, the fastest route back out to Leyton's suburbs. Never in the same order, though. He knows better than to set up a routine of his own.*

> *He'll be coming for me, but you'll be waiting.*

And I will be—I just have to narrow down where.

"Time," I say out loud as my eyes sweep the area once, twice. *16:48.*

Twelve minutes until the end of the workday . . . and I know it's too good an opportunity for my strike to pass up. Routine or not, if he's staking out the area on the off chance his Alt will give himself away, no way would he *not* wait outside his workplace. He has nothing to lose by covering his bases and spending a few minutes here to see for himself that his Alt really didn't go to work.

I decide on a trio of benches near the end of the path that leads to the main doors. Here I'll have a clear view of what's happening across the street—and of anyone there who's also taking advantage of the unobstructed sight line to look back this way, watching and waiting for one person in particular to leave Forester Finance.

It'd be better if the benches were empty, but they're not. A woman and two men occupy them. Three people to fool into thinking I'm someone I'm not: someone with time to waste. Someone waiting for a friend, or a boyfriend. Not a striker looking for her target.

Two quick, discreet slashes with the tip of the switchblade from my pocket as I walk over. I slip my thumbs into the holes in the sleeves of my new sweater, pulling at the fabric so it stays over my marks—even out in the open, I'm still hiding.

I sit down with an air of affected boredom, my bag hanging carelessly from one arm, my eyes carefully averted. To be noticed as an active would be acceptable; as an idle, I'd be even more nondescript. I pull out my cell, start punching out a text to myself. All the while, I'm aware of the revolving doors on my right, lazily shuffling people in and out, and the storefronts across the street on my left. A bank, a tablet distributor, a shop specializing in custom cells, a train stop.

The sun is lower, gleaming orange and sparkling off the edges of roofs. The edge of the barrier juts out into the sky, far off in the horizon, a giant black cuff.

Less than ten minutes now.

A Leyton Ward train pulls up to the station across the street and unloads a good dozen people. Around me, the benches clear as the lady and the two men get up, leaving to cross the street to board the train. I barely notice because my eyes are drawn to a couple making their way over from the train. They sit down on a now-vacant bench, whispering and laughing together, their shopping bags slipping to the ground as he holds her. They're young, but not younger than twenty. Completes then. Beginning their lives, with the world at their feet.

How easy it would be for me to say something. That it doesn't mean everything's going to be perfect, no matter how much we want to believe it. That life could still suck, that accidents and just plain bad luck still happen.

But of course I don't. Because I'm watching them and thinking of Chord and all that could still be possible for us . . . if only I could let it.

My shoulder's sore. I wish I thought of taking that bottle of painkillers with me from the apartment in Gaslight. I want to believe I would have, if I hadn't been so distracted thinking about Chord.

Then all thoughts wink out, carefully put away for another time. I see only the last person left standing at the train stop.

My client's Alt. Eyes half-shielded by a hat pulled low over his forehead, cheeks slightly more hollowed than those in my client's photo. I see the grip of his gun poking out from the top of his jeans as he lifts his arm to adjust his hat. He doesn't hide the fact that he's watching the building next to me.

Slowly, calmly, I tuck my cell back into my bag. Zip it up as

I run my fingers over all my pockets, checking as I always do. Yes, all there. I get to my feet, slide my bag on, check for traffic both ways, and step off the curb.

I'm still torn, even as I start walking. Use my gun, maintain a safe distance, call attention to myself. Or use my blade, a fast, clean stab or slash, hope he lets me get close enough.

Or . . . throw my blade. No risk of a PK since he's alone. No explosive boom. Only a flick of my wrist, a spin of steel, then simple retrieval of the weapon. Something I've done many times over.

Except—

Except—

I don't know if I can do it.

I can still see the look in her eyes—my first strike—knowing she's about to die, not fast, not clean, but painfully, slowly, and by my hand.

My hand, which now twitches against my leg. It slips free of my sleeve and reaches into my jacket pocket.

For my gun.

The decision's as fast as a breath, as fresh as a new bruise, and I'm only ten feet away with my hand already on the grip of my gun, drawing it out and up, my finger starting to squeeze the trigger with nothing in my sight except the vulnerability of his chest, when—

A girl darts out of the store behind him and runs, laughing and calling out my client's name, leaping for his Alt—

He turns at the sound, a snap of the head as fast as a reflex, as he tries to catch her—

Both of them, tilting forward, my strike, his distraction—

And I'm too late to take it back, too late to stop the bullet.

It hits the girl in the side. She spins from the force of it, falls to the ground, my strike going down beneath her.

My heart pounding furiously beneath my tainted skin, barely contained by my traitorous bones and inferior muscles, as I run up to see what I've done. Never before have I been so far off, miscalculated so badly, as to do a PK. Like Taje . . . like my mother.

But I can breathe again. Because she's not dead, or dying, just wounded. Flesh wound, shallow, not fatal. Her hand's clasped around her side, blood trickling through her fingers, but already she's trying to sit up, already she's trying to figure out what happened. Coherent enough, though she stares blankly at me, a dazed expression on her face.

My strike, looking up to meet my eyes as I turn toward him. And I can tell he's not confused at all about who I am, why I'm there.

I lift my gun again, point it again. I don't miss again.

Whatever relief I felt at the girl still being alive disappears. Has to in order to make room for dull, plodding determination, which will see me through this completion.

I lean down to check for a pulse. There is none. In the utter relaxation of death, his neck feels as soft as a little boy's. And his eyes are absolutely clear again.

I walk away, texting my client for the rest of my payment, reminding him to call clearing.

The sky is charcoal gray, almost fully dark. I don't think of much except that I need to keep moving. Soon I've left the business core and find myself closing in on Leyton's suburbs.

It would have been faster to catch the train on Fortis, but I couldn't. Too close to the scene.

And I'm too tired to get out of the ward tonight, I decide. I can sleep here as well as anywhere. Probably safer, too . . . farther from the Grid, from her.

Now I need to find a place to crash. There aren't many houses around here, only luxury apartments and high-rises for the most part. The lack of individual front entrances makes finding an empty much more difficult; if I even can get inside, it means wandering around all the floors hoping to find something, and still possibly ending up with nothing. I keep walking for a bit, wondering if I should simply suck up my fatigue and head back to Jethro. Then I see a clearing vehicle parked at the corner. In front of an apartment building that might very well be the site of a recent completion.

Drawing closer, I can hear the two crew members talking as they fill out the claim info on their Board-issued cells. They're standing at the side of the truck, and as I pass by, I bend down to tie my shoe.

"So we're at capacity right now, and the other ward vehicles are on site elsewhere." It's a lady speaking, tall and thin, her voice brusque. She's still keying information into her cell as she talks to her coworker, an older man with a slicked-back ponytail and arms the size of small tree trunks. "We'll have to come back in the morning."

"The body will be okay left in there overnight?" he grunts as he secures a full gurney to the interior so it won't roll.

She shrugs. "It's not going anywhere. And her Alt's already

free and clear. We'll just lock up, put the tag out, and come back tomorrow."

"Whatever you say, boss," he answers. He grabs a white tag from a hook inside the truck and twirls it around his finger. "Be right back."

"I'll just finish wiring everything over," the lady says to him as he starts toward the lobby doors.

But I barely hear her, because I'm walking fast now, staying ahead of her coworker. Thoughts are a flurry in my head. Only seconds to get ready.

By the time he gets there, I'm standing directly in front of the doors. My bag dangles off one hand and I'm searching inside with the other. Muttering to myself just loud enough for him to hear me.

"Where did I put them?" I shake my head in disgust. "I know I couldn't have left them inside. So stupid of me . . ."

"You live here?" the guy asks me.

I look up, hoping my feigned surprise reaches my eyes. "Um, yeah, but I can't find my keys."

"Well, I have to get inside, so . . ." He stops talking, clearly waiting for me to move to the side.

"Oh—*oh!*" I slide over hastily. "Sorry, I'm in your way."

"It's fine." He enters the Board-issued master key code and the lock tumbles, gives. He steps in, keeping the door open for me.

I take the door from him with a nod of thanks, feeling relief break through me like a cool tide. Almost there. He makes his way to the elevator, presses the call button, and I bend down, pretending to fumble with my bag. Only when the elevator doors open do I start walking again, following him inside just as the doors shut behind me. Make sure to let him punch the button for his floor first.

Ninth.

Again, not ideal. A higher floor means it will take longer to get down and out later.

The doors shut. I press the button for the tenth floor.

He gets off at the ninth floor without looking behind him. I'm of no importance, just another resident in another building in which another idle has become an incomplete and must now be tagged.

When the elevator doors open on the tenth floor, I step out and walk all the way down the hall until I get to the side exit. I push the door open and take the stairs down one flight. Reenter on the ninth, just in time to see the back of the crew member disappear into the elevator. The doors shut behind him and I'm alone on the floor, left to search in peace.

It turns out to be apartment 934. The white tag hangs limply from the front door. A press of my wrist through Chord's disrupter and the lock springs open. I slip the tag off, hang it on the knob inside, and flip the switch for the secondary lock.

The entrance hall opens up to a kitchen and a small front room on the right, and another, shorter hallway ends in a bedroom on the left. Small but clean—definitely one of the nicer empties I've ever found.

In the kitchen, the cupboards aren't too bad, so I'll have to remember to load up before leaving. I eat two slightly bruised apples from the fruit bowl on the counter and a few slices of bread from the loaf in the fridge. I finish off a bag of mini-brownies that don't contain an ounce of real chocolate, and wash all of it down with thinned milk.

In the bedroom, the body of the incomplete lies crumpled in one corner, a bedsheet hastily thrown over her so only her feet show. The work of her Alt, since clearing hasn't been inside yet. Her toenails are painted in jaunty blue-and-black stripes.

I want to think she wouldn't have minded an overnight guest.

As soon as I fall onto the couch in the front room, I close my eyes. With my bag on the floor next to me and my gun beneath the couch cushion I'm using for a pillow, I drift off almost immediately.

When the buzzing from my cell wakes me up, I realize two things before I even open my eyes. One: It's the middle of the night, but I feel like only minutes have passed since I first fell asleep. Two: I should have told Chord I was in Leyton—and safe. He'll have no way of knowing where I am, having figured out long ago that I've taken out the tracking chip. How else to explain why I'm apparently still in the apartment in Gaslight?

Another buzz, and guilt has me yanking the phone from my pocket.

Where are you? the screen shouts at me.

Chord.

Rubbing the bleariness from my eyes, I text back. *In Leyton be back tomorrow.*

I was worried you ok?

Yes I'm fine see you soon. I reread what I've put on the screen. Too late to take it back. I pretend it's because I'm still half-asleep that I've admitted I want to see him. Not since before I became a striker have I been the one to reach out to him . . . and especially not since I became active.

Chord's words flash back at me. *Sounds good we need to talk can we meet tomorrow?*

The idea of seeing Chord outside of what has become our crazy routine—him constantly shadowing me, me getting pissed off at him—could all too easily become natural again. Like it was never not that way. I don't know if either one of us still believes it's possible to cut the other loose . . . or if we even want to.

For a long minute, I hold the cell in my hand and stare at Chord's message. Such a simple question on the surface, but the answer he wants is too much for me to handle right now. I deflect it like a blow.

Sorry can't I just took another job, I text back. Necessary lies don't change the fact that they're still lies.

He doesn't text back immediately, and I know he hates me for what I feel I have to do, for what he can't understand. I don't entirely understand it myself. How can I kill Alts for strangers so they can live, yet keep running from my own? Endangering my own survival, even as my skills are getting stronger?

In my hand, my cell thrums with his reply.

Will you let me know once you're back? Nothing about me taking on another job. As if he knows there's no point in arguing with me, or trying to figure out anything beyond what I'm willing to give him.

Yes is all I let myself respond with.

A fast and terse reply this time. *Fine.*

As angry as he is with me, he can't be angrier than I already am with myself.

I'm putting my cell to sleep and sliding it back into my pocket when a sound comes from outside the apartment.

The elevator, on the move, being called to attention.

A flutter in my gut, mild and restrained as a bird's breath.

"Time," I ask out loud in the dark.

3:20.

I sit up on the couch, frowning. Press a hand to my gut.

There are so many reasonable explanations. A visitor, a resident, a night custodian. Any of these make perfect sense for an apartment complex.

Except that it's three-twenty in the morning. And this is Leyton. Wardwide curfew is at 23:00 in deference to the substantial business district. The ward doesn't so much cycle down for the night as *shut* down. And Leyton's custodians, keeping the ward as clean as they do, don't work in the middle of the night.

There's the distinct ping of the elevator doors as they open onto the floor . . . this floor. The soft, careful shuffle of shoes on carpet, moving down the hall. Getting closer.

When the sound stops right outside the apartment door, I know I'm in trouble.

Chapter 9

I give myself thirty seconds.

Instantly, I'm on my feet and moving away from the couch. I throw my bag on and shove my gun into my pocket.

The doorknob is being turned. Being tested. The white tag hanging off it shimmies just the slightest.

Twenty-five seconds left.

I run down the hall on my right into the bedroom and grab the body from the floor. She's small, so it's not too difficult to drag her onto the bed. My injured shoulder bellows in protest, but I can't stop now.

Ten.

I position her limbs just so and pull the blankets over her. Tuck them in around her, but not too neatly. There. It'll have to do.

Five.

As I run past the apartment's front door to duck around the corner into the kitchen, I pull out my gun so it's ready.

Zero.

In the dark, I hear another attempt at turning the doorknob, more aggressive this time.

There's a splintering crash as the door is kicked in. Shards of wood from the door frame fly in to litter the ground. When he steps inside, I know I'm not looking at a stranger. I've seen him before—once. On that street in the Quad, standing next to my Alt.

So she really did hire a striker for me. And now he's found me here in Leyton. But if he were any good, I'd have died many times over already. There were more than a few instances today when I was more vulnerable than I would have liked. And that very first time he went for me, when he shot at me in the alley . . . I would have made that shot.

He's probably a cheap hire if he's as green as he seems to be. Not all strikers are equal, and we charge accordingly. Though most of us get better with experience. We have to, or we don't last long. But some come by it more naturally, and I don't think he's one of those.

As it is, he barely takes the time to check the front room before heading for the bedroom. There's a glint off the gun he's holding in his hand. Covered by darkness, I move forward until I'm right behind him. He's breathing so heavily that there's no way he can hear me.

As a fellow striker, I feel some sympathy for him in his learning pains. But as his intended strike, I feel a curious mixture of emotions: relief that he's not as skilled as I am, stunned disbelief at being a targeted strike, and a renewed drive for survival, alive and screaming inside me.

The incomplete's body fools him. He shoots at her once, twice, three times. The bullets make a deep, thwacking sound as they hit flesh and bone. A streetlamp shines through the bare window, and I can see the lump of her figure jerk on the bed with each impact.

Without even giving him a chance to double-check that I'm dead, I press my gun into the side of his neck, right below his ear. Where it's soft.

He freezes. His heavy breathing stops midbreath, and everything is quiet again.

"Hey." My voice is as brittle as glass. "Surprise."

He says nothing.

"Throw the gun down on the bed. Now."

A second of consideration before he does. It bounces off and lands on the floor on the other side of the bed. Beyond reach now.

"You're her striker, aren't you?" I ask him. "The striker she hired for me."

Still nothing.

His silence is infuriating, and I drill the muzzle harder into his skin. To his credit, he doesn't give. *"Aren't you?"*

Slowly he nods. "I guess you do have some guts, then," he says. He wants to sound tough, but his voice is shaking. Way too fresh. What was Dire thinking, taking him on?

"Don't talk to me about guts," I spit out. "Who ran away that day, huh?"

"More like who should have shot her Alt when she had the chance."

My hand is clammy, sweaty, and feeling almost clumsy beneath the fabric of my pulled-down sleeve. I wasn't able to slip it free before he broke in. "There's still time."

He laughs, but it comes out too high. Still scared. "Not much. You should probably stop hiding now."

Now it's my turn to stay silent. There is nothing I can say that would change the truth of his words.

But he's not done, and he sounds steadier now. As if he's drawing guts from my lack of response. "It's not going to be you, you know. You're always a step behind. She's the one who's come to you, who's chased you from the Grid. She's the one who's watching your—"

"You don't know me," I blurt out. I can't listen anymore. My arm begins to shake, and I steady it with my left hand. Bright anvils of pain flare from my damaged shoulder. They pound a drumbeat into my fingertips. "You don't know anything about me!"

"I don't need to. I know *her.*"

"You don't know her!" My voice is rising. A bad sign, telling both of us I'm losing control. "She's nothing but another client! You shouldn't have even met! Does Dire even know what you've done?"

A pause, longer than it should have been. "Yes."

A lie. I know it before the word leaves his lips. And it hits me, then—what I should have caught that first time I saw him.

The fact that they were together, when strikers are supposed to remain faceless, even to each other. It's to keep both striker and client safe, in case the Board suspects an unnatural completion. Dire would have told him this.

The thought of Dire, again. Something there, wanting me to connect the pieces—

"How did you find me?" I demand, even as unease begins to set in. Because I'm already starting to circle the answer.

Another pause before he answers. "Through Dire's contract log."

Something nearly like betrayal is bitter in the back of my throat. "No *way* he would have let you see that."

"Not Dire. But Hestor would."

An image of the resentful salesclerk in my head, and I'm swearing silently.

"I saw the marks on your wrists that day, you know," he says, "back in that alley in the Quad."

"*You* saw them," I say slowly, a new thought taking shape. "What about *her*? Does she know she's just wasted a whole whack of money, setting a striker on another striker?"

"She doesn't know." A note of smugness in his voice, grating at me. "I didn't tell her, or she wouldn't have let me sign up for this."

The memory of her eyes, the utter determination in their depths.

"You sure about that?" I say to him. "What are the chances of her missing my marks if *you* saw them?" The memory of the two of them, standing across the street from me. How they disappeared into the darkness together. Like sylphs into thin air, I thought then. But more than that, I think now. Maybe not just friends. "Just who are you to each other?"

He's gone motionless at my words, gone silent. Listening to something he never fully considered before. The muzzle of my gun is absolutely still against the skin of his neck.

"Because if she *did* know I wasn't just a normal Alt, what

does that say about her putting *you* in danger?" I ask. "Maybe what she is to you isn't what you are to—"

Then he's swinging around, a yell on his lips. Lamplight glints off the switchblade in his hand, either pulled out of his pocket or hidden in his left hand all along, and I barely have time for either possibility to register before I'm lunging to the side, out of its path.

Balance tips. Feet stumble. My gun shifts and slips against a sleeve of cotton before being righted again. Almost too many seconds are lost—his blade comes within inches of my neck before I finally shoot him.

He collapses like a felled tree. I stagger back before his body has stopped rolling.

My harsh breathing fills the air now, overlapping with the sound of the gunshot still ringing off the walls. I sit down on the floor next to him. Look over with suddenly heavy eyes.

His sleeves are ruched up, and the sight of his marked wrists leaves no doubt that he was a real striker. I pick up a hand, rub my finger over one of his wrists. Raised, with still-healing scars. Proof of his willingness to skew the system and risk death—for *her*.

Dully, I wonder if he loved her. He must have, a lot. I wonder if she loved him, too. Maybe not as much as she let him believe, if she really did use him for this, knowing what I am. Or maybe she loved him too much to keep this away from him. My thoughts are muddled, going places I'm not ready to go.

I use his body as leverage to stand, and as I jostle him, something around his neck hits the floor with a small clink.

A necklace. A set of small, hammered-metal plates, all strung together on a thin black string.

I yank it free, feeling the slight weight of the plates against my skin. It's still warm. I slip my bag off my shoulders, shove the necklace inside one of the interior pockets, and slip my bag back on.

I'm not quite sure why I'm taking it. Maybe it's the satisfaction of killing someone who wanted me dead. Or some kind of twisted guilt, loved as he was by a person only a shade removed from me. I've just killed an Alt who wasn't my own, and I have no client, no one to answer to. But against the threat of death, I had no other choice.

Whatever the reason, I can sense a change. The last buffer between me and my Alt has been removed, eliminating whatever distance I've struggled to put between us, drawing us toward an inevitable final meeting.

I do a quick check of his pockets, seeking a clue to who he was. Nothing, except his switchblade on the floor next to me. Even in the dark, I can tell the blade is fine and straight, the handle a good fit in my grip. It's too sturdy to leave behind, no matter where it comes from. That it could've killed me doesn't change the fact that it's here for the taking. I snap it shut and slide it into the knife roll in my bag.

I close the apartment door as well as I can behind me (more like a propping up, actually), careful to replace the white tag on the outer doorknob. After making my way onto the elevator, I ride down, and then drift through the empty lobby. Outside, the wind plays with my hair and cuts right through my layers of clothing until I'm shivering. It pushes me along until I reach an outer ward train station. When I climb on the train heading back to Jethro, the wind can no longer touch me, but

I still feel cold inside. I huddle into a seat in the back, next to the emergency exit as always, my bag taking up the seat next to me.

As the train charges up and gathers speed, I take out my cell. With a shuddering sigh, I open the file I've managed to keep buried until now.

The file fills my screen. The details of my assignment. I read, deduce, decide.

When I'm done, I put my cell to sleep and tuck it back into my jeans pocket. Leaning my head against the window, I wait for the day to climb over the edge of the world and make its way up to where the city's barrier cradles the sky.

Five days left. It has to be enough for what must be done. But first, to convince myself I'm ready to do it.

Back in the Grid, it's sunny for the first time in days, and the streets and sidewalks seem even more crowded than usual. I walk out of the pawnshop and head toward the train station, rubbing my newly bare wrist. Where I wore Luc's watch these past couple of months.

The clerk must have sensed my desperation, because he had no problem ripping me off. And I had no choice but to let him. I guess that girl at the terminal was right—I did still need it, in more ways than one. A thin sheaf of bills is in my pocket now, hopefully enough to take me all the way to the end. And I know Luc would have wanted that for me.

But it's hard to let go of a piece of him that didn't hurt to think about.

I get in line for tickets at the outer ward train station. When it's my turn, I step up to the console and punch in the information it needs to get me where I have to go. Even though I don't select the free option available for actives, I still keep my eyes a safe distance from the scanner, in case of accidental contact. I feed some of my new cash into the machine, and when my ticket number appears on the screen, I hold my cell up to receive my two tickets. One for now, and one for boarding the second outer ward train to take me down to Calden. It's Kersh's southeastern ward, whose far borders stretch out long and thin, a swiping paw on a beast.

And it's where she grew up. My Alt's home.

When I was very little I used to think the world was a huge place, even if it was just one city, heavily gated and surrounded by an even larger entity. The idea of my Alt was hazy, vague, only a hint of a threat. But the closer I got to qualifying age, the more the walls started closing in—and the more real her presence grew.

Only now, reading the Point of Origin on my assignment and finding out where she lives, does it hit home just how small the world really is. How all that time I was thinking of her, she was probably thinking of me. Wondering what I was doing in any given moment, what I was feeling, imagining.

She won't be going back to the terminal now. Since I managed to track her from there to the Quad, her whole routine will have altered. So I have to start from scratch. Go back to the very beginning. *Her* beginning.

It's where I should have gone first, instead of making excuses to run and losing sight of what I needed to do. I know full well she's long gone from there, but if she's left any trace of herself behind, any sign of what she's thinking, maybe I'll find it. I have to start thinking like her—*be* her.

The train is only a bit more than half-full, and I find my seat near the emergency exit, my bag on the seat next to me so no one can sit there. I watch people slowly file in and make a note of them. A mother with a toddler and an overnight bag. A teenager, short and greasy-haired and an active from the sight of his eyes—not to mention the gun tucked beneath his arm. A couple sits close together on the bench seat, hands entwined.

Then we're moving, and I send a text to Chord. *On a job please don't worry about me. I'll let you know when I get back.*

I wait and wait, but he doesn't respond. I'm both disappointed and relieved. As the train lays down more miles between us, I refuse to allow myself to think about him anymore.

It's easy to see where Jethro ends and Calden begins. Factories and warehouses slowly give way to farms and barns, grain silos and rows of parked combines. Wheat and produce fields are brown, dormant, still wet from the rain. Greenhouses are everywhere, shapes and shadows of busy farmers moving within their translucent walls. Even inside the train, the smell of manure pervades, making my nose flare in protest.

The business center of Calden is made up of blocks of grocers, bakers, and butchers. When the outer ward train reaches the end of its line, I get off at the station along with everyone else. My stomach is hollow; I need to eat.

It's the third food stall I come to that finally doesn't demand an eye scan for making a transaction. The clerk is a young complete, too busy wrestling with a roll of locally woven flax to hang across the front window to press the issue. Flax fibers are milky, obscuring the view so that an active inside the shop won't be spotted by his Alt from outside. Such means attempt to keep any potential completion moving along, away from the premises. Half the businesses here opt for flax—the other half for middle-grade bulletproof glass—to protect their storefront windows.

I leave him to his work and eat my lunch: real chicken from a Calden farm. Slaughtered just that morning, cubed and roasted with fresh potatoes, it's whatever didn't make the cut for a Leyton delivery. And even though I had to overpay for something reserved only for completes, and even though it wasn't good enough for Leyton, it's hot and utterly delicious and makes it almost easy to forget for a few minutes how cold I am . . . why I'm even here.

Leaning against the side of a building with my food, I observe the crowd some more, the people milling about. There's an air of abundance here—not so much one of luxury or indulgence like in Leyton, but one of total satiety all the same. No one would ever go hungry living here. If whatever Calden produces is nothing even close to fancy, it can't be said that the most basic of human needs is not met, and met well.

Friends, families, couples. At a bakery across the street stands the couple I saw on the train. Their body language speaks volumes, the way they lean toward each other, touching without touching. Deep in conversation, when even the spaces between their words are understood.

The couple disappears around the corner. I recognize no one else, which isn't a surprise. But seeing all the bodies around me spins a new thought: if my Alt's parents were to walk by right now, would I recognize them? How much do I resemble either of them? More than my own parents?

The inner ward train pulls up to the corner, and I hurriedly sort what's left of my lunch into the proper garbage and recycling units. I give an automatic glance at the brass plate that's bolted onto the unit—REMEMBER PLEASE BE CONSIDERATE AND AVOID DAMAGING PUBLIC OR PRIVATE PROPERTY DURING COMPLETIONS THANK YOU THE BOARD—before getting on.

I slide into a seat near the back. Allow the train to wind me deeper into her world, leave my own farther behind.

Her house is in the suburbs of Calden, the equivalent of my neighborhood in Jethro. But these streets are wider, a bit less run-down, a small step up in the world. And while we have garages crammed full of industrial materials, here it's yard sheds spilling over with farming equipment.

Her house is a two-level, with a white stucco exterior and a picture window in the front. A row of skeletal fruit trees stands sentinel along the curb lining the front yard, their final harvest for the season long past. On the far side of the yard, a huge winter vegetable patch is swirling with pale shades of greens, creams, violets.

Everything is maintained. My Alt hasn't left behind an empty house, then. Parents, siblings . . . family.

No cars are in the driveway, but that means little since there is a closed garage. No lights are on in the windows, despite the darkness that's creeping in fast. I might be lucky tonight after all.

The gate at the side of the house is locked, but it's the kind of lock that's found at two houses out of three. It's easy enough to reach over and pull the latch. The gate swings open, and I slide through it to enter the backyard.

There's a small wooden deck with an umbrella and matching chairs, all covered up for the off-season. Their tarped shapes are hulking shadows, far from welcoming. A series of raised flower beds—probably filled come spring, the blooms reserved for the market—sit empty except for soil. The back door to the house is next to a large window that's bare, the curtains open.

I've never before broken into a house knowing that there could be people inside. It makes me nervous, like something wants to fly free from the pit of my stomach.

Just do it, already. This is nothing. Nothing.

I feel for Chord's disrupter along the outer side pocket of my bag. Slip it out so I have it ready in my hand.

Somehow, I make my feet start moving.

When I get within twenty feet of the house, the back door's overhead light switches on and I freeze. Suddenly the whole area is thrown into harsh brightness—anyone inside happening to look out the window right now would be able to see anything and everything.

It must be set to detect motion, and I need the light to turn off before anyone sees me back here. Which means either breaking the bulb and risking being heard or getting inside as quickly as possible.

Without even knowing I've already decided, I break into a sprint to cover the rest of the way.

I press the black strip hard against the lock, the seconds passing much too slowly. Listening endlessly and breathlessly for those tumbles, clicks, minute turns. I'm quiet enough, as quiet as I've ever been, but if there's someone inside—

There's a muffled thump, deep inside the lock, and it's done. I keep the disrupter tight against my palm and with one twist of the wrist of my other hand I'm in.

The lines of the kitchen are illuminated by the light coming in from the window. Linoleum flooring, dishes stacked high and messily in the sink. There's a dining room to the right, the table still uncleared, and a small family room off to the side of that. A short hall directly in front of me leads away to another room, what I'm guessing is the main front room.

Smells from that day's cooking linger in the air—coffee, spices, meat—all normal smells, routine smells. It reminds me of any house in the suburbs of Jethro. There's not much difference between this and those . . . except for the people who live here. My family, but not. Me, but not. Because I can only think of it as *hers*.

The light outside blinks off, and the room is thrown into darkness. But it's not whole, because on the side table in the hall, someone's left an open tablet behind. Images flicker on the screen, turning the ceiling into a spinning celestial design.

Acute curiosity springs to life, too pointed to ignore. I carefully put the disrupter back in my bag before moving closer to look.

Family photos.

It's weird to see my face with people I don't know, at events and places that don't exist for me. The sensation is unnerving, and I feel like a ghost, sliding through walls, unsure of my place. The life I know to be mine is suddenly less real.

In this life, I'm a privileged only child.

I was top of my year two class; we celebrated at a fancy restaurant last spring.

My date for last year's winter dance was a guy who's cute enough—in a bland, jockish kind of way.

I was presented with a trophy as the star forward on the school soccer—

Hold on.

My eyes scan back over, waiting for the photo of the dance to show up again. When it does, the confirmation of my suspicions hits me hard, clogging my breath in my throat.

It's *him*. The striker she had on me. The boy I killed. Her friend, boyfriend, someone she loved.

A deep and painful pang of regret has sudden heat flaring up behind my eyes. Why did she have to make me do it, when it should have stayed between the two of us? What if what happened to him happened to—

My mind automatically skitters past the thought, the way I used to hop over cracks in a sidewalk as a child. No, it's not going to happen. Not now, when I'm so close to the end. I shut my eyes, breathe out slowly. Open them again and look at the rest of the photos.

Concentrate.

In every picture, she has the same smile on her face, the same expression. Bright, lively, open. Her hair is always neat, her clothes never wrinkled. Even her posture is flawless.

"Great," I mutter under my breath. "Absolutely perfect." She's my biggest nightmare, a type A with real results. She's the kid in school who can't help but reveal just how much slower and clumsier and inadequate I really am, no matter how much I try to hide it.

She's the Alt who deserves to win.

I shudder and turn away, my gut clenched into a fist. However true that is, on the playing field of our assignments, things are level now. Her striker is dead by my hand. I refuse to believe she's better than me. I can't.

No more time for any of this. I have to get out of here as soon as I can. I don't know what would be worse—for someone to come in and think that I'm her or for someone to come in and know that I'm not.

A groaning creak comes from upstairs, directly over my head. Another creak, then a squeaking of floorboards as feet move across.

Someone's home, after all.

There's no use trying to calm the queasiness in my stomach, the nerves jangling in my blood as it races through my veins. None of it will go away until I've done what I need to do with this place.

Full dark outside now, turning it even darker inside. My hand uses the walls for guidance as I silently make my way upstairs.

I can see better up here. There's a large skylight in the roof above me, and it's raining again outside. Drops trickle down the rounded dome in rivulets. The sound wants to be soothing, but instead it ramps me up, each dull thwack winding me tighter.

Four rooms. One's a bathroom. Another is a home office, and through the doorway the sight of a desk; there's the faint outline of a high-backed chair behind.

Next to the office is the closed door of what must be a bedroom. A line of dim light shines through from where the door doesn't quite meet the floor. From inside comes the muffled reception of a show or program. Slightly louder are voices like the reedy buzz of insects.

Her parents' room.

My Alt's bedroom is at the end of the hall. There's an air of stillness that I can already sense. She's been gone from here for a while now. Most likely since the very beginning.

I step inside, past the threshold where the hall's blond hardwood meets soft carpet. Faint perfume reaches me. I wrinkle my nose in distaste. Too floral. I wish I could turn on the lamp, but I can't risk the light being seen. Well, it won't be the first time I've had to work in the dark.

In so many ways it's a completely typical bedroom for a fifteen-year-old girl. Pillows on the bed for lounging, bright walls covered with posters and static photos (including more of *him*, too, all over the place). Cosmetics and jewelry cover the top of the dresser.

Except everything is freakishly neat. Everything. The pillows are aligned, not tossed. The posters and photos on the wall are all at right angles to each other. The cosmetics are in perfectly measured rows, the jewelry in distinct piles.

That same odd sensation I had downstairs, when I came across the photos of her boyfriend. Both ice and heat running along my limbs, reminding me that I can never forget I'm in the home of the one person who wants nothing more than to see me dead.

Enough, West.

I begin to search.

It's hard to find something when you don't know exactly what you're looking for. Coming in, I had this brilliant idea of stumbling across an old cell with contact numbers, a list of close friends with whom she keeps in touch, maybe even discarded notes with jotted-down ideas for tracking me. Something, *anything* that would tell me how she planned to eliminate me.

I'm cursing myself even as I silently open drawers, sift through the neat, squared-off stack of papers on her desk, try to boot up a dead tablet. I saw her face, her eyes, didn't I? How could I have even begun to hope she would slip when it counted the most and leave a hint behind?

The door to the closet is open. As I run my hand over her clothing, I think of my own sweaty shirt, my jeans that are already creased with dirt. I can smell how unclean they are, how unclean I am. For a brief second I consider changing my outfit. I know everything would fit me as if it were my own. But the thought is gone before it takes hold. I can't do it. It would be too . . . close. Pushing a boundary that is already too blurred. To slip from one identity to another shouldn't be that easy. This is where she lived, slept, dreamed, the essence of who she was— and is. If I spent enough time here, would I become more like her and less like me? The idea is both exhilarating and disturbing.

Wait.

The voices from the other room are growing louder. There's the creak of a door swinging open, the sudden bright glow of a bedroom light before it's turned off, and the shuffle of feet in the hall.

Instantly, my back is against the wall, my bag caught in

between. My eyes are wide and staring, my breathing light and quick. Ducking into the closet, I fall to a crouch. Jackets hang in front of my face, boots and sneakers make the ground an uneven terrain. I place a hand on the wall for balance.

The footsteps are getting closer.

I free my hand from my sleeve and reach for my gun. When I feel the cool steel, I slip it into my palm. The comfort I feel is both wrong and right. Slowly I slide up until I'm standing again, leaning against the closet's door frame.

A large shadow emerges in the doorway of the bedroom. Then it splits into two. I can see the figures of the parents, backlit by the skylight. For a moment, they don't move, hovering in the doorway as if remembering how it once was. Wishing for it to be again.

A cold sweat washes over me, and I can smell the acidity of it in the air. The taste of fear in my mouth is sharp and bitter.

Someone comes inside. The steps are light and hesitant. The mother. She reaches over to touch something on the desk. The movement of her hand is like a ghost in the shadows, flitting. She's adjusting something I moved. I hold my breath, wondering if she can somehow sense there's someone else in the room with her. Not just any someone, but me—her daughter's Alt.

No. I'm safe. The moment passes, and she turns to face her husband, who hasn't moved from the doorway. It's eerie, her profile. There are echoes of my Alt there . . . echoes of me.

"Tell me that you believed her," my Alt's mother says quietly. "When she called you this afternoon. That she wasn't saying it just for our sakes."

"She knows what she's doing." A man's voice, sounding strained. The father. "She'll be home soon."

Hearing them, it's almost easy to imagine my own parents—if they were still alive, that is—having the same conversation about me. For a brief second, all four voices overlap, blur, become interchangeable in my head, before they sort themselves. I snuff out the twinge of sorrow that I suddenly feel for my Alt's parents, for putting them through this. It's weak of me to forget for even a second that the sadness surrounding them is not even remotely for me.

"For her to have made it this far . . . ," the mother murmurs. "I have to think she's going to be the one. And what about Glade? Has she heard from him?"

Glade. The striker. The boyfriend.

The father sighs heavily. "She said not yet, no."

"I *told* her to reconsider asking him to become a striker. Even if it did mean not having the Board classify it as an AK if it worked out . . ." She moves over to the bookshelf. Starts straightening some of the books absentmindedly as she continues to speak. It might have been something my own mother would have done—keeping her hands busy to lessen the significance of what she was actually talking about, the fate of her child. "And that boy she saw with *her.* How can she be sure he's not *her* hired striker?"

My hands clench at her words, and I almost drop the gun. My mouth goes dry instantly.

Chord. She's talking about Chord.

Images flash inside my head like bursts of wildfire. My bullet grazing her cheek. The expression on her face as she turns to run from Chord. His face, harsh with concern as he bandages my wound, the gentleness of his hands giving him away.

"Those photos she saw of him at her Alt's house, remember?" the father says. "No marks on his wrists."

My house. Is she there right now, just like I'm here in hers?

"Well, *she* wouldn't be anywhere near there. No one would be that foolish," the mother says, her voice hard, full of hate. Confusing me, bewildering me, because I know she's as much my mother by blood as my real mother was. Why does it seem both right and wrong for a deep ache of hurt to swell in my chest? How has it nestled itself so snugly alongside the growing panic I'm feeling for Chord?

"Did she say where she's planning on heading now?" the mother asks.

"She did, but she's waiting in Gaslight until she hears from Glade first. He's supposed to call her tomorrow, after he's completed a contract."

"Well, she can't wait for him forever!" Notes of hysteria, perfectly normal for any mother over her child. "She's running out of time!"

"We'll find out soon enough," the father says, trying to calm his wife. "C'mon, you should eat. Let's go downstairs."

With that, they both leave the room. They walk down the hall together, the sound of their feet moving down the stairs and soon dwindling to nothing.

I don't move for a few seconds, trying to pull myself together. Information pounds at me from all directions, threatening to blow me apart. I can't sort it fast enough.

Glade. My Alt, waiting. My house. Chord.

Somehow I have to find out where she's going to be next. And the one thing left connecting me to that answer is the fact that her father knows.

Slowly I step out from the closet, glide toward the doorway. Stand motionless and listen to make sure they're still downstairs. Only when I hear the clanking of pots and pans against the stovetop do I dare to finally move into the hallway. Toward the home office.

The skylight behind me gives me enough light to see what's inside. Carpeted floors. A bookshelf along one wall, a large whiteboard along another.

I move to the desk. Not just the briefcase on top, but also these:

An empty coffee mug.

A tablet.

Two books.

A cell.

And a pen. Lying on top of a single sheet of notepaper. Which has something scrawled across it.

Two lines, actually, the ink stark and heavy against the white.

It's not logical that my pulse picks up right then, becomes absolute thunder in my ears, but it does. Heart and gut leaping ahead of what my head doesn't want to believe. My fingers shake as they reach out and grab the paper.

Difficult to read. I pull out my cell with my free hand, tap it awake, and hold the lit screen to the writing. It doesn't register at first. Meaningless scribbles on paper, numbers and letters that have nothing to do with me.

Except they do. They have *everything* to do with me.

77513 Arcadian. My address. Which is understandable.

But then this below it. Which is not.

77561 Arcadian. Not my house, but the one five doors down.

Did she say where's she planning on heading now? the mother asks.

She did, the father answers.

When it finally hits me, it hits hard.

Chord. Suddenly the distance between us is unbearable, a test of my sanity. Never have I needed to see him so badly as I do this minute, this second.

I let the paper drop back onto the desk. Stride over to the office window. I'm on the second floor, but leaving the way I came in is no longer an option. I draw the blinds up, slowly and quietly, even as a voice sounds in my head, shouting at me to hurry, hurry!

Outside the window is the front yard. The bare fruit trees I saw earlier are small and distant and frail-looking, too far away for me to use as a way down.

Which means sliding down the roof and jumping. And the downslope of the roof is undeniably steep. Steep and slick with rain before it drops off into nothingness.

If I think about it, I'll waste time trying to find another way. So I don't let myself. Instead I picture Chord's face.

The window slides open along the metal track. Using both hands, I push at the screen until the whole square frame pops off with a mild twang. It lands with a clank on the roof shingles below and skates down until it flies off the edge. Panic has my pulse dancing, but I don't hear it land, so I'm spared that noise at least.

I climb out until I'm perched on the lip of the window frame. Take a deep breath, hold it, and start half crawling, half shimmying down, trying to keep the weight of my body from overtaking the hold of my feet.

I can't do it for long before gravity takes over and I start tumbling. Fast.

The roof catches at my hips, my knees and elbows. I see rough asphalt shingles; dark, cloud-filled sky; the pale flash of moon. Then I'm clutching the gutter that lines the edge of the roof. My breath is fire in my throat as my legs dangle over the driveway. My fingertips are painfully white, gripping the gutter with desperation. My shoulder throbs in time with my drumming heartbeat.

The rest of the way down is tame in comparison, a straightforward drop of about fifteen feet, from toes to ground. So I let go, careful to keep my knees bent just the slightest until I land on my feet. My jaw clicks together hard as I let my weight tip forward and enter a tumbling roll, just like we were taught back in kinetics.

My shoulder screams long and loud before slowly petering out. But that's it. No bones snap. No muscles twist. I can barely believe it.

Sprinting across the lawn and hitting the street at a full-out run, I stare straight ahead, making my way home to him.

CHAPTER 10

My neighborhood has become a minefield of shadow and danger and threat. In the utter darkness of night, I no longer know it. I stick close to fences and bushes, trying to disappear as much as humanly possible. The fact that she's supposed to be in Gaslight until tomorrow is only mildly reassuring. Things happen. People hear wrong. My Alt could figure out where Glade went, find his body, and race back to Jethro to destroy me twice over—once for each of them.

In the backyard of the house behind mine, the ground below the old tree house is sloped and soft—typical of the silt the ward sits on—and my feet are getting wet from standing in a rain puddle that never entirely dries out. I bend down to the fence that divides our backyards. Coming from the opposite side this time, so it's three boards over from the right. I slide the loose slat to the side and peer through.

My house is absolutely still. Asleep. Nothing obviously out of place—no lights in the windows, no doors left open. But my eyes have already adjusted to the lack of light, and it's the littlest of things that tell me someone's been here.

The blinds on the kitchen window are not twisted all the way shut. Almost, but not quite.

I feel the shadow of her presence here, a weighted heaviness in the air. It's ugly and unfamiliar and rings of confidence. Has she made it a part of her routine to come by, or is it only a spur of the moment thing? It's possible she's inside right now—if her parents are wrong about where she is, if her plans have changed.

I slip my bag off my shoulders. Holding it by the straps, I tuck it through the gap. It fits through easily enough, and I can't help but remember the last time I slipped through this same gap. How the bag got stuck, overpacked and fat with a past that I didn't know how to leave behind. It holds less now, but in many ways, everything that's inside has become *more*. The contents are what my life has been pared down to.

After stepping through the fence, I slide the loose board back to close the gap behind me.

I'm home.

I don't even breathe, not daring to risk that telltale white plume of warmth from my mouth. When there's no movement, I slowly make my way along the side of the house, heading out toward the front yard, staying so close to the siding that I'm nearly rubbing against it.

When I get to the front yard, I stop, lean against the corner of the house, and silently count to fifty. Still no movement—no sign of anything at all. I can hear the constant rumbling hiss of the inner ward trains in the near distance as they cut through the suburban streets of Jethro. The low clank of the factories working the graveyard shift.

It's no more than thirty feet to the end of my yard from here, where a row of hedges separates the property from the public sidewalk just beyond it. When I reach the yard's edge, I crouch down behind the hedges, keeping low and flat, and try to let some of the tension seep from my muscles, to let my spine go loose and soft. I count to fifty again before slowly turning to look back at my house, still staying as low to the ground as possible.

It appears the same as it always has, but I know it's been changed by her touch. Will I ever be able to fall asleep in my own bed again without dreaming about being hunted, chased by someone who is too much of me?

The dull glint of the steel garage door. Concrete front steps lined with wooden railings. The large picture window on the main floor, two more on the upper level. They're black and silent, their drapes drawn all the way across. In the moonlight, they look like funeral shrouds, as if the house is in mourning.

From here, I can almost see Chord's house. Five houses down.

I was so close to texting him about what I heard while at my Alt's house. I sat on the outer ward train with my cell shaking in my hand, my chest pounding with dread and pure, cold fear for him. I punched in the message, was about to hit SEND, when it hit me that telling Chord he was in danger might only set things in motion. Down paths I didn't want to go.

It played out in my head, the worst that could happen, whichever way he might react. He could charge after her without thought, blinded to everything but the knowledge that my

Alt is coming for him. If he knows there is even a chance he could somehow get to her before she gets to me, he will take it in a heartbeat.

Or he could try his very hardest to act like nothing has changed—that he isn't aware of the fact that he is holding a grenade primed to blow—if only to keep her from suspecting that he knows. But if he fails, she could slip away, the hunt beginning all over again . . . and with less than five days left.

So I did the only thing I could do—nothing. My Alt is using him to get to me, after all. It is me she wants, not him. I trashed the unsent text, tucked my cell away, and waited for the excruciatingly long train ride to come to an end. By the time I got off the train and hit the ground running—in the direction of my house—I was a mass of nerves, every system in my body sizzling and at the ready.

Now as I near Chord's house, I crouch down low against one of the cars lined up along the curb and reach for my cell to call Chord's number. It rings more times than usual for him, but it's late. And I don't feel the least bit guilty for waking him up. I can't wait till morning to see him. To see for myself that he's really okay.

"West? What's wrong?" His voice is husky with sleep. Relief flows through me. He's fine. He's safe.

"I'm right outside," I hiss into the phone. "Open the door, okay?"

"What? You're where?"

"Chord, I'm at your front door." I say the words slowly, trying to be patient. "Open it."

"Okay, I'm there." A click as he hangs up.

I take a deep breath and move away from the car. I'm at the door within seconds, and even as I step onto the landing, Chord's waiting for me. He pulls me in with an arm around my waist, and as he slams the door shut behind us, I can't help but let him close the space between us. It feels good to lean against him, if only for a moment.

His thick hair is wild, brown-black curls everywhere. The look in his eyes is a combination of pleasure, worry, and exasperation. "Hey" is all he says.

Needing an excuse to not move just yet, I let myself simply absorb the fact that I'm finally here. Where we're both safe . . . for now.

The front room is neater than it might have been, considering how much Chord would rather do anything else than clean. Couch, two armchairs, a television. A coffee table covered with what's probably Chord's homework. A colossal stereo system Chord and Luc pieced together. The heavy iron-framed mirror my mother found for Chord and Taje at a vintage sale a few summers ago placed over the fireplace. A worn patterned rug strewn over the pitted wood floor.

Then the kitchen and eating area on the other side of the house, with the stairs in between. All the details are a comfort to me, a solace, an extension of Chord himself.

I lean my head back so I can see his face. "There's something you need to know," I begin. "My Alt. She's been—"

"Watching me," he finishes. "I know. I told you, I've been watching her, too."

My mouth drops open. Of course he knows. "Why didn't you say any—"

"I said I wanted to talk, didn't I?" he replies. "When you were coming back from Leyton, remember?"

Chord's words play again in my head, and I push a hand against his chest as I drop my bag down on the floor. "You should have made me—"

"Listen? I tried, West. But you still needed to figure some things out. So I thought maybe you shouldn't come near here until you were sure you were ready." He blows out a sigh. Reaches over my shoulder and hits the light switch. Yellow gold from the overhead lamp shines down on us. "Besides, I knew that as long as she was close to me here, she couldn't be near you. After all, you've been doing your best to stay far away from me."

I can't help but wince at the bluntness of his words. He's right. I wasn't ready to see him. Not then, at least. Though I wanted to, badly.

A recollection of what happened after our last cell conversation flashes in my head. The striker she hired crashing into the apartment. The body on the bed that endured a second death. The gun in my hand, the bullet in Glade's head.

Chord must see something in my face because his eyes narrow. "Where were you, West?"

No point in lying. "Calden," I say cautiously.

"Calden." Instantly, he's suspicious. "It wasn't a job, was it?"

I shake my head. "I wanted to see where she lives."

I can see the shock go through him. "Are you crazy?"

"I know, it was stupid. And risky and dangerous and I'm an idiot. I know all that. But I had to go. And that's how I found out what she—that she's been—"

"Using me to get to you." He doesn't sound scared so much as still pissed off at what I did.

I nod, my throat suddenly too tight to speak, because I have more than enough fear for both of us. I've been so wrapped up in the idea of Chord getting hurt simply for being too close. Caught in the middle, a senseless PK. Never would I have guessed she'd think to use him directly—the last person I have left whom I can call family.

Chord's hand grabs mine. Like a reflex, I squeeze back. How long before it's not so strange anymore? To feel someone else's skin next to mine, someone who's not there to hurt me . . . or for me to hurt them?

"She's coming tomorrow," I say, my voice raspy, the words hard to say out loud. "I found that out, too. Here or my place, I don't know which."

He pulls me back until I'm close again, his arms around me, and I don't fight it . . . or him.

"So we have until tomorrow," he says quietly. "But right now you're tired. Let's go get some sleep."

But now we're both too wired from a sense of things starting to wind down. However things are going to unfold, it has to be soon.

And I'm starving. So Chord passes me what's left of his dinner from the fridge—half of a sub, still wrapped up, and a container of pasta salad.

I lift off the top half of the sandwich (the bread's made from wheat, speckled throughout with grains, and still soft) to see what's inside. Actual vegetables, real mayo, meat that wasn't extruded through a machine and then mashed into sheets. I stir the salad with a fork, noticing the herbs, chopped-up bacon, a dressing that doesn't smell just slightly off.

"Pass inspection?" Chord asks. He's sitting next to me, instead of across the table as I would have expected.

Way too aware of his nearness, my nerves still scrubbed raw from everything that's been happening, I take my time to swallow. Use the action to pretend I'm too focused on the food to notice anything else.

"How could it not, right?" I say to him with a shrug, concentrating on spearing the last of the bacon. It'd be easier to see if we turned on the kitchen lights, but neither of us has bothered. There's something oddly soothing about sitting in the half dark together, with only one lamp in the hall turned on, wrapping us up in its cocoonlike glow.

"If you were around more, I'd get stuff like this for you all the time," he says.

I know he would. Even at the risk of getting reprimanded by the Board. "It's not worth getting in trouble for, Chord."

"I think it would be," he says, mildly enough but not quite able to cover the steel beneath. Not fed up with the rule but with me, if I had to guess. One more example of West refusing to give.

Disgust at my own inability to bend kills the rest of my appetite.

"I'm sorry, that's not what I meant," I say to him. I ball up the sub wrapper, snap the salad container shut. Nothing else to do with my hands, so I sit on them. Finally peek over at his face.

"I really did just mean that. About you not getting in trouble." I take a deep breath, slowly let it out. "Not about not wanting to be around here . . . more . . . with you," I finish haltingly.

Chord keeps his gaze on me. "I knew that was what you meant, West," he says in a low voice. "So you didn't have to explain yourself."

Heat flames up along my cheeks and ears even as I freeze inside. My mind has gone absolutely, completely blank.

"But thank you for doing it, anyway." A hint of a smile now, lurking at the corners of his mouth.

I blink at him, then glare at the grin that breaks out on his face. "So great of you to let me finish, really."

He touches my shoulder and I'm grateful he knows me well enough to change the subject without me having to ask. "You need some more pain meds for this? I could help you change the bandage, if you want."

Memories of his hands on me, the look on his face as he leaned over me on that bed.

"No, it's okay, I'll be fine," I say quietly.

Chord shakes his head. "So you'd rather do it one-handed instead of letting me—"

"No to the pain meds, Chord," I interrupt him, trying not to rush the words. "I don't want to risk being groggy right now. But yes to your help with my shoulder, all right?"

A flash of surprise in his eyes, then something hotter, and all he says is "Okay."

"But I need a shower first."

"Okay."

"And can I borrow a T-shirt or something? This one's pretty much had it."

"Okay."

Small steps. Take enough of them and they add up.

"Do you think she'll find someone else?" Chord asks from where he's sitting behind me on the couch. He cuts off more tape and lays the strip over the edge of the fresh gauze pad that's covering my wound.

I roll up the sleeve of my shirt higher over my shoulder— Chord's shirt, to replace the one I've already tossed in the garbage. Getting dressed, I could still smell him on it, even beneath the heavier scent of laundry detergent.

"You mean hire another striker?" I ask him. His hands are cool this time, my skin still heated from my shower.

"Yeah. Because it won't be long before she finds out Glade is dead. What's stopping her from getting another, right?"

"I guess it's possible." I do my best to ignore how close he is to me. "But I don't think so. I think . . . I think she *wants* to finish this herself, now. Like, it's *supposed* to come to an end this way."

Chord gently presses another strip of tape down. "Do you want that, too?"

I slowly shake my head. Unable to tell him that everything I've learned about her tells me she's meant to be the one, not me. "I don't know."

"Either way, it's a huge risk to assume she's going at you alone from here on out. You could be walking into anything."

I have to laugh. "Same goes for you, the way you keep wanting to hang around me."

"It's not me she needs to eliminate," Chord says. He snips off yet another piece of tape, smooths it down. "I would just be an accident. Collateral damage. A classic PK."

A chill at his words. "I shouldn't even be here right now. She would never have noticed you if I'd just stayed away."

"You did stay away. I was the one following you, that day she saw me. If you have to blame someone, blame me." From behind, I can hear him put the scissors and the rest of the tape back in the med kit. He leans forward and places it on the coffee table. Sits back on the couch, just as close to me as he was before. Begins to roll down my sleeve for me.

I snort. "Fine. I blame you for being there to save my life."

"I don't want to have to save your life," Chord says softly. "Not when you can do it."

For a long moment I don't speak. I'm thinking of my shoulder, which still sings its pain all too easily, my Alt's cold eyes, and fresh doubt steamrolls through me. "I could have bled to death, Chord." My voice is miserable, defeated. The sudden need to see his face has me turning around. "I blew it, didn't I?"

His eyes flash, the glint sharp beneath the lamplight. "Don't do that."

"Do what?"

"Talk like you're the one who should die."

"Well, I *could*," I snap at him. "I'm human, aren't I?"

"And a striker," he retorts. Suddenly he's moving back just the slightest, his shoulders stiff. "If there's any good that's going to come from you being one, it's now."

"If I'd done it sooner, then who knows how things might have turned out. *Who* might still be here."

"You don't know if you could have saved them, West. And they wouldn't have let you fight for them, anyway."

I bring my knees up and hug them, protection against his frustration, my own thoughts. "I hated your Alt for what happened to Luc," I say. "I even hated *you* a little bit, too, at first. But it wasn't just your Alt that killed Luc. If I hadn't walked into that house . . . if I'd just stayed in the car like he'd asked me to . . . he'd still be here." My breath hitches dangerously. "No matter how many ways I want to pick it apart, it all comes back together the same way."

Silence. "Maybe *I* wouldn't be here, then," Chord finally says. "Would that have been easier?"

"You know it wouldn't have," I whisper, my voice splintered.

"And it wouldn't have changed you getting your assignment, either. West, I blamed myself at first. And you too. But it wasn't our fault. Luc would have wanted us to know that, don't you think? Stop blaming yourself and realize it's your own life at stake now."

I can feel my eyes get hot, sting and blur with the weight of his words. "I'm just scared I'm going to screw up again, when it matters the most."

"How can I have so much faith in you, when you have so little?" He swears under his breath and looks at me; the anguish and anger on his face terrify me in a way his anger alone never could. "West. *Please.*"

My heart beats fast in my throat. "Chord . . ." But I can't say anything else, paralyzed by how much he expects of me, what he thinks I'm capable of.

"If not for yourself, then for me," he says roughly. "Would that be enough for you to try?"

Each word tears at me. It seemed so simple in the beginning—to keep Chord away from whatever crossfire that might erupt. I believed he wanted to be there only because of guilt and a promise. How to accept that he's already made me vulnerable by making me love him . . . and that I might be stronger because of it?

I hear him exhale at my silence. Heavy with exhaustion, the endless chore of dealing with me. But it's only the most intense kind of grief I hear in his voice when he stands up, shoves his hands into his pockets, and says in a low, uneven voice, "I can't make you fight, West, or feel like you're the one who deserves to live. But for whatever it's worth, I do love you." Then he's out of reach, pulling away from me and heading up the stairs.

The sound of his bedroom door, slamming shut.

The sound of his words, echoing in my mind.

I do love you.

My Alt, coming here tomorrow. Four days left.

And things have never, ever been clearer. They align, fall into place, make absolutely and completely perfect sense. Leave me wondering how I could have ever, for one second, with one breath, with any one part of me, thought otherwise.

When my cell buzzes with a fresh striker job, I don't respond, barely even hear the ring or glance at the screen. Too frantic and fevered as I mentally work things through, lay it all out, plan my steps. It's the most important contract I'll ever have in my life, after all. And it's going to take everything I have to pull it off.

When I sneak out the back door, the cold, white light of the moon is still bright. Far over the horizon I can see the very first pink tint of day. Crowning it is the high, jagged edge of the iron barrier, thin and spidery in the distance. It's absolutely freezing out. My breaths are thick puffs of steam.

If Chord notices I'm gone, the note I've left him on the couch will have to be enough. I just hope he sees it before he freaks out.

I'm giving myself five minutes. Five minutes to get inside, get what I need, and get back here. Five more minutes I need to keep believing that she's still all the way over in Gaslight, sitting somewhere and patiently waiting to hear from a dead person.

As soon as I hit the front curb, I take off. My gun is in my hand as I run down the street, ready to jump at any movement that might or might not be a threat. No longer simply houses and windows but faces with deceptive eyes. Not just trees and bushes but perfect hiding places for a slim fifteen-year-old girl. A girl with hair dark enough to melt into shadow, nothing like the glowing blond of mine.

From the moment you get your assignment and you make the decision to run, life changes in the most momentous of ways. It's no longer a question of what you're going to do that day, what you're going to eat, who you're going to see. It's how you're going to survive until the next day comes. That you were stressing out about some exam or essay means nothing. Instead you learn how to be paranoid. You learn to distinguish between the echoes behind you. You learn how to beg and sneak and how to move in the dark.

You learn that you can never go home again. At least, not until you're complete.

As I near the front of my house, I take a second to make sure there are still no signs of life inside. I can't go in blind—*because* it's my own home, not in spite of it. My house has become a trap, a potential converging point where ninety-seven times out of a hundred things are not going to end well. Not leaving home is surrender; returning is suicide.

No lights. I have to go for it.

I dart to the side of the house and keep running until I reach my backyard. Moving to the back door, I punch in the code with hard, practiced jabs of my fingers. When the lock clicks free, I turn the knob and push the door open. And it's still swinging on its hinges when I realize I shouldn't have even needed the entry code because the door shouldn't have been locked.

She got in *somehow*. Wouldn't it have had to be here, through the back, out of sight? So then how to explain her being able to lock the door behind her when it's just not possible? Not without the code or the backup manual key that I lost long ago—

Still unsure but already aware of how there is no time to think about it anymore—not right now, at least—I step inside and shut the door behind me. Lock it and release a breath I didn't even know I was holding. It stirs the stale air. And beneath the staleness, the smells are the same, in the way that every house has its own unique scent.

I can smell the eucalyptus of my mother's hand cream, the tang of the metals my father could never seem to wash off his hands, the oil Aave would use on his knives. I can smell the lingering sweat of Luc's dirty sports equipment, the citrusy shampoo he liked to use. I can smell Ehm's candy lip balms, the menthol-mint gum she was addicted to. All of it gone, but still here. Leaving this house, I felt nothing. Now I feel too much.

Standing there in the kitchen, I let it wash over me—the shadows and shapes of all that is familiar, of everything that I've ever known—and I'm unable to stop tears rushing to my eyes. It's at times like this, when it's more pain than good, that I could all too easily slip back into that safe numbness . . . if it weren't for having to leave Chord behind again. I can't go back to not feeling if it means I would have to stop loving him.

I pass the dining table where my father would often clean his gun, taking the time to show us how to do it properly, how it all came apart and then together again like an intricate puzzle. The kitchen island, corners gone round and soft with the years.

Then the front room. And as caught up as I am in the past, my hand is still clasped tightly around my gun. Safety is not an absolute, not here, not yet.

The bookshelves that line the far wall are filled with my parents' collections of paper books and assorted flexi-readers. The striped couches on which many of my brothers' friends crashed, after it was too late for them to catch the last ward train home. The coffee table, forever too short after my father hacked at the legs in his attempts to fix the wobbliness.

There's something . . .

I bend down to the coffee table, studying its glossy surface now covered with a layer of dust.

It's a water ring. From a careless cup or mug. It cuts through the dust right down to the wood, so I know it's recent.

I straighten, my heart pounding just a little bit louder now, a new thought forming in my mind. In the wake of my discovery of her ability to make herself at home here, I go to the front door.

It's unlocked.

I open it and examine the lock from the outside. Run my thumb along the faceplate, close to the area around the manual key override, because it's too dark to see much, especially something as small as scratches from a wayward lock pick or screwdri—

The raised edges and jagged grooves around the slot are my answer, and I think of Chord's key code disrupter. How it's only fitting that she'd have her own system of getting in, too. Both of us, slowly canceling each other out—advantage for advantage, strength for strength.

I shut the door and leave it unlocked, just the way I found it. No reason to let her know anything's changed, if she comes back early. No reason to not take any advantage I can find.

Nearly all the bedrooms are clear. My parents' bedroom is still the way my father left it. The bed covered with their sheets, the unfolded laundry a mountain in the basket. On his bedside table is a book, still open to mark his page. He was only three-quarters of the way through.

Aave and Luc's bedroom, Luc's half still messy with his stuff. I wasn't able to make myself go inside afterward, before I had to leave altogether.

It's my bedroom—the one I shared with Ehm—that shows signs of intrusion.

After Ehm died, I spread out her ruffled yellow quilt over her bed and placed her favorite stuffed animals alongside her pillow. It was the way she liked to keep them—saving good dreams for her when she went to sleep, was what she said. And I never touched her bed again. Or even really looked at it. It was too painful to still see her there, safe and sound, when she was buried beneath six feet of dirt and reduced to no more than dust and hair and bone.

But it's been touched now. Her animals have been swept to one side, the pillow askew, the blanket tucked in but mussed.

And my bed has been slept in. Not just sat on like Ehm's, but the covers pushed back, the pillow indented with the shape of her head. There's even a lone black hair left on the pillowcase, longer than any of mine, even before my hasty chop-and-bleach job.

I take in everything at once, frantic to see what else she's ruined. The desktop is a different sort of mess than before. Not the controlled chaos I've gotten used to, but a scattered kind of carelessness. My pens and brushes and paints shoved in the wrong pails. Art books and sketch pads stacked in the wrong piles. Drawers left open a crack. I can smell the faint whiff of turpentine seeping out from inside.

Fury is a red film over my eyes. My Alt sleeping here with my things, finding shelter in a place where Ehm's scent still lingers, is the same as being attacked, a personal violation. A furious sob breaks through my throat, and the sound of it cracks open the quiet.

Breathe. I just have to breathe. Because my five minutes are quickly running out.

I sprint to my parents' bathroom. The half-used tube of toothpaste on the counter . . . my father's shaver . . . my mother's favorite beaded necklace in its little tray that my father never put away . . .

I feel a distant ache at the normalcy of the sight, an ache that's always eager to grow bigger. But I stifle it and then I'm searching through the medicine cabinet like I'm hunting for a fix.

Bottles clank and fall onto the counter. They roll off to spill open on the floor. Pills scatter like cheap pastel candy. It has to be here. I remember putting it—

Then I see it. My father's sleeping pills, prescribed to him after my mother's death. A small bottle, easy to miss, easy to underestimate.

I pry off the lid and peer inside. There's enough. Not much after what my father used them for.

Suicide.

It's a dead word in Kersh, foreign and nearly obsolete. Like a sore on my tongue, no matter how many times I try to equate it with my father's death. For an idle to fail to understand the fundamentals of combat, for an active to never actually manage to engage, is one thing. For a complete to decide survival is not worth it in the end is another.

It's what my father decided when he downed his pills. That in the end, life with me and Luc wasn't enough to make up for a life without my mother, without Ehm, without Aave. And I hated him for it . . . then. Now, when I think of what I have at stake myself, I still might not understand it—and maybe never will, I don't know—but I don't hate him for it anymore.

I pour all the pills into my palm and tilt them into the pocket of my jeans. Chord's too sharp. If he's awake when I get back, no way he'd miss the bulk of the bottle, no matter how I try to sneak it in.

Nearly out of time now, and I leave the same way I came: down the stairs, out into the kitchen, and through the back door. Then along the side of the house, through the front yard, and onto the street. Day is slowly filtering through the house, shadows withdrawing by degrees. I need to hurry, before I become a target that's all too visible.

Back inside Chord's house, I stand at the door for a minute, positive he knows I slipped out. Half of me is dreading him asking me where I've been. And the other half almost wishes he would, if only so I wouldn't have to do this. So he could convince me of some other way.

But Chord's still asleep. The door to his bedroom remains shut.

I get to work.

• • •

It takes me a long time to make breakfast. Not only has it been forever since I've cooked anything, but combine that with my already less than stellar skills in the kitchen and I'm lucky I don't burn the house down.

I do a quick visual check of the food. It actually appears edible. Eggs, toast, bacon, orange juice. Nothing's too black or too raw. It'll pass. I give the orange juice another stir, just to make sure the crushed sleeping pills have all dissolved. I know I've already stirred it half to death, but I can't help it. If Chord even suspects what I'm planning, this won't go much further.

Taking a deep breath, I pick up the tray with hands as steady as they're going to get and head upstairs toward his bedroom. I don't even bother knocking. I can't. I can't afford to hesitate, to let myself doubt.

Muted gray light flows in from the window. On his desk is a pile of the old tablets and cells that he and Luc used to mess around with, the ones they lifted from recycling units to refurbish or mine for parts. There's also a separate stack for school stuff—the tablet he set aside for his own use, some textbooks, papers, a flexi-reader.

He's still in bed, but he's not asleep. I can tell, despite the arm thrown over his face so it's hidden from view. I wonder if he's actually slept at all.

"Chord." My voice is hoarse and so tentative it doesn't even sound like my own. I clear my throat and try again. "Chord."

I'm met with silence. Then, quietly, "What is it, West? You okay?" He moves his arm and slowly sits up. No shirt, despite it being winter outside. His shoulders are broader than I'd have ever guessed, cut and defined by angles both soft and sharp.

I can't miss the slow, languid play of muscle and bone within them as he turns to face me.

For a long moment, I just let myself look at him. Completely overwhelmed that he wants me, loves me, still stunned that I'm actually going to meet him halfway.

"Yeah, I'm fine," I say. I can't remember the last time I was so shaky inside, more than walking into any strike. And not just from what I'm about to set in motion. From the way he's staring back at me, his eyes unreadable. "How'd you sleep?"

"All right, I guess," Chord says lightly, almost lightly enough to convince me that he's forgotten what happened last night. Unsure of what to say, I hold my breath as he points to the tray I'm still clutching. "What's that?" he asks, sounding immediately suspicious.

My shoulders stiffen. "Food. What does it look like?"

He laughs. "You? Making me breakfast? In bed?" He shakes his head. "No way this is happening, West Grayer."

"Shut up," I mutter. I'm too uncomfortable to laugh at his reaction, even though it makes total sense. Never in a million years would I have done this before today. But I don't have any other choice.

I walk over to the bed and slap the tray down in front of him. Too hard. I almost swear at how the food jostles dangerously. But the orange juice doesn't spill. I take another deep breath, try to calm down. "Here, eat. I just . . . I thought you might be hungry."

He glances down, then back up at me. "Where's yours?"

"I've been up for a while, and I was starving, so I already ate. Sorry."

"Oh. Well, thanks, by the way. It looks good."

I watch him pick up the fork. I can't leave until I know for sure it's worked. But instead of eating anything, he puts it back and reaches for my hand. Tugs me down until I'm sitting next to him. There's heat coming from him, and I lean in closer, wanting to thaw out the chill that's in me, even if it's what is going to get me through this.

"I'm sorry," Chord says suddenly, very softly. His eyes are dark and luminous and full of the same sadness that's been there for too long. "About last night, I mean."

"It's fine, Chord."

"It's not. I had no right to . . . push you that way."

Unable to meet his eyes, I can only look at his shoulder. But I entwine my hand with his so he knows I'm listening, even if I can't speak. Whether he's talking about me finally finding the guts to kill my Alt, or him telling me how he feels about me, or both, I'm not sure. But I can't let myself think too much about anything right now. I just have to . . . do.

"West, you're almost out of time." His voice is low, trying to hide the desperation there so he doesn't send me running. He knows me too well . . . but not completely, not yet. He doesn't know how far I can go.

"I know."

"Before it self-detonates."

"I know."

"When it won't be up to you anymore. Or her."

"I know."

Chord starts to say something and then stops himself, before finally asking in a tight voice, "So what are you doing today? Not sticking around, I'm assuming? Got a job lined up?"

There's a giant lump in my throat, heavy with sorrow and everything I wish I could tell him. I cover it up as best I can and pick up the orange juice. Hold it out to him. "Something like that. Here. Drink this, okay?"

It's the perfect response. The typical West nonanswer that he's heard for years. His face harsh with impatience, he grabs the glass from my hand and chugs the orange juice down.

"There. Happy?" He slams the empty glass on the tray. It falls over.

Gently, I set it upright again. I hope that I calculated the dose correctly. Too little, it won't do anything but make him groggy. Too much, and he goes into a coma from which he might never wake.

A feeling too close to grief is already clouding my mind. It's squeezing my heart with vicious relentlessness, making my insides ache. Silently, without looking at him, I lift the tray from the bed and place it on the bedroom floor.

Chord glances over at me. "What are you . . ."

I can't stop myself from sliding under the covers until I'm next to him. I push him down until he's on his back. Curling myself up against him, I press my face into his neck, smelling his skin. Feeling safe for as long as I can.

He turns toward me and wraps his arms all the way around. Weaves his fingers into the hair at the back of my neck. "Hey, you okay?" he asks. Husky again, but this time not just from sleep.

I can only nod. I don't trust myself to speak. And I need this. The calm before the storm. *It's not good-bye, Chord. It's just see you later, okay? I swear.*

For a few minutes, neither of us says anything. I hear nothing but the whistle of the wind outside and the steady, drumming beat of his heart through his chest. Still strong.

"Talk, West," he murmurs. "You're starting to freak me out."

I breathe out a sigh. Sounding far from steady, however I try to convince myself. "Sorry, I'm just . . . tired."

"Yeah, me too," he says. And he does sound tired. It's not my imagination, I'm sure of it.

"Go to sleep, then," I tell him.

Chord shakes his head. Even in the faint light, I can see the first glint of confusion in his eyes. His words are starting to slow. "Can't. We need to get moving before it's too late. It's not safe here . . . for you. Not if . . . she really means to . . . come back." He frowns, moves to sit up, as if it's possible to get rid of the sudden blanketing fog that way.

I pull him back down with my arm. "Stay, Chord. I don't want to get up yet."

He squints as me. "What? You should know we . . . can't stay. . . ." He rubs his eyes with his hand. "Man, I'm beat. I feel . . . weird."

I stay quiet, my leg lying over his. I touch my hand to his cheek and turn his face to me so I can see him and he can see me. Already his eyes are blurring, and he's fighting the urge to close them.

I run my hand along his jaw. "I'm doing it for myself, and for you," I say to him. "For both of us together, all right?"

I can see he doesn't understand at first, but then his eyes go bright with alarm, even as they're starting to fall shut. I press my mouth to his, the softness of his lips heartbreaking. "For what it's worth, I love you, too, Chord."

I don't know if he hears me, or if he's already gone too deep. I think in some ways, it's better not to know. I'll have something to ask him when I get back, then.

I've got about twelve hours, give or take, if I'm not too off my guess of Chord's weight. Now I just have to pray that she shows in time.

I kiss him once more before pulling myself off the bed.

As I smooth the blankets back on top of him, I give myself over to the coldness again—closing myself off, shifting back to that earlier numbness in which I nearly lost myself . . . lost Chord. What's left is West the striker and the pure, distilled instinct to kill or be killed.

It was always Chord who yanked me back from drowning, no matter how much I fought him. This time, I'm jumping back in to save us both.

CHAPTER 11

A quick but thorough check of my house and I know she's not anywhere inside.

Alone in the kitchen, I lock the back door behind me. The motion is almost lazy, careless, as if I have all the time in the world. The day no longer exists within normal boundaries. Nothing matters beyond what happens in the here and now, this chunk of time that has been cut out and set aside for just the two of us, my Alt and me.

My usual seat is the one that faces the kitchen window, where I can look out and see the backyard. Walking over to the table, I slip off my bag and place it down. Then I pull out my chair and slide in, as smoothly as if I never left.

The past tries to sneak in—the way the dawn's light is eking in through the partially open blinds reminds me of thousands of early family breakfasts that will never happen again—but I shove it away with an ease that both surprises and reassures me.

Unzipping my bag, I pull out my gun and my switchblades and lay them out in front of me. The shapes of them, all menacing lines and deadly curves, stand out against the warm amber grain of the beaten pine tabletop.

I stare down at what has become my life. Other than Chord, they are the only constants I have left. What frightens me is that I don't know if I can ever let them go, even if I do manage to survive the day. Lifeboat, anchor . . . I can't decide which I would rather they be. If I even have a choice.

With quick, sure movements of my fingers, I reload the gun. Place the remaining ammo back in my bag.

Next are the switchblades. I examine them in the cool, gray light. The handles are grotty and embedded with dried blood gone black. But none of that is important. Appearances mean nothing, as long as they won't fail me when I need them. I open each one in turn, searching for nicks, bends, sticking joints. Nothing.

The last switchblade is Glade's. It stands out from the rest, simply because it's virtually brand-new. Given that and his fresh marks, I'm almost positive I was his first assignment, off the books or not. And it's hard to pinpoint exactly how I feel about it. Satisfaction that I beat my Alt in some way, was the one to take away *her* Chord. And sorrow, too. For making her hurt in the worst way possible . . . she who is nearly me.

The quality of the blade is excellent, so it's not a hard decision to make. I slip it into the right front pocket of my jeans—backup if my gun should ever be lost to me. Another blade is in my right back jeans pocket, as always. My left shoulder is still sore enough to give me doubts about relying on it as I normally would. Still, I shove another blade in my left jacket pocket. Just in case.

I push back from the table and stand up. My mind races as

I do a slow turn, taking in the layout of the room, the positioning of the windows. I've lived here for my entire life, but now I'm seeing it through the eyes of an active, a striker, and someone with more than her own life at stake.

It's going to have to be the window over the sink.

It's the smallest window in the room, which is both good and bad. Good because once I see her through the paned glass, I'll know I have the best shot I'm going to get. Bad because it's going to limit how much I can track her movements before she gets there. It'll be as if she's popping out of nowhere, like a jack-in-the-box springing up, sadistically gleeful.

But there's no way around it. Not if I want to do this as cleanly as possible.

I move over to the window and pull the string to the blinds.

Fake wood slats roll up with a screech. Dust motes fly everywhere, a delicate shimmer stirred to life by my rude disturbance. As I've done for as long as I can remember, I peer through the window, and look out at the same view I've seen for years.

Our backyard, butting up against the backyard of the house directly behind us. The house is the same as always—white siding, dark red brick accents, brown trim that needs to be repainted—so my eyes don't bother to linger. Instead they zero in on what's in the far corner of their yard, slightly off center and to my right.

The old tree house. A very old, very well used, and perfectly situated tree house.

I hope it can still hold my weight.

I head back to the table and reach for my bag again. Feel inside for the interior patch pocket, the one that contains what

I need. Seconds later, it's in my fingers, nearly weightless but at the same time heavy with significance.

A tangle of black and silver, of string and hammered metal. The sight of it reminds me how I snapped it free from around Glade's neck without even knowing why I wanted it. Or maybe I did know why, deep down. Because here I have the necklace in my grasp; it's closer to a talisman than I ever guessed it would become.

My last strike in Leyton Ward nearly slipped away from me, and I came within inches of making a mistake that could have been a million times worse. Because of a freak diversion that came in the form of a girl who was in the wrong place at the wrong time.

But a diversion can be turned into a decoy—and work for me rather than against me this time.

I move back to the kitchen counter and gently place the necklace down, right in front of the window. It'll call to her, draw her exactly where I need her to go. If he was anything to her, it should be enough.

The one last thing left to do has me walking to the front room, over toward the picture window that looks out onto the street. Whether she means to come here or go to Chord's, I know without a doubt she'll be coming for us from that direction again. My Alt's slept in my bed, sat down on the couch with a drink—how could she not be confident enough to keep taking the most direct route?

And if it's Chord she's looking for today, I'm going to head her off at the pass.

At the window, I draw back one of the curtain panels, parting it from the center so there's a gap. Only about a hand's width—large enough for her to notice from outside . . . and small enough for her to see as sloppy carelessness on my part.

If I can make her think I'm starting to break down and am hiding in here from her . . .

If I can make her believe she simply has to come in and find me . . .

If I can make her forget about Chord entirely . . .

Back in the kitchen, I go to the pantry, wolf down granola bars, dried fruit, juice concentrate—anything that can be done standing up. The act is mechanical, all the food tasteless, nothing more than pure sustenance. When I'm done, I grab my bag from the table, zip it up, and sling the straps over my shoulders. One final glance at Glade's necklace on the counter beneath the bared window and I know I've set the stage as well as I can.

I step outside through the back door. The day is brand-new. Everything is tinged with the gray haze that belongs only to early-winter mornings. I'm careful to stay off the thin strips of grass along the sides of the backyard. They're crusted with frost, and I don't know how long it would take for my footprints to disappear.

At the back fence I slide the loose slats of wood over again, slip through, and replace them carefully. When I turn my head to see that the old slab of plywood we used as a climbing ramp is still there, leaning against a different section of the fence, it's almost like I'm going back in time. A little kid again, here to play, not to kill.

I drag it over and lean it against the base of the tree house. It's rough with splinters and mildewed, but whole. In my head I hear the young voices of my brothers, arguing about who's going to go first. I see them crawling up, careful to keep each other from spilling over the edges to the soggy ground below even as they yell at each other to hurry the heck up.

Climbing up now only takes me a few strides. I think of that fire escape in the Grid, the way it led me to a clear sight line as well. When I hit the landing, I immediately fall to a sitting position, testing the floorboards.

To call it a tree house is not a lie; it is a house, and it's in a tree. But it's absolutely nothing like what they describe in books, and worlds apart from those do-it-yourself kits you can order online. Seven gapped wide cedar planks for the base, more planks nailed lengthwise to form walls about four feet high. Roughly notched-out holes for windows. And that's it.

But it's enough. I slide over until I'm next to the window that faces my house and peer out for the clearest line of sight between me and the enemy.

Everything squeezes in and shuts down to a vivid pinpoint. Sound disappears except for the evenness of my own breathing. I try to break down the shadows inside the house. I can see the light fixture that hangs over the dining room table. The round knobs of the cupboards that line the wall.

Nothing moves, all is still. But soon. Anytime now she'll be back in Jethro, back at my house.

I rest the barrel of my gun along the jagged bottom edge of

the cedar sill. The muscles along my arm bunch, as do those in my gut.

I wait.

Time plays with you, toys with your mind. Sometimes it flows slow and languid, sometimes so quick that if you dare to blink you'll miss it all.

And it can hurt . . . if I let it. I can decide to think about the sharp crick in my neck that's starting to jab, the pounding ache in my skull that threatens to drum out everything else. I can wallow in the spasms in my hand from clenching the gun too hard, the raw, still-healing heat in my shoulder. I can replay the memories of that first stakeout, too, when I crouched beneath the bushes of that house in Jethro, waiting and waiting even as my body wanted to do anything but.

I've learned now. I made myself eat so hunger would become meaningless. I tell myself the aches of muscle, bone, and limb are phantom pains of a body not really mine.

Be numb, a striker.

The sun is making its daily climb in the sky. Without a watch, I can only guess what time it is. It's been a while since I left Chord, and the inside of my house is lighter yet.

Ten, I guess from the position of the sun in the sky. Rising steadily, it should make me warmer, but instead there is nothing. My skin, impenetrable.

She's not there. Not yet.

And time passes. It clings and drags, but passes all the same. Ten o'clock becomes eleven. Twelve. Then it's two o'clock, maybe three, maybe even four. The sun is falling. Slowly, but definitely, falling. That pale, ashy light of a dying winter's day is darkening to speckled granite, swirling with cloud now. Thin shadows of the last stubborn leaves still clinging to the maple tree drift overhead and are gone.

And I'm getting tired, no matter how much I fight it. It makes me less sharp, slowing my reflexes. Eventually it will lead to mistakes. At one point, the barrel of the gun slips, the dull clatter of metal against wood very loud in the quiet. It takes me longer than it should to bring it back into place. Panic works its way through my exhaustion, piercing it like an arrow through prey. Thoughts scrabble and wander down prickly paths, drawing blood that is full of pain and uncertainty, and I'm simply unable to stop it. Unable to stay numb.

Two hours until he wakes up from the drugs. Maybe as little as one.

What will I do if I actually complete? Could I go on to be anything but a striker, when it's all I know now, its shadow blotting everything else out? Turning my back on it would not keep everyone else from turning their backs on *me*. Even Chord, eventually, in the worst of my nightmares. Being with a striker might wear him down. Or what if I screw this up and she runs? Every minute that she's alive—that *I'm* alive—he's in danger. He's complete, but he still has a death sentence hanging over him. Because of me. What if time runs out for both of us? What if—

Chord.

It hurts how much I want him. How much I want us to be given new lives again, both of us completes.

But the thought dissipates, disintegrates, falling away even as breath deserts my lungs, taking with it any more capacity to think.

Because someone is inside my house.

The shadowed figure is moving along one side of the kitchen, so I see no more than the slight bob of a head along the far edge of the window frame. But it's her. It must be.

She's twenty-four feet away.

I automatically tilt the barrel up by a small fraction. A bullet will start to fall as soon as it leaves the muzzle of a gun.

Then a cool wind flutters against my cheek. It's gentle enough but has the impact of a hard slap.

The sudden image of my strike, that boy in Tweed's back lot, appears in my mind's eye. How that first bullet was supposed to be enough. How I underestimated space and wind and let it go astray, adrift.

Not this time. I tilt the barrel up another fraction.

Then my hand is shaking again, the gun making little tapping sounds against the wooden sill. I lift my left hand to steady my grip. Ignore the snap of pain in my shoulder.

I imagine Chord's voice in my head. *Breathe, West. Just breathe.*

Twenty feet apart now. The space between us. From limbo to life, active to complete.

I know you're there. Come closer.

As if she's heard me, my Alt steps forward. She's inside the frame of the window now. I get a glimpse of her familiar profile.

The damage to her cheek from that afternoon on the streets of the Quad has become a purple gash. I'm happy to see it— it makes her look less like me.

As I watch her slowly pick up the necklace from the counter, I can almost feel her initial confusion. It's a stumbling thought process, she's seeing something so completely out of context. *Isn't this Glade's necklace? How did it get here? Why is it here?* When realization hits, it's like a tidal wave. Her devastation grows, compounds, feeds into itself.

I wondered how much he loved her, whether she loved him in return. How maybe it wasn't as much as she let him believe, if she let him do what he did. Or perhaps it was the opposite, and it was too much to keep him away. Now I know the answer. And knowing I've played a part in her grief, Alt or not, is hard to live with.

A cloud breaks. A ray of weak light winks off the smooth metal of my gun. It sparks. Catches. She looks out the window at the flash of silver.

Her eyes go blank with shock as they meet mine.

A muscle in my hand betrays its weakness, twitching once, and the gun jerks just the slightest.

The sun flicks off the metal again, a twin flame to the first one.

She moves like a cat, beginning to dart away.

I squeeze the trigger. The bullet drives through air and glass before it buries itself in the side of her neck.

I don't even see her fall, because suddenly tears are burning my eyes. My lungs are gasping for breath, my throat scorched as I choke on wild, unchecked sobs.

It's over.

Chapter 12

Like any professional striker, I'm compelled to make sure the assignment really is complete.

On shaking legs I climb down from the tree house, my sneakers landing heavily on the soggy ground. Mud squeaks and squelches as I hurriedly work my way through the fence, across the yard, and back into the kitchen.

Death must be confirmed.

The replay of it is vivid in my head, like a garish oil painting with too many colors. I see the bullet hit her in the neck, an intricate web of vessels and tissues and connections that can so easily be broken. I've done that, without a doubt.

And yet—

Yet—

She's gone. The kitchen is empty except for a pool of blood in the middle of the tiled floor. She's not here, where she is supposed to be.

I stare down at the blood. I don't know what to think—*how* to think. My mind is racing for an answer, a galloping horse blind with the need to keep running for the finish line.

How is it possible? There's no way. No way she could have survived that.

I'm turning in circles, crazed and panicked. What surrounds me is so familiar, but it only makes it worse. That I can know where everything is in this house except the one thing I'm searching for.

West.

Not Chord's voice this time, but Luc's, an oasis in the storm that's raging in my head. So calm, even while he was dying. *West, slow down. You're moving too fast. You always have.*

Mistake number one.

I squeeze my eyes shut.

Now look. Really *look.*

I look. And I see it. It's so obvious that I can't believe I didn't notice it right away. I really *was* blind.

There are tiny droplets of blood next to the pool on the floor. They lead away in a trail, not a neat one but chaotic, jagged, zigzagging. As they leave the kitchen, their shape changes just the slightest, growing thinner, more elongated.

She's moving. Fast.

It's easy to picture it. My Alt staggering to her feet, hand pressed against her neck to stanch the bleeding. She's thinking it's a miracle she turned her head at the last second. It was just enough for the bullet to miss anything vital. What should have killed her is instead a messy flesh wound. Her face is drawn with pain. She was sure it was the end. Glade's necklace might still be hanging from her fingers.

But now she needs to get out of the house because I'm on the way. She's half stumbling, half running to the front door, and she yanks it open, furious and desperate and wanting to end this just as badly as I do. She runs outside, toward—

It hits me with the force of a giant bunched fist. Hot, acidic bile strains to climb up my throat. The truth of it is undeniable, indisputable.

Because it's exactly what I would do.

"No," I breathe into the silence of the room. Incapable of screaming. Only barely hanging on.

Then I'm running as fast as I can, racing through the kitchen, down the short hall, and across the living room. I crash through the front door, leaving it open and swinging behind me. Only one thought fills my head as my feet hit the pavement, the chilled winter air on my face, its thin, factory stink singeing my nose.

Chord.

Down the street, five houses down. So close. So incredibly far.

Chord!

I'm only halfway there when I hear it. Exploding glass, shards of it crashing onto concrete. She's breaking the window to get inside.

The sound of it won't be enough to wake him, though. Even with the drugs starting to cycle out of his system. By trying to keep him safe, I left him more vulnerable than ever.

Mistake number two.

Hurry. You've got to hurry. No one's voice in my head now except my own. Hard, cold, without feeling. Me as a striker, moving in on a target. The way I was always supposed to be for this.

The front door of Chord's house gapes and is just beginning

to drift shut when I get there. More blood on the steps, the scattered droplets turning into little puddles and smears. Even more along the splinters of glass that line the smashed-in side window, where she reached in for the knob.

As I'm rushing up the front steps, I hear my voice inside my head again, cool and calm. Telling me to move carefully, to think things through, to—

But I can't listen, even if I wanted to.

I push the door open with a foot, then throw myself to the side of the entrance, expecting anything and everything to come at me: the whoosh of a bullet, a wild slice of a blade, *her*—

And . . . nothing.

My breath is fire in my throat, my gun slick with sweat in my hand as I lean back over and peer into the front hall.

Absolutely silent and almost wholly dark all the way through. The last light of the day is falling away fast. I see nothing, and for a heartbeat, I'm literally unable to move. Held prisoner by the weight of the moment.

Fight, flight, freeze. A fresh active will almost always freeze. But I'm not new to this, not anymore—and only one choice is left.

I step over the threshold, past the still-open door. Sweep the wall alongside me with my arm for the light switch. When I find it, I press my palm down, desperate for eyes again.

The overhead lamp turns on, and its muted light trails into the front room, peeks into the kitchen, slides up the first few steps of the staircase. It was comforting last night, almost like being wrapped up and shielded. No more. Now it's weak, a sham, not nearly enough to ward off the bad.

My Alt is somewhere in here. This one place where she can hurt me the most. Dread's a beast now, its teeth and claws and stench already deep inside me. Its face is the look in his eyes as he went under, a blend of love, panic, betrayed trust.

Chord, no. Not this way. It can't end like this.

I take a step, another, then another, and with darting, fevered eyes scan the deeply shadowed front room on my right.

Empty, just as I left it that morning. The couch with my blanket tossed on top, the pillow still creased with the restlessness of my plotting. The coffee table with the med kit sitting on top, dangerously close to falling off. The mirror over the fireplace, where I can see the reflection of my shadow.

And her shadow moving in behind mine.

Only reflex borne on a shot of pure adrenaline has my left leg snapping outward to kick the front door back against the wall, keeping her stuck between both. Where she was hiding, waiting for me. Where I didn't even think to look.

Mistake number three.

I kick it again, snapping her head once, twice, against the wall. In between the sounds there's a sharp clatter. Her gun, falling to the floor and careening toward the kitchen.

Both hands freed now, she shoves hard at the door, and my leg can't hold her or the weight of her rage. She springs loose and lunges at me. We crash to the ground, hitting the edge of the coffee table. My left shoulder convulses, its fire rekindled with each pound of my pulse. The med kit slams down next to us, scattering its contents. Silver tools and bandages go flying—along with my gun, breaking free of my slick grip with the impact. Like my Alt's gun, it glides over the hardwood and hits the far wall before coming to a stop. Too far for me to possibly reach. It's gone.

Mistake number four.

She's a fireball of hate and desperation and broken flesh as she reaches for my eyes, fingers clawed. I can smell her blood like fresh sweat, all copper and salt as it streams from her neck. The fact that she's bleeding so much sparks hope inside me. It's not too late. Maybe.

Both of us gasp as we struggle. There are no words that need to be said.

She's on top of me, but all I can see as I'm trying to get a grip around her neck is a flurry of narrowed, twisted features, long black hair twisting everywhere like gothic ribbons, her blood soaking into my clothes. In this instant, we look nothing like each other, but we are one and the same, both of us crazed with the need to live beyond the next breath. This is the worst kind of battle; it's come down to muscle against muscle, will against will, whose synapses and neurons fire the best.

Her hand reaches for something on the floor next to my head. Then sheer fire burns the side of my face as she drags the tipped point of the med scissors from my temple to my chin.

I scream. Bring one hand to my face, instinctively trying to ward off any further injury. The other swings blindly at her and makes hard contact with the side of her throat, where she's already hurting from my bullet. I swear I feel the heat of her damage along my own neck, as if I'm wounded there, too.

A short burst of a word from her throat—maybe a plea, maybe a name, whose I can't tell—and the hair rises on my arms at the sound. It's garbled and thick with blood, and it's the first time I've ever heard it, but I know it just the same. Her voice—the way I must sound to someone else.

Then she's on the move. Staggering wildly across the floor, going for her gun, only inches away from her fingers. I'm left watching, waiting, a lick of pure terror unwinding in my gut, filling my mouth with the sharp taste of it—

I drag myself to my knees. My right hand dances and skitters along my thigh, looking for the groove of the pocket of my jeans. Finding it, digging in.

Only a second now.

One last chance.

Be the one, be worthy.

She's barely turned around, her gun pointed at me, when my switchblade spins free from my fingers, smoothly and deftly. With zero hesitation, it drives into her chest.

A long, airless second. Breaths hold, eyes lock. The moment stretches between us, my Alt and me, full of understanding.

Then she's no more than a heap on the floor. A burst of icy heat shoots through my eyes and I know they're clear again, my assignment number dissolved into nothingness. Her life ending so I can have the rest of mine.

But I'm also falling. So incredibly tired, drained, stretched thin. I land hard. Close my eyes as I curl over, curl up. Only dimly aware that nothing hurts anymore. Not my face, not my shoulder, not any other part of my body that's fought so hard.

How long I lie there before sound breaks the silence, I don't know. The click of a switch and new, brighter light floods through my eyelids. Halting footsteps come toward me.

I open my eyes. Just a crack. Too heavy, still.

Chord, finally safe.

"West?" His voice is groggy, confused.

I'm finally safe.

"West!"

And I open my eyes all the way, as wide as I can. Because I don't want to miss anything, not anymore, not ever again. Because it's Chord I see rushing straight toward me now . . . and no one else.

CHAPTER 13

My fingers weave through Chord's, holding on tight. As we get closer to the classroom, I can't help but squeeze his hand. I'm nervous.

"Ouch," Chord says, laughing. "West, the hand. You're going to bust it."

"Sorry." I loosen my grip without letting go. It feels good to be so close to him without being scared.

Suddenly Chord's guiding me to the side of the hall. We cut across the flow of students, all rushing to get to class before the final bell rings, and duck into the shadowed doorway of an empty classroom. Almost alone as bodies continue to stream past. A few faces turn to look at us, but I ignore them, too caught up with Chord. The fact that we're both here, alive and together.

He pulls me close, wrapping his arms around my waist. "Are you sure you're ready?" he asks. "You know there's no hurry. He did say however long it takes before you're better."

I lift my left shoulder to show him. "No, it's okay. It doesn't hurt anymore."

"Liar."

I scowl. He knows me too well. "Fine, but only sometimes. Like when it rains."

"It rains three-quarters of the year around here."

"Chord, it's fine, really. I'll rest it when it acts up, okay?"

He leans down, his dark eyes simmering, and kisses me until neither of us wants to come up for air. Only the ringing of the bell tears us apart.

"Damn bell," he says softly. He places his hand along the scar that rides my face from temple to chin. A slash of purple, it's never going to disappear. But it doesn't bother me. When I look at it, I only think of how I won.

"And this feels okay?" he asks.

"Yeah, it's good."

"Good." His hand moves to the back of my head and tilts my face up for another kiss, but I dart to the side with a laugh.

"Chord. The bell. *Go.*"

He sighs and drops a kiss on the top of my head. "Only if you're sure. It's been a while, you know."

It has. It's no longer winter but full-fledged spring now, and months after the completion of my assignment.

And it's time. My injuries are pretty much healed, and I want to know what it feels like to grip metal and steel again—without knowing I have to kill.

I hold both sides of Chord's face and gently pull him down. If we were truly alone, my sleeves wouldn't be pulled down, and I could feel his skin next to mine, but we both know there's no choice about me keeping my marks covered. I will always have to do it, for the rest of my life. I press a brief kiss on his mouth, which has to be enough for now. I need to get going before my nerves start jumping again.

"Meet me right after class?" I ask him. "I told Dess we'd help him shop for a new cell. He still can't find his." Dess, who ended up completing on his own after all, and with more than a week to spare. Dess, who has somehow carved out his own special space in my life, one that helps me think of family without hurting as much anymore.

"Where? Someplace in the Grid, then?" Chord asks.

I nod.

"Yeah, of course," he says. "We'll pick him up from school, if he wants." He reluctantly lets me go to lift his bag back over his shoulder. "But about this . . . you'll be great, West."

"I know." I say it with a smile and hope it hides how nervous I am.

I adjust my new bag, smoothing my hand over the soft camel leather. Overloaded as always, but not like it is on Saturdays, when I cram it full of supplies for my internship at the gallery in Leyton.

Chord bends down for one more kiss, faster and more fleeting, but no less felt by either of us. "Love you. I'll see you soon." He gives me a slow grin that makes my chest ache. "And don't hurt anyone." Then he's off, walking down the hall, late for his own class.

The class waiting for me is right around the corner. When I reach the door, I take a deep breath and nudge it open.

Baer is at the front of the classroom, looking just as tough and surly and brusque as I remember him. He's balancing the point of a switchblade on the tip of one finger.

"So it's not just about learning how to properly use a weapon, but also understanding the weapon itself, the properties of it, why it works the way it—"

Thirty pairs of eyes leave Baer's face to see who is at the door. All of them are idles. Their expressions, full of innocence and inexperience, make me feel very old. So many questions behind those stares, and I can feel my face get hot, my mouth dry.

Baer turns his head at the intrusion. When he sees me, he makes the motion to come in, his pale blue eyes as warm as I will probably ever see them.

Without saying anything or giving even a hint of warning, he tosses the switchblade toward me.

My hand catches it exactly where I want to, as if it hasn't been months since I've held a blade this way. But it feels lighter than I remember, no longer such a weight. Just a knife. No more life or death . . . at least not for me. I've got a different job now.

I look down at the switchblade in my hand. A perfect catch—because the tip of it is pointing straight at Baer.

There's an actual smile on his face as he turns to the class and says, "Everyone, please welcome West Grayer—our new weaponry assistant."

Baer turns back and gives me a brisk, satisfied nod. With that, I know he's never doubted for a second.

That I am the one. That I am worthy.

Acknowledgments

My hugest thanks to:

My agent, Steven Chudney, for believing right from the
beginning.

My editor, Chelsea Eberly, whose brilliance helped me turn a
book into a dream come true.

My family at Random House Children's Books: Ellice Lee
in Design and illustrator Michael Heath of Magnus
Creative, for envisioning a phenomenal cover concept
and bringing it to life; Alison Kolani and her copyediting
team, whose attention to detail continued to amaze me
throughout the final stages of *Dualed;* my publicist, Paul
Samuelson, for helping me achieve a million times over
what I couldn't have done on my own; Rachel Feld, Linda
Leonard, Julie Leung, and Tracy Lerner in Marketing,
for loving this story and helping to make it a success;
and Richard Vallejo and Deanna Meyerhoff in Sales, for
noticing *Dualed* from the very beginning.

My friends Ellen Oh and April Tucholke, two truly talented YA authors whose generosity in both spirit and time also make them great people. I'm so very fortunate to have them in my life. You guys, we did it!

My online families at Friday the Thirteeners and the Lucky 13s, for being such a joy to hang out with as we all go on this incredible journey; the many authors, bloggers, and members of the kidlit community on Twitter who have very much become my friends; and the true treasure that is the Absolute Write forums, for getting me started.

My parents, Bak and Hing, for the early encouragement and for always letting me read at the table.

My parents-in-law, Ray and Peggy, for the constant support and enthusiasm.

And Wendy, Heather, Terry, Ashley, and Dallas, for everything else that counts, in ways both big and small.

About the Author

ELSIE CHAPMAN grew up in Prince George, in British Columbia, Canada, before graduating from the University of British Columbia with a BA in English literature. She lives in Vancouver with her husband and two children, where she writes to either movies on a loop or music turned up way too loud (and sometimes both at the same time). *Dualed* is her first novel, with its sequel, *Divided*, to follow. Visit Elsie at elsiechapman.com.